TO CATCH A

Poisoner

A Pride & Prejudice Variation Mystery

by

Renata McMann & Summer Hanford

ACKNOWLEDGEMENT

With special thanks to Doris, Colleen, and Linda, and to our wonderful Beta Reader Team.

Dear Reader,
After enjoying our story, consider signing up for our mailing list, where you will have the opportunity for free gifts, information about new releases and in person events, and more. Join us by visiting
www.renatamcmann.com/news/

By Renata McMann and Summer Hanford
Charitable Endeavors
Pride & Prejudice and Planets*
To Fall for Mr. Darcy*
Mr. Collins' Will
More Than He Seems
After Anne
Their Secret Love
A Duel in Meryton*
Love, Letters and Lies
The Long Road to Longbourn*
Hypothetically Married*
The Forgiving Season
The Widow Elizabeth
Foiled Elopement
Believing in Darcy
Her Final Wish
Miss Bingley's Christmas
Epiphany with Tea
Courting Elizabeth
The Fire at Netherfield Park
From Ashes to Heiresses*
Entanglements of Honor
Lady Catherine Regrets
A Death at Rosings
Mary Younge
Poor Mr. Darcy
Mr. Collins' Deception
The Scandalous Stepmother
Caroline and the Footman
Elizabeth's Plight (The Wickham Coin Book II)
Georgiana's Folly (The Wickham Coin Book I)
The Second Mrs. Darcy

*available as an audio book

Collections:
A Dollop of Pride and a Dash of Prejudice
Includes from above: Their Secret Love, Miss Bingley's Christmas,
Epiphany with Tea and From Ashes to Heiresses.

Pride and Prejudice Villains Revisited – Redeemed – Reimagined
Includes from above: Lady Catherine Regrets, Mary Younge, Mr. Collins'
Deception and Caroline and the Footman, along with two additional flash
fiction pieces, Mrs. Bennet's Triumph and Wickham's Journal.

Georgiana's Folly & Elizabeth's Plight: Wickham Coin Series
Includes from above: Elizabeth's Plight and Georgiana's Folly.

Pride and Prejudice Variations by Renata McMann
Why Wed?
Is Esteem Enough?

Heiress to Longbourn
Anne de Bourgh Manages
Three Daughters Married
The Inconsistency of Caroline Bingley
Pemberley Weddings
The above five stories are collected in:
Pride and Prejudice Variations: A Collection of Short Stories

Pride & Prejudice Variations by Summer Hanford
Mr. Darcy's Bookshop*
The Adventures of Anne de Bourgh of Rosings*
Mr. Darcy's Matchmaker*
Once Upon a Time in Pemberley*

*available as an audio book

TO CATCH A
Poisoner

Chapter One

Pemberley, 1784

Mr. Albert Wickham looked out the carriage window, taking in a pleasantly situated, well-kept stone dwelling far larger than anywhere he'd yet lived. And this was only the steward's house, where he and his wife would dwell. The manor house at Pemberley would surely be something to behold.

Turning from the view as they drew to a halt, he smiled at his wife and their wetnurse, Henrietta, who held baby George, and said, "It is a very amiable appearing dwelling."

They disembarked and Clara Wickham took baby George, for Henrietta was unwell and not up to carrying him about. Leaving the wetnurse in the care of the competent seeming staff who greeted them, Albert and Clara explored the house, Clara holding baby George close. They went from room to room, guided by a maid, more overwhelmed every moment by the grandeur of their new home.

When they reached the nursery, which the staff hurried to make ready for they had not been informed that a baby would arrive with the couple, Clara hugged George and whispered, "This will be such a magnificent home for you. You will be so happy here with us."

Albert took in the joyful tears that gleamed in his wife's eyes and smiled. It seemed as if, after years of hard work coming up through the ranks in Wales, they would finally reap the reward for their diligence and service. He had secured an unparalleled position, they had a beautiful son, and life seemed suddenly perfect.

Tugging free his timepiece, he consulted it, then said, "I am due at the manor house to meet Mr. Darcy. I will return shortly." He placed a kiss on his wife's brow, tickled baby George under the chin, and left them with the maid.

He asked directions and walked to the house, the rented carriage having already departed, the way short, and the day fine. When he came through the copse that shielded the two dwellings from sight of one another he was, indeed, stunned by the grandeur of Pemberley's manor house. So much so as to render him slightly nervous to approach.

But when he arrived, he was treated respectfully, not talked down to or made to feel inferior. His meeting with George Darcy went well, and Albert returned to his new home even happier than when he'd set out.

Cheerfulness still permeated Albert's mood the following day at breakfast, taken in a sunny little parlor with his wife, while the baby was in Henrietta's care with a maid from the household to assist her. Albert was reaching for a bowl of boiled eggs when one of the footmen entered, the taller of the two, as he thought of the man, having forgotten his name. He would have to ask Clara, who was better than he about such things, for not knowing wouldn't do.

"Mr. Darcy is here to see you, sir," the man said.

Before Albert could reply, George Darcy strode in, his brow furrowed and his demeanor unsettled.

Albert and Clara rose, one to bow and the other to curtsy. Clara cast him a worried look, as surprised as Albert to see his new employer during breakfast and in a state of agitation.

As he straightened, Albert said, "Mr. Darcy, may I introduce my wife, Mrs. Wickham?"

Mr. Darcy peered at her, looking her up and down with odd intensity. "You appear well, Madam."

Clara exchanged another confused glance with her husband. "Thank you, sir. I am well."

Mr. Darcy harrumphed at that and turned back to Albert. "I have been informed by the servants that you have a son, something you failed to mention in your many correspondences, and that he still has an umbilical cord. Is that correct?"

"It is," Albert replied, worry knotting in his stomach.

Mr. Darcy's mouth pulled down in a scowl. "I am letting you go. The position is no longer yours."

"What? Why?" Albert exclaimed, panic shooting through him.

"I am no expert, but either you brought a nearly newborn infant on a journey from Wales or your wife gave birth on the road. My wife is lying in, and I wouldn't let her travel four hours from home, much less make a journey of days."

Albert opened his mouth to protest.

"Not only that," Mr. Darcy continued, not permitting Albert to speak. "I am told you traveled with an ill servant. A wetnurse who is all but bedridden. You are not the kind of man I want for a steward."

"Albert," Clara said weakly into the stillness that followed that declaration, punctuated by Mr. Darcy's slightly labored breath, winded as he was from the vehemence of his speech.

"I have an explanation," Albert said in a quiet but firm voice.

Mr. Darcy drew his shoulders back and thrust out his chin. "There can be no explanation. You are leaving within a fortnight. The only thing preventing me from ordering you out today is an innocent babe, who should be home in Wales."

"You would let me go without a hearing?" Albert asked, trying to tamp down the desperation that welled in him.

"Perhaps if I fetched Henrietta and George?" Clara suggested tentatively.

Albert nodded. "That would be best. If Mr. Darcy will hear us out, he will want to meet them."

Silence returned to the parlor. Mr. Darcy studied Albert, then Clara again. Finally, some of the grimness eased from his features and he said, "Tell me."

Relief flooded Albert. "What I will say must be kept private."

"I will bring George and Henrietta," Clara said and slipped from the room. Albert could hear her gathering the waiting servants as she went, assigning them tasks that would keep them from the parlor door for some time.

Albert turned to his employer and gestured to the seat beside his at the table. His expression stony, Mr. Darcy came around to sit. Retaking his chair as well, Albert gathered his thoughts. The silence in the room was not comfortable.

"Well?" Mr. Darcy demanded.

Albert drew in a deep breath. "I ask that you keep this secret."

"That will depend on what you tell me," Mr. Darcy said with no trace of discomfiture. "Regardless of what it is, I will almost certainly tell my wife, who is as concerned as I am. She will undoubtedly tell her sister Lady Catherine, who is visiting us."

Dismay settled in Albert's gut. Must he choose between his new son and his employment? He'd hoped to give little George such a grand future. He shook his head. "Then I cannot tell you. It is too important to me and to Clara."

Interest glinted in Mr. Darcy's eyes. "I assure you both my wife and her sister can keep secrets."

Albert considered that for a long moment. Finally, feeling he had little choice for they could not return to where they'd lived in Wales, at least not with the baby, he nodded. "I suppose I must trust you." He glanced at the closed door. "My wife and I have been married for four years. She has never been with child."

Mr. Darcy's brows drew together in confusion. "Go on."

"On the way here, we stopped at an inn. Henrietta, our ill wetnurse, worked there and was obviously very pregnant, but she waited on us. Her water broke. The innkeeper struck her and told her to clean up the mess and continue serving us." Albert held up his hands, shrugging. "I couldn't let that stand."

"The child is hers?"

"Yes. The babe was born the following morning."

"My servants said he is yours."

"He is now," Albert said firmly. "My wife cannot have children. This way, we have a son."

"And this Henrietta, she agreed to this?"

"To escape her employer and see her son raised in a place like this?" Albert's gesture took in the room. "She was overjoyed to accept our proposal."

Mr. Darcy sat back in his chair. "You expect to succeed in this ruse?"

"We hope to. When we registered baby George, Henrietta posed as my wife. We put her arm in a sling so I would have an excuse to write for her." Quiet desperation in his voice, Albert continued, "We do not want George to ever know he is not legitimate."

Footfalls sounded in the hallway. Silent, they turned to the door. Clara and Henrietta came in, Clara cradling baby George. Both men stood, Mr. Darcy pulling out a chair for Clara and she came around the table to sit beside him. Albert seated Henrietta, wide-eyed, worried, and twisting her hands together in her lap. Albert went to the door to look up and down the hall.

"I have given the staff tasks which will keep them employed for some time," Clara said.

With a nod, Albert returned to the table and sat. Baby George gurgled, evoking a smile from him. Clara looked down at the baby tenderly.

"Miss Henrietta, is it not?" Mr. Darcy asked in a kinder voice than Albert had yet heard from him.

Henrietta nodded, staring down at her hands.

"Do not worry, Henrietta, you are not in any trouble."

She glanced up at him, and Albert tried to see Mr. Darcy as Henrietta must. A gentleman of middling years, dressed very sternly, who exuded wealth and power.

But also kindness, as he regarded the girl with steady eyes and a warm expression.

"Now, Henrietta, please tell the truth. Is baby George yours?" Mr. Darcy asked.

She gave a jerky nod. "I birthed 'im, sir."

"And how old are you, Henrietta?"

She studied her hands again. "Seventeen."

"Henrietta." Mr. Darcy's voice held patient disbelief.

The girl darted a look up. "Fifteen, sir."

"That's better. Now, I do not mean to pry and please do not feel the need to delve into specifics, but how came you to be working in an inn and with child? Is the baby's father not about?"

"I don't know who the father is, sir." Henrietta looked down, her ears and cheeks red.

"How can that be?" Mr. Darcy cast Albert a questioning look as he asked that, but Albert nodded to Henrietta, who had already explained her circumstances to them the night before she gave birth.

"The innkeeper took me on when my family died of a sickness when I was seven, sir. I've been working for him since then, and it wasn't so bad except for he's quick to set to if I'm slow, but then…" She trailed off, darting a glance at Mr. Darcy.

Adjusting George, who took in the gathering with wide eyes while he blew bubbles of spit, Clara freed a hand to reach across the table to offer to the girl. "You do not have to go on if you do not want to. I can tell him."

Mr. Darcy cast her a narrow-eyed look but still spoke gently as he said, "But I would rather hear the tale from you, Henrietta."

Henrietta took Clara's hand, squeezing tight, and continued, "A—about a year or so ago, men started taking notice of me. Men passing through, and the innkeeper, he started t-taking their coin…" Henrietta continued on in this vein, revealing the details of a horrifying life that had Mr. Darcy vowing aloud to send men to see what could be done about this innkeeper…permanently.

But he continued to be nothing but kindness to Henrietta as her story revealed that there was really no way to know who baby George's father might be, or much hope of tracking anyone down who would be willing to admit to even the possibility of fatherhood. In the end, what happened with the babe must be Henrietta's choice. She, undisputedly the mother, was the only connection the child had.

"And you wish to give the Wickhams your son," Mr. Darcy asked in the gentlest voice he'd yet used. "You are certain of this?"

Henrietta nodded vigorously. She pulled her hand free of Clara's and waved it, the gesture taking in the room. "They can give him such a good life. So much more than I ever could, and they said I can be his wetnurse, and then his nanny, and that we can say as I'm a widow who lost her baby, so I won't have to be so ashamed anymore all the time."

"You should not be ashamed," Clara said quite firmly. "That man you worked for should be." She turned to Mr. Darcy. "And I do hope, whatever decision you make regarding us, you mean your words about seeing that something is done about him."

"I do," Mr. Darcy stated.

Clara nodded and turned back to Henrietta to pat the hand she now rested on the table. "Whatever you choose to do, we will do our best for you and baby George."

Earnestly, Henrietta replied, "I want you to have him, ma'am. I want him to have a good life, and I want to stay here and work and see him every day. I don't want to raise him on my own, and I'll love him and him me, every bit as much as we would if we was somewhere starving together, even if he won't know I was his mum."

"Well?" Albert asked, raising his chin defiantly and turning to Mr. Darcy.

Mr. Darcy considered the four of them for a long moment. "It seems to me that everyone is pleased with the arrangement, and entering into it of their own free will, except of course for the baby, but that cannot be helped at this time. Once he is older, he will, of course, need to be told."

"No," Albert said firmly. "We do not want him to live with that stigma. He will believe he is ours."

Mr. Darcy's eyes narrowed. "He has a right to know where he came from."

"He has a right to be free of the circumstances of his birth, a gift we can give him."

The two men stared mulishly at each other.

Clara and Henrietta looked between them in worry. The baby let out a contented sigh, unwittingly breaking the tense silence.

"We can discuss this another time," Mr. Darcy said, the hard lines on his face relaxing. "For now, little George is falling asleep, and Henrietta appears quite wilted. Perhaps it is time for both to rest."

Taking that cue, Clara stood, causing the men to rise. She said, "Thank you, Mr. Darcy," a sentiment echoed by Henrietta, and the three left the parlor.

Albert glanced down at his barely touched breakfast, a bit sad to see such fine food going to waste but with no appetite. Not after the trials of the morning.

Mr. Darcy cleared his throat. "I am sorry I misjudged you."

"And I am sorry I misjudged you as well," Albert replied.

"How so?" Mr. Darcy asked.

"It did not occur to me that you would take notice of George's age, let alone be angry with me. Most people aren't as caring."

With a snort of amusement, Mr. Darcy admitted, "While I do care, I do not know if I would be quite as caring if my wife hadn't got wind of George's age."

Albert chuckled. "They do make us better people, do they not?"

"Indeed." Mr. Darcy turned to the door, then swung back. "The name George. Is it a family name?"

Albert couldn't suppress a grin. "We thought you would be more amenable to a child who bears your name."

Mr. Darcy glanced at the parlor door, where the women and George had long since disappeared. "I am. If you do not mind, I will become his godfather."

Chapter Two

Pemberley, 1788

It was nearly four years since Albert took the position of steward for Mr. Darcy, and as he and Clara sat with Mr. and Mrs. Darcy, chatting and playing cards in the storm-swept garden, he still could not believe his good fortune. When he'd applied for the position, his main concern had been where he and Clara would live and what sort of income he could bring in. He hadn't dreamed he would be living in a lovely eight-room house, have a beautiful golden-haired son, and be on such good terms with his employer and his wife that the four of them could only be called friends.

"Albert." Clara tapped the table to get his attention. "That's a six to you."

"What? Oh, yes, dear, so it is." He played a card, too content to have much care for if he lost or won. His gaze swept over the lawn, where some rather large branches were being cleared by the garden staff, and to the manor house, near which little George and Fitz played. Henrietta usually had them at this hour, keeping the rambunctious boys entertained with rolling balls down the lawn or rollicking in Fitz's playroom, but the weather was so fine after the night's storm that their mothers had wanted to spend time outdoors with them.

Noticing the lines of rope coming over the roof, Albert asked, "Did the storm cause any damage to the house?"

"I worry it did," Mr. Darcy replied, playing a card. "I sent some men up to check the roof."

"Saving me the trouble?" Albert asked, uncertain if he was quite pleased to have his role usurped.

Mr. Darcy shrugged. "It needed doing."

Clara and Mrs. Darcy exchanged amused looks, for they often claimed that Albert and Mr. Darcy bickered as if they were an old married couple. Mrs. Darcy played a card.

"But the roof is probably still wet," Albert felt obliged to point out. "It might be slippery."

"I had not thought of that," Mr. Darcy admitted, squinting at the roof. "But they have, obviously. Hence the ropes."

"They would employ ropes regardless. There is no reason to enhance the danger with wet slate." Albert studied the mansion speculatively. "Perhaps we should call them down until later this afternoon."

Movement caught his eye, and he lowered his gaze to see Henrietta rapidly approaching, concern pinching her features. A glance showed George and Fitz still sat near the house, cheerfully engaged in some sort of game with rocks, toy soldiers, and twigs, so he couldn't imagine what troubled her. Henrietta had grown into a stern young woman and a valuable member of their household, with a tendency to worry.

"Is something amiss, Henrietta?" Mrs. Darcy asked when the wetnurse turned nanny stopped beside the table.

"The boys are playing too close to the house," Henrietta said. "I'm afraid something might fall on them." She twisted her hands together, a nervous affliction she'd yet to outgrow. "The workers are careful and using ropes, but people err."

"Yes, people do," Mrs. Darcy agreed. "Please attend to it."

Henrietta dipped a curtsy. "Thank you, ma'am."

After Henrietta left, Mrs. Darcy said, "I am going to give her a bonus for that."

"And I am going to call those men down off the roof, once the boys are clear," Albert said, setting down his cards. "I do not want to startle them into dropping anything while George and Fitz are playing there."

The four of them, their card game momentarily forgotten, watched as Henrietta strode briskly back up the lawn, calling to the children. George walked reluctantly toward Henrietta. Fitzwilliam began collecting the toy soldiers and rocks, the sticks apparently not important, but he could not hold them all. Setting them back down, he tried to shove a soldier head first into his pocket.

"Go to your mother, George," Henrietta said when George reached her, turning him to face Clara.

Nodding, he started in their direction, his short, chubby legs carrying him careening through the thick grass, made more wild than usual by the passing storm.

After watching George for a moment to make certain he'd listened, Henrietta set off up the lawn in the direction of the house. "Master Fitzwilliam, come here."

He looked up at her, then resumed attempting to shove rocks and toy soldiers into his coat. Henrietta reached him and crouched down, casting him a reassuring smile as she helped him gather the toys. George arrived at the card table, and Clara picked him up to sit on her lap. She pulled out a handkerchief, fussing over his grubby little hands, dirty from playing with rocks and sticks. Albert smiled at them, his heart overflowing to see his beautiful wife and son together.

A shout sounded from the roof.

Albert whipped his head around, his gaze snapping to where Henrietta and Fitz gathered the toys.

Tiles clattered down the roof, the men at the top pointing and shouting.

Mrs. Darcy yelled. Mr. Darcy jumped up from his chair.

Henrietta looked up. She threw Fitz, sending him flying out onto the lawn in a shower of toy soldiers and little rocks. Tiles crashed down around her. Henrietta went sprawling.

Albert was on his feet, racing after Mr. Darcy as he ran up the lawn. Mr. Darcy dropped down by a bawling Fitz, checking him for injuries, and yelled to Albert, "See to Henrietta."

Passing his friend and employer without a word, Albert reached the young woman who'd given them George. He dropped to his knees beside her, heedless of the rubble of shattered tile or the potential for more to fall. Above, workers gathered near the edge of the roof, peering over with white faces.

Henrietta lay limp and pale, a gash on her neck bubbling blood. Albert pulled out his handkerchief and applied it to the wound, but he knew there was nothing to be done. Not with how quickly the blood flowed, and how much already pooled about her among the broken tiles.

"Mr. Wickham," she whispered. Tears leaked from her eyes, and she plucked at his coat sleeve with nervous, weak fingers. "Fitz? Did I save Fitz?"

Mr. Darcy appeared, a squalling Fitz in his arms, a bloodied handkerchief swaddling one grubby hand. "He is here, Henrietta. See? He is well. You saved him. You have my gratitude."

She smiled, her hands stilling, and her eyes drifting closed.

Albert exchanged a look with Mr. Darcy. He could read in the other man's face that he, too, knew there was no saving the girl. She let out a long sigh. Albert dropped his gaze, tears in his eyes.

Her hand latched onto his arm.

His attention snapped to her face. He'd thought her already dead.

Wide, panicked eyes looked from him to Mr. Darcy and back. "Take care of George. Please."

Her hand fell away, sliding to lie beside her among the rubble of tile. Albert reached out and closed her eyes, for they now stared sightlessly at the blue sky. Footfalls sounded in the stillness, the ladies approaching.

"Albert?" Clara's tearful voice asked.

As one, he and Mr. Darcy stood, coming shoulder to shoulder to shield their wives from the sight of Henrietta's still form. Darcy handed a now quietly crying Fitz to his mother. Both women looked to Albert.

He shook his head. "She's gone."

"Oh," Clara gasped, choking back tears. She hugged George to her.

"She died saving Fitz," Mrs. Darcy murmured, appearing stunned.

"She did." Mr. Darcy's face was grave. "All the more reason for me to take the utmost care of my godson."

Servants were rushing from the house now, soon to reach the grisly scene. The men on the roof were calling out questions, filled with worry both for what they'd accidentally done and what retribution they would receive. Albert could have reassured them on the latter, for all could see the falling tile was an accident.

But he did not. He simply stood with Clara, Mr. Darcy, Mrs. Darcy, and the two boys in a silent gathering of grief. One thing he knew for certain, they would all take care of George, and Fitz. They would ensure that only good ever happened to the two boys. Out of love for each other, their sons, and for George's real mother.

Chapter Three

Pemberley, 1808

Fitzwilliam Darcy cast his good friend, George Wickham, a grin as Darcy's father raised his glass for silence among those gathered to celebrate Wickham's achievement. He'd been ordained that day, after years of hard work, and Darcy knew his father was about to commemorate the occasion by revealing that the living in Kympton was Wickham's. Darcy eagerly anticipated his friend's joy at the news.

"Thank you all for joining us in this celebration," Darcy Sr. said, glass held high.

The room was full of Darcy and Wickham's friends. Of Darcys, Fitzwilliams, and de Bourghs, and several of the senior members of the staff at Pemberley, who had helped to raise both Darcy and Wickham, especially after first Darcy's mother, and then Wickham's parents, had died. Even Darcy's sister Georgiana was there, with her governess, permitted to join in this evening's celebration despite being only eleven.

"George," Darcy Sr. continued, meeting Wickham's gaze across the full sitting room, the largest at Pemberley. "I am so proud of you. Of the work you have put in. Your dedication to your calling. I only wish…" He broke off, swallowing, for even after so many years, Darcy's father could rarely speak of his lost wife and dear friends without the deepest sorrow. "I only wish your father and mother, and my dear wife Anne, could be here to see all you have accomplished." He cleared his throat. "They, too, would be happy to learn that I am gifting you the living in Kympton. I cannot think of a better man for the position. I know you will be the very best rector and will continue to make us all proud."

Cheers rose about the room. Darcy slapped Wickham on the back, still grinning.

Wickham let the cheers go on for a moment, then raised his hand. Talk fell to a cheerful murmur. His voice pitched to carry, Wickham declared, "Of pride in me, sir, I hope you can be assured, for I will strive every day to deserve this most generous gift. To shepherd and cultivate the souls of my congregation, that all may pull together and prosper, as befits a holding of Pemberley's."

That elicited more applause, and Wickham let them continue a moment before raising his voice again. "Moreover, it is you who deserve acknowledgement and praise, Mr. Darcy. What other man would take such stalwart care of his godson? Would ensure I have been clothed, fed, and educated as well as your own son? I deem it few, if any, who would have been so good to me as you, sir." He looked about the room, somehow solemn and joyous at once, a gift Wickham had. "Let us all give praise to my dear benefactor. Mr. Darcy, thank you. I can only strive to be worthy of your affection and care."

More cheering filled the room. Darcy Sr.'s eyes glinted with happiness and a shimmer of tears. With no more speeches forthcoming, the swell of chatter returned.

Darcy grinned, filled with joy for his friend. "How long have you been saving up that speech?"

"How do you know it did not come to me on the spot?" Wickham asked with a chuckle.

"Wonderful speech," Richard Fitzwilliam, Darcy's cousin and a Lieutenant Colonel in the regulars, said as he and his older brother Henry joined them, glasses in hand.

"Indeed," Henry echoed. "Top notch." He looked from Darcy to Wickham and back, taking in their empty hands. "But what is this? You made a toast without a drink? That's bad luck, Wickham."

Wickham shrugged. "I am afraid I do not often imbibe."

"Be that as it may, this is your celebration, man." Henry tipped back the remnants of his drink. "Come. You must have a glass. I insist you celebrate for once. You've been studying for years."

Wickham cast Darcy a pleading look. Although the Darcys, Fitzwilliams, and de Bourghs considered Wickham family, he remained cognizant of the difference in their ranks. He didn't like to go against Henry's wishes.

"Leave the man be," Richard said lightly.

"We have an early morning ahead of us," Darcy added. "Wickham and I are riding out to inspect his new parish tomorrow."

Wickham appeared startled, for they had not agreed on that, Wickham having just been given the living. "We are?"

"I imagine so," Darcy said with a shrug. "That is, you do want to, do you not?"

Wickham grinned and Darcy could tell it was all starting to sink in. The fact that Wickham's years of study had come to fruition. That he had been given a wonderful living. He nodded. "Indeed, I do."

"The two of you are depressingly responsible," Henry muttered. "Well, I will have to have a glass for you." With that, he wandered away.

"Don't mind him," Richard said once Henry was out of earshot. "He will never get to celebrate anything other than being born first, so he likes to make a fuss when others succeed."

Before Darcy or Wickham could answer, Sir Lewis and Lady Catherine de Bourgh barreled up to them. Both were formidable of stature and tended to stand a touch too near and speak a bit too loudly, but Wickham's smile was as warm for them as for anyone, and Darcy knew they regarded him as part of the family.

"Wickham, my boy," Sir Lewis boomed. "Fine occasion. All felicitations on your success."

Wickham bowed. "Thank you, sir. I owe it all to Mr. Darcy's patronage."

"Nonsense," Lady Catherine snapped. "Did he read all those dry old tomes for you? Did he sit for exams for you?" She shook her head. "No, my boy, you were born for the role and have honed your natural talents through hard work. The accomplishment is yours."

Red raced up the back of Wickham's neck and he bowed again. "You honor me, Lady Catherine."

Darcy exchanged an amused look with Richard. Their aunt rarely heaped such praise on anyone but Wickham had always been a favorite of hers. He was generally quick-witted and managed to be frank without giving offence, yet also to compliment without kowtowing. Lady Catherine respected that.

As his aunt and uncle chatted on with Wickham, Darcy scanned the room for his cousin Anne, the de Bourghs' daughter and only child. She stood with her companion, Mrs. Jenkinson, as well as Richard's sister Elinor. Elinor had recently married Colonel Christian Newcomb who stood out in his uniform and was the only officer in the room aside from Richard.

Despite Richard's dedication to serving King and Country, Darcy's uncle, the Earl of Matlock, had not been pleased for his only daughter to marry a military man. Especially not one as active as Newcomb, who was often away for extended missions that somehow took him to places from which he could not write, nor receive letters. Darcy did not know the particulars, but Richard had hinted at rumors that Newcomb worked covertly, gathering information about the French.

But he was present tonight and, catching Darcy's eye, he raised his glass in salute. Darcy nodded back, then turned to bow to his aunt and uncle as they excused themselves.

Richard's father, the earl, approached next, then several members of the community. Wickham was a popular young man and his appointment met with universal approval. He received many well wishes and compliments and met them all with genuine pleasure and modesty. Darcy had never been prouder of his friend than he was that evening.

Eventually the party wound down. Those not staying at Pemberley departed. Darcy's sister had long since been escorted away by her governess, and Lady Catherine, Anne, and Mrs. Jenkinson retired, as did Elinor. Henry had sneaked off somewhere, Darcy fervently hoped not imposing on any of the female staff, and Richard and Colonel Newcomb stood on the veranda speaking in low voices about the troubles of the Continent.

Wickham stifled a yawn, then turned to Darcy. "I think I will bid your father a good night and retire. We truly will ride out early tomorrow to see my new parish, will we not? I would value your opinion on what we find there, though I am certain all will be in order."

"I would like nothing better," Darcy agreed. "I believe I will retire as well."

They approached Darcy's father, who stood speaking with the Earl of Matlock and Sir Lewis. All three appeared oddly intent, their voices too low to overhear. Wickham exchanged a look with Darcy, obviously wondering, as he was, if they should interrupt.

Glancing up, Darcy's father spotted them. He waved them over, raising his voice. "Fitzwilliam, George, come here."

They exchanged another look, for Darcy's father sounded rather grim, but did as ordered.

None of the tension left the three older men as Darcy and Wickham approached. Darcy's father said, "Please join us in my study. There is something we must tell you."

Sir Lewis and the earl both appeared quite aggrieved at that.

The earl caught Darcy Sr.'s arm as he made to lead the way. "You are certain, George?"

Darcy's father nodded. "He has the right to know."

That cryptic remark only increasing Darcy's disquiet, he and Wickham followed the three to the study. There, Darcy's father dismissed the footman who had trailed them, with orders that they were not to be disturbed and that none were to even enter the corridor in which the study stood. Alarm raced through Darcy. Wickham's features pulled tight with worry.

Once they were all settled in the study, the earl, Sir Lewis, Wickham, and Darcy employing the sofas that faced each other at one end of the room, Darcy's father came to stand before his desk, his attention on Wickham. "Now, George, the first thing you must decide is if you would like Fitzwilliam to remain. What I have to say concerns him, but it much more so concerns you, and it is your choice if you wish him to hear the details of it from me."

"How can he possibly decide that when we have no idea what you will say?" Darcy protested on behalf of his friend. "You must give him some hint. Some clue."

"There is no need," Wickham said firmly. "No matter what will be said here, I will want you to know." He turned to Darcy's father. "I want Fitz to remain."

Darcy Sr. nodded. Leaning against the desk, arms folded across his chest, he studied the floor for a long moment before looking up with haunted eyes. "You are not the son of Albert and Clara Wickham."

Darcy's breath left him as harshly and quickly as if he'd taken a blow to the gut.

On his side of the couch they shared, Wickham gripped the arm tightly. "I am not?"

Darcy's father shook his head. "Your mother was an orphaned girl of fifteen who worked in an inn. The innkeeper, who I had removed to one of the penal colonies, may he rot there, sold her favors to passing customers. He also beat her. Mr. and Mrs. Wickham took her away from there and took you as their own. They could not have children, and your mother, Henrietta, wanted the best life for you that she could give you."

"Henrietta?" Darcy repeated, shock racing through him. "Is that not the name of our nanny who died when we were not yet four?"

His father nodded. "She was a wetnurse to both of you, and then your nanny. She was a wonderful young woman and loved you both."

Darcy dared not look at Wickham, worry clenching his gut. "But…there are rumors about how she died. Why she died."

Though he had no recollection of the woman who had cared for him and George when they were babes, Darcy had heard the whispers over the years. They both had.

"They say she was hit by roof tiles while…" Wickham trailed off, darting a glance at Darcy.

Darcy's father sighed, scrubbing both hands over his face. "I had hoped to spare you both this part of the story, but as I can only conclude that idle tongues have already imparted much, I will give you the truth of the matter."

"No good will come of this," the earl muttered.

Seated beside him, Sir Lewis cast him a quelling look.

"You were both playing near the house," Darcy's father began. "There had been a storm, and I had men up on the roof. George's father—" Darcy Sr. broke off. "That is, Albert, said I should not have sent them up yet. He said the roof would be too wet still and there might be an accident." Darcy's father shook his head. "I should have let him handle the matter. That was his job and he was good at it." With another sigh, he continued, "Henrietta worried that if something fell off the roof, you two might be hit, so she went to collect you. George, you did as you were told, but Fitzwilliam, you tried to gather up your toys. You were always good about collecting your toys."

Pausing again, Darcy's father studied them in turn, the silence strained. Harsh breathing reached Darcy's ears. His own, he realized. Beside him, Wickham was as white as bed linens.

"There is not much more to tell," Darcy's father said sadly. "Henrietta went to gather you and the toys, son, and some tiles fell. She pushed you out of the way and they hit her. Her…the end came quickly." He crossed to Wickham, reaching to clasp his shoulder. "You were already my godson, and Anne and I loved you nearly as much as the Wickhams did, but from that day forward I made certain you lacked for nothing."

Silence overtook the room. Darcy Sr. squeezed Wickham's shoulder, then moved back to lean against his desk again, his face creased with worry.

"I see." Wickham's voice was soft. He looked up, meeting the eyes of Darcy's father. "Thank you for telling me. A man has a right to know who he is."

"Who you are is George Wickham," Sir Lewis said firmly. "Precisely who you were before we entered this study." He cast Darcy's father an angry look.

"Yes. Certainly." Wickham stood abruptly, causing them all to rise. "If you will excuse me. It is late." He bowed low.

"George," Darcy said, reaching out as Wickham walked past him to the study door.

Wickham looked back, his eyes haunted, then slipped from the room.

"Excuse me Father, my lord, sir." Darcy rushed away after Wickham. He could hear his uncles' voices rise almost immediately, querulous, and his father answer.

Darcy followed Wickham through Pemberley's halls, lengthening his stride to try to overtake his friend. Their silent chase ended when Wickham spilled out onto the now-empty veranda. He came up against the balustrade and braced his hands on the wide stone railing, raising his gaze to the stars.

Moving slowly now, as if Wickham might bolt like a skittish colt, Darcy joined him.

After a long silence during which Darcy wrestled with what he might say, Wickham whispered, "What am I to do now?"

"What you have worked for years to do," Darcy said quickly. Guilt washed through him as he grappled with his father's revelations. He'd caused Henrietta's death. That was the truth behind the staff's whispers about her. Darcy had killed Wickham's mother.

"How can I guide a flock when I do not know who I am? When I am the son of a fifteen-year-old girl and the sort of man who would…who would pay money to lay with her?"

"That is not who you are," Darcy said fervently. Within him, a battle waged, for he wished to beg Wickham's forgiveness for his role in Henrietta's death. Was now the time? He did not want to further burden his friend.

"Is it not?" Wickham's knuckles were white upon the balustrade. "All I know of my father, all anyone knows, is that one truth. If that is the man he was, what sort of man does that make me?"

"You are a good man." Darcy turned to face him, more earnest than he'd ever been. "You are defined by what you do, not by what some…some…" He could not think of a word that applied and yet wouldn't play into Wickham's newfound revulsion for himself.

"Miscreant? Savage? Immoral filth?"

Darcy flinched with each word, well aware that Wickham was applying them to himself.

Wickham sighed, sagging, his head dropping. When he raised it, he whispered, "You are not to wallow in guilt, Fitz. You were a child. It was an accident. There can be no blame where there is no malicious intent."

Darcy turned to the railing and the darkness in the garden. Shoulder to shoulder with his friend, he squeezed his eyes closed. How like Wickham to think of Darcy's pain when he was full to brimming with pain of his own.

Visible even by moonlight, Darcy looked down at the scar on the back of his right hand. Whenever he'd asked about it, he'd received vague replies about an accident involving tiles falling from the roof. Now, he knew why his parents had never been more specific. "I will come to terms with my guilt, and you must come to terms with the truth that you are George Wickham, the son of the couple who raised you."

"But I am not." Wickham rubbed his forehead. "I do not know who I am, but I know that nothing will be the same again. Nothing." This last, he added forlornly.

"It is very late," Darcy said, wishing he could think of something, anything, helpful to say, but George was the insightful and eloquent one. "You should sleep. You need rest, and to think."

"Yes. Likely I should sleep, but I do not think I will." His expression grim, Wickham turned from the railing. "What I think I will do is find that drink now." With that, he strode back into the house, leaving Darcy staring after him in worry.

Chapter Four

Hertfordshire, 1811

Elizabeth Bennet sat at the breakfast table with her family and toyed idly with a roll, contemplating her day. She would mend, perhaps. September had not yet been cold, but the weather would eventually turn, and she had not repaired a small tear in the hem of her cloak, got while walking months ago in the spring when she caught it on some thorny brush.

Mending was so boring, though. Life, in truth, was a bit boring of late. Nothing interesting ever happened at Longbourn, or even the nearby market town, Meryton. Every day was the same.

Her roaming gaze found the back of her father's paper, held open before him as he read, and alighted on an article about a group of militia members who had fallen ill. The title was, *More Militia Murders? Are Spies Among Us?* But reading onward showed that while a regiment stationed outside Bath had grown ill, none had died, much as with the last such 'poisoning,' up in Lancashire, where there were only a few fatalities.

Not like the terrible incident that winter. That had been horrendous and splashed all over the papers, mostly due to the fact that the daughter of an earl and her husband, a decorated colonel in the regulars, had died along with the officers of the local militia they'd hosted for supper. The food had also been served to the troop as a special Yuletide treat, meaning more than just officers died. The reports had been quite gruesome.

To add to the suspicion and gossip surrounding the event, the couple had employed a new chef, who had turned out to be a Frenchman in disguise and who had fled after the deaths. He'd been found, but not before taking his own life. The papers, and gossip, speculated he'd done so to avoid revealing his fellow conspirators. The story had occupied the interest of the entirety of England for months.

The subsequent illnesses, the one in Lancaster, where two men had died, and now this one near Bath, where it seemed no one had been more than ill, likely would not have made the papers if not for the first, terrible incident. Rumors abounded, some that the Frenchman had secretly escaped capture and claims of his death were crafted merely to soothe the populace. Some that his fellow conspirators had silenced him, making the wounds appear self-inflicted, and still hid among them. Some, even, that the murdered colonel had been a spy for the Crown and the sole target of the poisoning, and the rest of those at dinner merely collateral.

Elizabeth didn't believe anything beyond the fact that people had died, a peer's relations among them. The rest was gossip and speculation, but she must admit that thinking about the possibilities behind the murders and subsequent failed poisonings was more interesting than mending.

Her father turned the page, folding his paper in such a way that the article was obscured, and Elizabeth returned to tearing up her roll and contemplating another day of stitching.

She took a walk after breakfast, then read for a time, though Longbourn held no books she had not already enjoyed at least once, except those on husbandry. Then, finally, she settled into the parlor, peaceful for the moment with only her father and older sister Jane there, to mend.

In short order, her mother and three younger sisters returned from making calls, and Mrs. Bennet bustled in with the news that Netherfield Park, the largest estate in the local area, had been let by a young, unattached man of considerable means, named Mr. Bingley. Rumor had his income as four or five thousand a year, and Elizabeth could see the avarice and hope in her mother's eyes as she scanned the five of them. To be certain, her gaze paused longest on Jane and second longest on the youngest of the sisters, Lydia. Mrs. Bennet made no secret of thinking that her eldest and youngest daughters were by far the most attractive of the five and that she did not believe Elizabeth, Mary, or Kitty would marry as well as Jane and Lydia would. Elizabeth imagined that when this Mr. Bingley arrived, they might learn the truth of her mother's idea.

***

Several weeks later, the arrival of Mr. Bingley and his sisters, one married and one not, along with his brother by marriage and his friend Mr. Darcy, certainly added interest to the neighborhood. For his part, Mr. Bingley was amiable and universally liked, especially by Elizabeth's sister Jane and by Mrs. Bennet, who saw a match for the two. The married sister, Mrs. Hurst, was tolerated and her husband, Mr. Hurst, readily accepted by the menfolk, in large part due to his propensity to lose at cards while gambling. The unmarried sister, Miss Caroline Bingley, was a terrible snob who considered the society about Netherfield Park to be quite beneath her.

But she was not the worst of the lot. That honor went to a Mr. Fitzwilliam Darcy. A handsome and very wealthy gentleman from Derbyshire who held himself aloof and looked down on all as if he were royalty. He scorned the presence of any but the Bingleys and Hursts. He refused to be sociable. He had insulted Elizabeth in public, saying she was not handsome enough to dance with where all could hear.

In short, he was the most disagreeable gentleman Elizabeth had ever encountered. She disliked him excessively.

Still, she had to admit, life was not so dull any longer with the addition of the party at Netherfield Park. It grew even less dull with the arrival of a local militia in late October. To universal delight, they were to be stationed in Meryton for some months. Soon, young ladies all over town, including Elizabeth's youngest sisters, Kitty and Lydia, were swooning over redcoats.

And then, come November, life became even more interesting. Perhaps too much so. Their cousin, a man named Mr. Collins, came to Longbourn. A cousinly visit might not be an interesting occurrence to many families, but to the Bennets it was. For Mr. Collins, who none of them had before met, would someday take their home from them, Longbourn being entailed away from them upon their father's hopefully-far-off demise.

Mr. Collins was an utter oaf. He spoke endlessly of his vaunted patroness, Lady Catherine de Bourgh. He insulted at every turn, while managing to fawn over all. And worst of all, he had every intention of marrying one of them. Elizabeth could only pray it was not her who he asked.

All of this occupied Elizabeth's thoughts as she and three of her sisters, their middle sister Mary having remained behind, walked to Meryton with Mr. Collins. As he prattled on about his garden, speaking too loudly for any other conversations to take place while they walked, it was not lost on Elizabeth that mere months ago she had been hoping for more interest in her life. Knowing her fables, she smiled, well aware that she should have a care making wishes. She did not want to be one of Aesop's frogs who wished for a king.

"So, you see, fair cousins, that Lady Catherine said to plant more carrots and, to be certain, she was correct," Mr. Collins was saying as they reached Meryton's central street. "Lady Catherine knows a great deal about vegetable gardens. She often relates how accomplished a gardener she would be if she had ever taken up the task. Her daughter, Miss Anne de Bourgh, as well—"

"Oh, Kitty, look at that muslin," Lydia interrupted, pointing. "That is new, is it not? We must see it."

"Lydia," Jane said with mild reprimand for interrupting their cousin.

Lydia did not appear to hear, grabbing Kitty's hand and pulling her down the street to peer into a shop window.

"I beg your pardon, Mr. Collins." Jane gave their cousin an apologetic smile, though Elizabeth could not blame Lydia for wanting to escape Mr. Collins' speech. "You were saying? About carrots?"

"Not about carrots in particular, my fair cousin, but about Lady

Catherine's excessively good advice in the realm of vegetable gardens."

"Yes. Vegetable gardens," Jane agreed.

"I prefer parsnips, when it comes to root vegetables of an elongated, rather than round, state," Elizabeth put in. She had no such preference and did not usually spout nonsense simply to hear herself speak, but she did not know how much more of Mr. Collins' voice she could endure. "On the other hand, when it comes to rounded vegetables, there is always the glory of the turnip."

Mr. Collins shook his head. "I must disagree, fair cousin, though it pains me to do so. Lady Catherine greatly espouses the potato. Such a useful, ubiquitous vegetable, which grows so readily in English soil."

"That is true," Elizabeth said with great solemnity. "Potatoes do grow."

On the other side of their cousin, Jane cast her a quelling look, quite aware that Elizabeth was coming close to openly mocking their relation.

"You can steam them, mash them, add them to a stew," Mr. Collins elaborated, as if none of those treatments could be applied to other vegetables. "They are delectable warm or cold. With heavy sauces or light seasoning. Eaten alone or added to a dish. Truly, a vegetable for all purposes."

"Not for sleeping on," Elizabeth stated, unable to resist, as they reached Kitty and Lydia. "So perhaps not all purposes."

Mr. Collins turned to her, blinking in confusion. The man had not an ounce of whimsy in him.

"Who is that?"

The covetous, speculative quality to Lydia's voice, not the volume, caught Elizabeth's attention. She looked to see her youngest two sisters staring across the street and followed their gaze.

Mr. Denny, one of the officers newly come to Meryton and a particular favorite of Lydia's, walked down the street with a man Elizabeth had not seen before. Tall, fair of features, and in all ways amiable looking, the unknown man strode beside Mr. Denny with an air of easy confidence.

Grabbing Kitty's hand again, Lydia pulled her across the street on the pretense of something glimpsed in a window there. Exchanging a slightly alarmed look, Elizabeth and Jane followed, bringing Mr. Collins with them.

Mr. Denny obliged them by approaching with his friend and reached them to the exclamation of, "Denny," from Lydia. "You are returned from London, and not alone, I see."

Mr. Denny bowed. "Miss Lydia, Miss Kitty." He looked past them as Elizabeth, Jane, and Mr. Collins joined them and more greetings were exchanged. Finally, Mr. Denny gestured to his handsome companion. "And this is Mr. Wickham, soon to be Lieutenant Wickham. He is newly up from London to join us."

Mr. Wickham bowed with practiced smoothness. "Had I but known Hertfordshire to be populated by such loveliness as I find before me, I would have striven to be stationed here far sooner."

"Then you are here to join the militia, Mr. Wickham?" Lydia asked eagerly.

For once, Elizabeth couldn't blame her sister for her show of enthusiasm. Mr. Wickham was upright, comely, and seemed all things amiable. He would be a welcome addition to their society.

The slightest of tremors went through Jane, an expression of emotion that would be unremarkable in one of Elizabeth's younger sisters but which caused her to turn to her eldest. Jane's attention was riveted on two riders coming up the street behind the gentlemen. Mr. Bingley, accompanied by the always dour Mr. Darcy. Delight clear on his face, Mr. Bingley locked gazes with Jane.

Upon nearing, the two dismounted and secured their horses a short way up the street, continuing on foot. Jane watched their approach eagerly, and Elizabeth watched Jane, delighted by her sister's interest in so fine a gentleman.

"What do you think, Miss Elizabeth?" Mr. Wickham said, his question drawing her back to the conversation her younger sisters and Mr. Collins were having with the two officers.

Elizabeth turned to him, at a loss as to what they'd been speaking about. She was saved by the arrival of Mr. Bingley, who came around the officers to bow to Jane and said, "Miss Bennet. How fortuitous. We were even now on our way to Longbourn to enquire after you."

Elizabeth cocked an eyebrow at Mr. Darcy, wondering at his true reason for accompanying his friend on a call to Longbourn. It certainly was not to seek the company of any who dwelled there. He'd made it quite clear that he had no use for their society.

But Mr. Darcy, teeth clenched and white about the mouth, was looking at Mr. Wickham. Elizabeth was surprised to see a flush overtake that man's countenance. He shrugged slightly and tipped his hat to Mr. Darcy. Mr. Darcy just deigned to return the salutation.

"...to hear you are so well," Mr. Bingley was saying as Elizabeth returned her attention to the conversation once more.

"But this is lovely," Lydia said loudly. "We're on our way to visit our Aunt Phillips and she adores callers of all sorts and in any number. You must all join us."

"We cannot," Mr. Darcy said immediately, even as Mr. Bingley opened his mouth to speak.

Mr. Bingley cast him a startled look and clamped his mouth back closed.

"We are sorry to lose your company, then," Jane said, her words aimed at Mr. Bingley.

Elizabeth cast Mr. Darcy a sardonic look. If they had been on their way to call on Longbourn, they could not possibly have any pressing business to which to attend.

He met her gaze evenly, as if daring her to speak.

"Oh, but you will come, won't you, Mr. Wickham? Denny?" Lydia beseeched, turning to the two officers. "It is monstrously unfair that we should meet so many gentlemen and be unable to convince any of them to attend us."

"Yes," Kitty echoed. "You must join us. It will be ever so fun."

"It is the duty of gentlemen to attend ladies," Mr. Collins intoned. "One of their paramount duties, Lady Catherine always says. When her husband, Sir Lewis de Bourgh, was alive, he was a very attentive gentleman."

Mr. Darcy eyed Mr. Collins as one would a dead fish on a beach.

"If nothing else, we will walk with you the remainder of the way," Mr. Wickham allowed. His gaze slid to Mr. Darcy and away again. "Every man should do his duty, and there are few duties as pleasant as attending to the ladies."

Mr. Darcy pressed his mouth into a hard line. He bowed to them, his attention fixed on Elizabeth as he straightened, before flicking back to Mr. Wickham. "Until next we meet." Pivoting, he strode back in the direction of the horses.

"Ah, yes, it's been a pleasure," Mr. Bingley said quickly, his manner so conciliatory as to be fawning. "If you will excuse me." He, too, bowed and departed.

How singular these men were, Elizabeth reflected as the seven of them, Kitty and Lydia clinging to Denny and Mr. Wickham, started up the street once more. She looked forward to learning more about them, especially Mr. Wickham. Perhaps he could shed some light on the character of the dour Mr. Darcy of Pemberley.

Chapter Five

Not two weeks later as she readied for the ball to be held at Netherfield Park that evening, Elizabeth couldn't help but reflect that Mr. Wickham had, indeed, shed light on Mr. Darcy's character. He'd proven full of tidbits about the Darcy family, their general hauteur, and their poor treatment of him. Elizabeth had developed quite a dislike of the tall, austere Mr. Darcy.

She'd also developed a not insubstantial amount of esteem for Mr. Wickham. He'd proved every bit as dashing and charming as their first meeting suggested. He was amenable to playing cards, walking about town, and to dancing. That last, especially, Elizabeth looked forward to at the ball that evening. Standing up with Mr. Wickham would be a pleasant change from the general dearth of partners in Meryton society, and certainly better than hanging about waiting to see if Mr. Darcy would insult her again.

Elizabeth had some small hope, as well, that Mr. Wickham's presence might mitigate her cousin Mr. Collins' attention. More and more, he made it clear that he had selected her, among her sisters, to be the focus of his quest for marriage. Insofar as she could without departing the realm of civility, Elizabeth endeavored to give him no encouragement. Despite that, he'd already claimed her first set.

Still, the prospect of an evening of dancing and socialization, coupled with Mr. Wickham's charming presence and the delight that a celebratory Netherfield Park manor house was certain to bring, saw Elizabeth dressing quickly. Her finery donned, she joined her father in the small front parlor to await the others.

"You are ready early," Mr. Bennet observed, looking up from the book he held.

"As are you, Papa."

He peered at her, assessing. "May I assume from your apparent exuberance that you look forward to this evening?"

"May I assume from the lack of yours that you do not?" Elizabeth countered, certain he did not.

In affirmation of that, Mr. Bennet grimaced. "What I have to look forward to is being kept from my home for far more hours than I appreciate, perhaps a card game or two that lack in challenge, though Mr. Hurst might give away more of his money, and another of Mr. Goulding's rails against the waste of porridge."

"Waste of porridge?" Elizabeth repeated, chuckling. "Whyever is Mr. Goulding worried about porridge?"

"You know Goulding. As magistrate, he feels everything is his business."

"Yes," Elizabeth agreed. "But there must be a particular reason he is worried about the militia's porridge."

"Have you not heard? The militia's cook sleeps while their meals simmer. Mr. Goulding, since taking note, has apparently walked right up to the pot and stirred the porridge no fewer than four times without being noticed. As magistrate, he seems to feel it is his duty to root out such negligence. He is quite convinced that once word gets out about this lax supervision, porridge theft will be on the rise."

Elizabeth shook her head. "But, is he not the one putting out the word?"

"He is, and I will be forced to endure another rendition, I am certain."

"I am sorry about your porridge woes, Papa, and about how late we will stay out, for I have every expectation that you are correct on all counts."

Lifting his book, Mr. Bennet waggled it at her. "Never fear. This volume is suitably small enough to secure in my pocket."

Elizabeth made no reply to that, secretly wishing her father would not sneak off to read. Were his absence noted, it would be embarrassing. Better he should use his presence to curtail some of her mother and sisters' less desirable behavior.

Elizabeth kept that hope close as they departed Longbourn and still held it when they entered Netherfield and joined the gathering there.

But Mr. Bennet did no such thing, instead adding to Elizabeth's consternation by humiliating Mary when she overstayed her welcome at the pianoforte. In contrast, Mr. Bennet did not intervene at all as Mrs. Bennet boasted that Jane would marry Mr. Bingley and reap all the ensuing financial advantages, even though there was no engagement.

Then, seemingly from nowhere, Lydia suggested that some officers tour the kitchen. This was met with loud agreement and, while Lydia did not leave the ballroom, laughingly declaring that she was too busy dancing, four officers did. When they returned from their tour of the kitchen, where they undoubtedly disrupted the preparation of the food that would be served soon, it was with excited reports of the late arrival of fresh salmon, which the kitchen staff was scrambling to prepare.

To cement the failure of the ball in Elizabeth's eyes, Mr. Wickham was not in attendance, and Mr. Collins was. He hung on her, dancing so terribly so as to dissuade her from wishing to ever partner him again, yet interfering with other opportunities to dance. Worse still, when dinner was served, she was unable to escape him. It seemed she would not even be permitted to enjoy the treat of fresh salmon in peace.

As dinner commenced, Mr. Collins proved to be as attentive as ever, in just as annoying a fashion. He gestured for the staff to take her hardly touched soup away the moment he'd slurped down his, then served her duck ragout without asking if she wanted any, which she did not. Having had it at Netherfield Park previously, she knew it was far too spicy for her taste. He also refused to serve her potatoes, which she desired but could not reach, citing her flippant claim to prefer turnips. Did she not know him incapable of subtlety, Elizabeth would suspect him of deliberately punishing her earlier cheek.

Fortunately, Elizabeth's good friend Charlotte Lucas sat on Mr. Collins' other side, and she procured his attention, drawing it from Elizabeth as she had very kindly been doing for much of the evening. Relieved, Elizabeth pushed the unwanted duck about on her plate and waited for the opportunity for salmon while other conversations at the table washed over her. On her other side, Captain Carter was engaged in speaking with Miss Harriet Harrington, one of Lydia's friends.

"Are you enjoying the ball, Lady Lucas?" Mr. Hurst asked, seated across from Elizabeth at the matron's side.

"Oh, I am. Never have I seen Netherfield Park look so lovely."

"Then you have attended balls here before?" Mr. Hurst asked before shoveling a large forkful of duck ragout into his mouth.

Elizabeth knew it to be a favorite of Mr. Hurst's and suspected he'd asked the question to gain time to eat while Lady Lucas reminisced.

"Oh, not since my youth," she said and obligingly went into detail about seeing the ballroom decorated for Christmas.

What Elizabeth knew, but Lady Lucas conveniently left out, was that the lady had not attended that ball as a guest. The daughter of a local shopkeeper, and the wife of one before her husband's elevation, she had likely supervised the delivery of goods to so important an event.

Up the table from them, Mrs. Bennet exclaimed loudly, "Mr. Bingley, this is by far the best salmon I have ever tasted," speaking to their host even though she did not sit near him. "You must have your cook give our cook the recipe."

"My patroness, Lady Catherine de Bourgh, decries salmon as a glorified river fish," Mr. Collins said, speaking every bit as loudly as Elizabeth's mother had. "Lady Catherine extolls the virtues of mackerel."

"Then Lady Catherine should try Mr. Bingley's most excellent salmon," Mrs. Bennet cast back with annoyance.

Elizabeth wished she could slide under the table and hide.

"Thank you, Mrs. Bennet." Mr. Bingley's smile was strained at the edges and Elizabeth winced at the censure she noted in his gaze. "I usually permit

Caroline to handle all preparations but a connection extended the offer and I was quick to take him up on it."

"Well, it is delightful, sir," Elizabeth's mother replied, all but shouting down the table. "There is nothing like the freshest ingredients, but then, as wealthy as you are, I am certain you know as much."

"Everything served here is fresh," Miss Bingley said stiffly as she stabbed a piece of duck.

"Yes, certainly." Mrs. Bennet adopted a mild expression, as if blameless for Miss Bingley's ire. "But it is good to know that Mr. Bingley is the sort of gentleman who will make the effort to procure what he most wants." She slanted a look at Jane, who sat staring down at her plate, obviously too embarrassed to eat.

Across the table from one another, Miss Bingley and Mrs. Hurst exchanged disgusted looks.

"Mrs. Bennet is very impressed with Mr. Bingley," Lady Lucas said quietly to Mr. Hurst. "She is certain that if Jane marries him, the other girls will meet wealthy people. Maybe even people of rank."

Mr. Hurst swallowed, then reached for his wine to rinse down the duck he'd been eating. "Wealth isn't the only way to get to know people who matter. Darcy's cousin is heir to an earl and I see him quite regularly. He enjoys having me as a partner for card games. He's more likely to win that way. Unfortunately, he's so bad a player, I lose more than I like. Louisa is always on about that, but a little debt is worth the cultivation of a relationship with a future earl."

Elizabeth wondered what Mr. Hurst considered a little debt.

"Oh, I daresay it is," Lady Lucas readily agreed. "Perhaps your relations will gain from your connection, and then Mrs. Hurst will be more accepting of the tactic."

"Perhaps?" Mr. Hurst shook his head. "They already have. That's how Bingley met Darcy, you know. Through me, this summer. Darcy is nephew to the earl, cousin to the heir, and I brought Bingley along to a game."

Elizabeth had not known the friendship between Mr. Bingley and Mr. Darcy was so new. No wonder Mr. Bingley had not realized his guest would be so aloof at the assembly where Mr. Darcy had insulted her. But then, if Mr. Wickham's reports and Elizabeth's observations were to be believed, Mr. Darcy must require new friends regularly. He obviously drove them off with his highhanded, supercilious ways.

She looked down at her untouched duck. Perhaps it wouldn't be as spicy as usual, as this was a large gathering. It was silly not to at least taste it. She took a forkful.

"Do not eat anything," a man's voice cried.

Fork poised, Elizabeth looked up to see Mr. Wickham struggling against a footman who had a firm grip on his arm.

To say Mr. Wickham wasn't dressed for the ball was an understatement. His uniform looked like it had been worn all day and his boots were crusted with dirt. His hair was disarrayed, and his face blotchy and sickly looking. He was almost unrecognizable.

"Wickham," Lydia cried into the stunned silence.

Mr. Darcy stood so abruptly that his chair crashed backward. Elizabeth watched, along with everyone else, as long, rapid strides brought him to Mr. Wickham's side. Her eyes widened. Was Mr. Darcy going to attack Mr. Wickham?

Reaching him, Mr. Darcy grabbed the other man by the shoulders, the footman moving back out of the way. "What has happened?"

Mr. Wickham slumped, seeming certain that Mr. Darcy would sustain him. "Poison."

"What?" Colonel Forster exclaimed.

A glance showed that he, too, was on his feet. He started around the table.

"I think," Mr. Wickham amended. "I am not certain. Many of the men are sick, but so far only the ones who ate after morning training. The half who didn't go out on maneuvers this morning seem perfectly well."

"They would have eaten earlier," Colonel Forster said, reaching Mr. Darcy and Mr. Wickham. "While you oversaw the training."

"Bad food," Sir William Lucas said sagely.

Murmurs sounded around the table; the other guests agreeing.

"Why was I not informed of the illness?" Colonel Forster asked.

Mr. Wickham shook his head. "No one realized anything was wrong until after you left for the ball."

"I do not see what a batch of bad porridge has to do with anything here," Miss Bingley said loudly, sounding very displeased.

"I told you all, did I not, that someone should watch that porridge," Mr. Goulding put in. "And now look what's come of it. Bad food."

"Why do you believe it is poison?" Mr. Darcy asked Mr. Wickham, studying his face intently. "Aside from the obvious reason."

Elizabeth wondered what the obvious reason could be, because it was certainly not obvious to her.

"We called in the local man, Jones," Mr. Wickham replied. "He's not certain what it is, but he said it is not anything he's seen before, and he's seen the results of spoiled food."

"But why do you believe it might be here?" Elizabeth's father asked.

"Really, this is hardly the thing to discuss at a ball." Mr. Bingley raised his voice to carry over the worried babble of conversation swirling around the table. "I suggest the people who wish to speak about it go elsewhere."

"Yes," Miss Bingley seconded. "This is an outrageous interruption to an occasion I have devoted weeks to planning."

"I agree," Mr. Collins added, though no one sought his opinion, and they did not dine in his home. "Lady Catherine would not countenance talk of poisoning and illness at a ball."

Mr. Darcy glanced at him, his expression devoid of warmth. "The interruption is warranted if the food here is poisoned." He turned back to Mr. Wickham. "How much of it did you eat?"

Mr. Wickham shook his head. "Enough."

Paling, Mr. Darcy helped Wickham over to the chair he'd vacated, which he rightened for Mr. Wickham to sit in.

"Our food is not spoiled," Miss Bingley said. "My cook is careful."

"The other cases, and the let—"

Colonel Forster cut off what Mr. Wickham was about to say with a slashing gesture and a quelling look.

"Other cases?" Miss Bingley scoffed. "Of soldiers who ate bad porridge? Any other cases there are have nothing to do with the food here."

"What other cases?" Elizabeth's father asked, strain in his voice.

Silence filled the room as everyone waited for an answer.

Chapter Six

His expression tight with worry, Mr. Darcy poured Mr. Wickham some wine, but Mr. Wickham waved the proffered cup away, looking ill.

Colonel Forster turned from watching them to face the room. He cleared his throat. "You will all have read in the papers, or heard tell of, the speculation about several poisonings in militias. Those reports are more than rumor, and in all cases, the officers and the men were both poisoned, even if they did not dine together."

"And what better time to poison the officers than here, at a ball to which they were all invited," Mr. Darcy added.

"Now hang on," Mr. Hurst said. "According to the papers, the officers were poisoned at the same time as the men. That is, they may not have sat down to the same table each time, but they dined simultaneously."

"This morning, this evening. That is close enough," Mr. Darcy said. "The symptoms seem to take hours to appear, thus the simplest thing is not to eat the food. We cannot be certain it is not poisoned."

"You want me to tell my guests that they cannot eat food so lovingly prepared?" Miss Bingley demanded. "This is ridiculous."

Elizabeth realized she still held her fork, though most of the duck had fallen off it back onto her plate. She put the fork down. With worry, she thought of the soup, suddenly relieved that Mr. Collins had ordered hers to be cleared before she could eat much. Had it tasted odd? Mr. Collins had devoured his bowl and eaten at least half of the large helping of duck ragout he'd served himself. On her other side, Captain Carter set aside his fork. He stared worriedly down at his plate, which held some of the salmon Elizabeth had hoped to ask him to serve her when the talk at the table officially turned.

"And why should we listen to this man?" Miss Bingley continued, her voice high and aggrieved. "He is no one. The son of a steward." She glared down her nose at Mr. Wickham.

Mr. Bingley turned to Mr. Darcy. "I confess to some confusion, Darcy. I thought you and Mr. Wickham were not on good terms."

That was a tactful way of putting it. Elizabeth had been certain they hated each other.

Colonel Forster waved that off. "It was a ruse to frame Mr. Wickham as a victim. Once we had reason to suspect that this unit might be in danger, we brought in Mr. Wickham. We wanted him to be considered someone who could be easily suborned to act against those in authority."

"A ruse?" Elizabeth blurted, hardly aware she spoke until heads turned to regard her. Meeting her gaze, Mr. Wickham offered an apologetic grimace.

How readily she had believed this so-called ruse. She'd lapped up every awful detail of Mr. Darcy's ill treatment, happy to have her impression of him confirmed after the way he'd behaved at their first meeting, a local assembly, insulting her and refusing to dance with anyone outside his own party. He'd been the very image of landed arrogance.

Had that been part of the ruse? But why so blatantly insult her as he had?

She sought back in her memories of Mr. Darcy, attempting to find other instances of bad behavior. Ones after that first meeting at the assembly, when he'd cemented local opinion against him.

By her recollection, he'd been aloof, but never again boorish.

"So what, then?" Mr. Hurst asked, looking from Wickham to Darcy to Colonel Forster. "Mr. Wickham here is some sort of spy?"

"I can assure you that Lady Catherine does not hold with spies at dinner," Mr. Collins stated.

Elizabeth wanted to kick him under the table, but she would not care to be that familiar with him, and it likely would not help. On his other side, Charlotte began speaking to him in a low voice.

"I don't know as I would go so far as to label myself a spy," Mr. Wickham said weakly. "It was merely our hope that the poisoner would seek out my assistance and be caught."

Elizabeth's father rose to his feet. "But he did not and was not. Mrs. Bennet, Jane, Elizabeth, Mary, Kitty, Lydia, you will not eat another bite of food."

Elizabeth tried to remember the last time her father had put so much authority in his voice. She couldn't.

"But Papa," Lydia whined. "We're at a ball."

"And it may be your last if you do not obey me, young lady," Mr. Bennet said firmly. "Furthermore, if I see any of you consume anything more, I will remove us all directly."

"Really, Bennet," Sir William said with a slightly forced sounding chuckle. "You're making a great deal of fuss about possibly poisoned food. I've read the papers. The poison was always added to one dish before, shared between all." His gesture swept the table. "I see no porridge here."

Lady Lucas nodded along with her husband's reasoning. Taking in the faces about the table, Elizabeth realized that most of the guests agreed with Sir William. She conceded he had a fair point, for she had read about the other incidents as well, but why take the risk?

"Precisely," Miss Bingley said contemptuously. "Possibly poisoned porridge served to soldiers this morning has absolutely nothing to do with a ball held here this evening. I will not have my careful preparations ruined because of a wild guess."

Mr. Hurst raised his glass to that, Mrs. Hurst appearing pleased, and Mr. Bingley thoughtful.

"Be that as it may," Colonel Forster said into the ensuing silence. "My officers and I will be departing. It is our duty to investigate this incident."

"Our carriages won't come for hours," Captain Carter said.

"We will walk. It is two miles, and the moon is out." Colonel Forster looked from officer to officer. "You are members of the militia, after all. The men do five miles a day, at a run."

Mr. Wickham started to stand but was pushed back into his chair by Mr. Darcy who said, "Not Wickham."

Colonel Forster turned to him. "I agree. Wickham, you do not look fit for duty."

"But sir—"

"My decision is final," Colonel Forster interrupted. To Mr. Darcy, he added, "I will be writing to Colonel Fitzwilliam immediately." A sweeping glance took in his officers. "The rest of you, with me." Colonel Forster pivoted and marched from the room.

The officers, including Captain Carter, followed, some with obvious reluctance. Elizabeth could hear Kitty and Lydia lamenting their departure.

From his place at the end of the table, Mr. Bingley looked about at the empty chairs. His gaze settled on Mr. Wickham. "Mr. Darcy, do you think you could arrange for Mr. Wickham to be taken to, ah, someplace he will be more comfortable? His presence is putting a pall over the gathering."

"Somewhere away from here," Miss Bingley added, her eyes as wide as if Mr. Wickham threatened her with a pistol rather than his presence in her home. "He is not even fit for one of the servants' rooms. He is covered in dirt and he is obviously ill."

Mr. Darcy cast her a look of contempt before scanning the room. His gaze settled on a footman. "Jackson, have Stevens pack my belongings."

Elizabeth realized her eyes were now as wide as Miss Bingley's as she struggled to contain her shock that Mr. Darcy knew the name of a footman.

Mr. Darcy turned to another footman. "Harry, see that my coachman and grooms prepare my carriage and pack their belongings as well."

"You are leaving?" Miss Bingley gasped.

"Obviously."

"Where are you going at this time of night?" Mr. Bingley sounded angry.

His gaze flicking between Miss Bingley and Mr. Bingley, Mr. Darcy said, "Somewhere Mr. Wickham will be welcomed."

"You are both welcome at Longbourn," Mr. Bennet said.

Elizabeth's mother shook her head. "But where? We do not have room."

Mr. Bennet frowned at her. "You will move to my room, Jane and Elizabeth will move to your room, and Mr. Darcy and Mr. Wickham will share Jane and Elizabeth's room."

Pulling away from his quiet conversation with Charlotte, Mr. Collins stood. "I will not stay in a house with a man who is obviously ill and deranged, and a spy to boot. And who knows? What he has could be infectious."

That started a commotion with many people rising from their chairs. Those near Mr. Wickham and Mr. Darcy backed away. Mr. Bingley called for order, but that command made little impact on the chaos of the room.

Where he sat with Mr. Darcy hovering over him, Mr. Wickham squeezed his eyes closed, looking quite ill indeed.

Elizabeth's father moved around the table, pressing through agitated partygoers until he reached Mr. Darcy. Though he spoke quietly, Elizabeth made out, "I have a carriage and a rented vehicle, but they will not return for some time."

"If I may, I will take Wickham to Longbourn in my carriage," Mr. Darcy said. "We can accommodate two others. Perhaps someone with the authority to make arrangements about the rooms?" His gaze found Elizabeth.

Did his eyes hold…hope? He wished for her to accompany them?

But Elizabeth's father was watching her mother, who still sat, fanning herself and expounding on the woes of the evening to all those near her. "Jane is the best choice for that, and her mother can go to chaperone her," Mr. Bennet said. "I will remain to ensure my younger daughters obey me in not eating anything more."

"Will it be possible to cancel your rented carriage?" Darcy asked.

"No," Mr. Bennet said.

"Then I will ask Miss Bennet to instruct your staff not to turn out your carriage. Mine will return with the rented vehicle for the remainder of your party."

"Please, everyone, do sit down," Mr. Bingley called over the ruckus.

Mr. Collins, who had been standing at his place before the table, left Elizabeth's side to lumber up to Mr. Bennet and Mr. Darcy, seeming not to care that doing so brought him near Mr. Wickham, whom he'd declared contagious. "I repeat, I will not remain in a house with that individual. As future master of Longbourn I—"

"As present master of Longbourn, I will see that your luggage is packed for you," Elizabeth's father snapped.

"And I will have it returned here and see that a carriage is made available to you, sir," Mr. Darcy added.

Mr. Bennet cast him a pleased look.

Mr. Collins studied Mr. Darcy for a moment, likely weighing his claim to Longbourn against aggravating the nephew of his vaunted patroness Lady Catherine de Bourgh, as Elizabeth knew Mr. Darcy to be. Finally, Mr. Collins bowed. "Very well. I thank you, sir." To Elizabeth's sorrow, he then returned to his seat between her and Charlotte.

"Will everyone sit down?" Miss Bingley cried in a tone a hairsbreadth from a shriek. Everyone turned to look at her except Elizabeth's father, who moved around the table to collect Jane while Miss Bingley continued, "The food here is not poisoned, that man is not contagious and is being removed, and we are all going to continue to have a lovely evening."

People began retaking their seats, conversation dropping to a quieter murmur once more. Mr. Darcy helped Mr. Wickham to his feet, bracing him as he swayed. Jane and Mr. Bennet reached Mrs. Bennet and began speaking to her softly.

"Send Elizabeth." Mrs. Bennet's angry hiss carried across the now quieter room. "Jane and I must remain until Mr. Bingley proposes."

Heat surged into Elizabeth's cheeks.

"That is certainly not taking place this evening," Miss Bingley snapped. By her expression and the look she exchanged with her sister, it would not be taking place at any time, if they had a say in the matter.

Mr. Bingley looked down at his plate, his ears scarlet.

Jane dipped her head as well, but not before Elizabeth noted the mortification on her face. Farther down the table, someone tittered. Elizabeth suspected her youngest sister.

"Come," Mr. Bennet ordered, the word clipped, and helped his wife to her feet.

Along with Mr. Darcy and Mr. Wickham, Jane and Mrs. Bennet left the room. His expression set, Mr. Bennet returned to his place. Elizabeth could tell by the aggrieved look Mr. Bingley cast him that he wished her father had departed as well.

"This duck is delicious, even a bit cold," Mr. Hurst declared loudly. "Always a favorite of mine." He hoisted his wine glass as the few stragglers retook their seats. "Here's to Caroline and a fine party the likes of which we will not soon forget."

That got a smattering of laughter and Mr. Bingley's shoulders returned to a more normal angle. Elizabeth lifted her glass along with the others but, exchanging a look with Charlotte across Mr. Collins, did not drink. She noted her friend did not either.

As the gathering settled back into a semblance of normalcy, Elizabeth wished she had gone with the first group, even if sharing a seat with her mother and Jane would be a squeeze. An evening observing the interactions between Mr. Darcy and Mr. Wickham would have been much more interesting than an evening sitting here not being allowed to eat.

Mr. Collins was almost too busy eating to talk, not that she welcomed his conversation. Charlotte, not eating and sitting on his other side, caught the small amount of his attention that wasn't on food. Even so, Elizabeth decided the empty chair left by Captain Carter was a boon. She would much rather listen to the opinions around the table, especially as Mrs. Hurst left her place to speak with her sister.

"Caroline, you must do something for the guests who are not eating." Mrs. Hurst's low words barely reached Elizabeth's ears.

"If they choose not to eat, let them go hungry," Miss Bingley responded. "I doubt they would trust anything I offer, so why make the effort?"

"I can arrange for safe food."

"The food is safe," Miss Bingley snapped back and shoved a forkful of salmon into her mouth.

The look Mrs. Hurst cast at her younger sister crackled with so much annoyance that Elizabeth's eyebrows rose. Mrs. Hurst closed her eyes for a moment as if seeking fortitude, then opened them to say, "I can arrange for food that people will trust enough to eat."

Miss Bingley pursed her lips, then muttered, "And what would that be?"

"Boiled eggs served in their shells."

"If you must," Miss Bingley said on a sigh of annoyance.

Mrs. Hurst left.

Elizabeth turned from watching her depart to find Mr. Hurst's gaze on her. "I see you have not touched your duck." He gestured to her plate with his fork. "It is very good."

"I prefer the salmon," Lady Lucas said, the two apparently deeming the occasion informal enough now to speak across the table. "But the duck this evening was so excellent I ate more than usual, I admit. I must get the recipe for my cook."

Elizabeth looked down at her plate, concealing her amusement at that statement. Charlotte did much of the cooking at Lucas Lodge, with the assistance of several of the maids.

Mr. Hurst nodded. "I was impressed with Bingley's resourcefulness in procuring salmon so late in the season, but not enough so to forgo my duck. That salmon was quite the surprise, I can tell you. Normally, the ragout is Bingley's favorite as well. Caroline was rather put out that he threw off her plans, but Louisa went down and reordered the kitchen and put all to rights."

"Oh, but salmon is such a treat, how can Miss Bingley be angry?" Lady Lucas protested, then lowered her voice to add, "And I hear salmon is so very expensive in London."

Mr. Hurst chuckled at that. "So Louisa is always telling me, but we serve it regularly while in town. I insist. What is wealth for, after all, if not to enjoy life?"

Based on what Elizabeth knew of him, apparently wealth was for gambling, not only expensive victuals, but Elizabeth would never voice that observation.

"Oh, I could not agree more," Lady Lucas replied, and they fell into a discussion recounting the most delectable meals they'd had. Hungry as she was, Elizabeth attempted not to listen, her mouth watering.

About half an hour later, eggs appeared. Charlotte took one, as did Elizabeth. Kitty and Lydia each took two, and complained loudly about eating them. In addition, unopened bottles of wine were set on the table and fresh glasses brought. Elizabeth noticed her father drank a glass but refrained from mimicking him. With only a few spoonfuls of soup and a single egg in her stomach, she did not fancy the lightheadedness wine would bring. So she remained in her seat, dreaming of what she might find to eat when she returned to Longbourn and wishing for the ball to be over.

Chapter Seven

Leaving Wickham slumped and asleep in his carriage, Darcy followed a nearly hysterical Mrs. Bennet and a silent Miss Bennet from the carriage when they reached Longbourn. Darcy longed for Miss Elizabeth's presence instead. Her steady wit would be a salve to his fears, whereas Mrs. Bennet's keening grated and he had no notion what to expect from Miss Bennet.

They entered to the sight of two footmen and a maid, all obviously coming to see who had arrived and why. Darcy studied them, trying to decide how best to frame his requests without sounding as if he thought he were the master of the household. Looking past them through the open door, one of the footmen made to slip out to assist Darcy's driver until grooms could be summoned.

Miss Bennet stayed him with, "Peter, Mr. Wickham is asleep in the carriage. He is not to be disturbed. We will fetch him in momentarily."

The footman dipped his head and left.

"Oh, this is terrible," Mrs. Bennet moaned, flapping a much-abused handkerchief. "This was to be the most wonderful of evenings. How could this happen? My poor, sweet Jane. Oh, my dear—"

"Sally," Miss Bennet said to the maid, speaking over her mother. "Please take Mama up and help her to move what she requires into my father's chambers. Elizabeth and I will be using her room."

Nodding, the maid wrapped an arm about the weeping matron and urged her up the steps.

Miss Bennet started to work off a glove as she turned to the final footman. "Robert, find Missy and go to Mr. Collins' room to pack his cases, which I would like brought down. Send me Mrs. Hill and Mathew while you're about it."

"Yes, miss." The footman hurried away.

Miss Bennet then turned to Mr. Darcy. "It seems to me that my father and sisters will all fit in your lovely carriage, Mr. Darcy, the use of which it was very kind of you to offer. I am certain Mary, Kitty, and Lydia can share a seat. I will have the rented carriage sent back with Mr. Collins' luggage and put at his disposal for the remainder of the night."

"I believe you are correct, Miss Bennet," he replied, bemused. He had not thought her the silly sort, but he had not expected such efficient practicality.

"With Mr. Collins' departure, I am able to offer you your own accommodations. Would you prefer the larger or smaller room?"

"The smaller, and there is no urgency. I will remain with Wickham until I am satisfied he will be well."

She nodded, her blue eyes calm and serious, not a hint of hysteria about her, though she must understand that he feared for Wickham's life. As Darcy could not credit her calm to a lack of feeling, knowing her to be quite kindhearted, he could only attribute it to impressive composure.

Miss Bennet turned as the sound of footfalls announced a matronly woman and a footman coming down the hall and said, "Mrs. Hill, you recall Mr. Darcy?"

If the housekeeper felt any surprise at finding the two of them in the entrance hall, she was too polite to show it, merely replying, "To be certain I do, miss."

"He and Mr. Wickham will be staying for the night, perhaps longer. Mr. Collins' possessions are being removed and Mr. Darcy will take the guest room, but our priority is to ready my and Elizabeth's room for Mr. Wickham. He is indisposed and waits in the carriage. My father and sisters will be collected once Mr. Wickham is brought inside."

Mrs. Hill nodded. "Yes, miss."

"I will come collect my and Elizabeth's possessions after I see Mr. Darcy settled in the parlor." Turning to him she added, "Mr. Darcy, do you require anything?"

"I may require assistance with Mr. Wickham."

"I suspect you will," Miss Bennet said before turning back to the housekeeper. "That will be all, Mrs. Hill."

"Yes, miss." Mrs. Hill dipped a curtsy and retreated back down the hall.

Darcy eyed Miss Bennet with respect. She had obviously felt no need to add that the arrangements were at her father's orders. Nor had the housekeeper sought such reassurance from her. That spoke well of both.

To the footman, Miss Bennet said, "Mathew, please collect Mr. Darcy's outerwear and then return. He may require assistance bringing in Mr. Wickham, and the fire in the front parlor should be stoked."

"Yes, miss."

Turning her calm smile on Darcy, she continued, "If you do not mind a few minutes alone in a dark parlor, I believe I should go check on my mother's progress and assist Mrs. Hill."

"I do not mind in the slightest," Darcy replied, still off kilter after Wickham's appearance, the chaos that had sparked, and now Miss Bennet's transformation from quiet to commanding. Though, he reflected, she still spoke softly, just with the assurance that her decisions were correct and that her requests would be carried out.

She gestured to the parlor in question, curtsied, and left him to hand off his outerwear to Mathew.

Darcy went into the parlor but did not sit, choosing instead to watch his carriage out the window on the chance that Wickham might wake and disembark. He fervently wished for that, in fact, for his friend's pallor and shallow breathing alarmed him. So much so, he would have assured the staff they need make up no room for him at all, for he foresaw a long night of sitting by Wickham's bedside.

Not that the staff would go against Miss Bennet's orders on his say, Darcy mused. They were obviously hers to command. Based on what he'd heard of Bingley's propensity to fall in and out of love, and what he'd seen of the way the man bowed to the wishes of his sisters, he didn't deserve a woman like Miss Bennet.

Darcy grimaced. Bingley. That was a bit of a mess. Though not the brightest individual Darcy had come across, Bingley would surely sort out that Darcy had befriended him at his uncle's home, who was the Earl of Matlock, specifically for the purpose of being invited to Hertfordshire.

Mathew returned then and they gathered Wickham from the carriage. He managed to walk, aided by Darcy's support with Mathew opening doors, but his white face and glazed look worried Darcy. They got him into the parlor and a chair, where he promptly closed his eyes and slumped back into sleep.

After hovering over him for a moment and covering him with the blanket Mathew offered, Darcy returned to the window. While Mathew stoked the fire, Darcy watched his carriage depart and reflected that if Wickham died, it would be Richard's fault.

Wickham's presence was entirely the doing of Darcy's cousin, Colonel Richard Fitzwilliam, and his elaborate plan. So elaborate, in fact, that Darcy had not believed it would work. He'd thought the complexity of the plan a symptom of Richard's obsession.

Nearly a year ago, Darcy's cousins Colonel Newcomb and Lady Elinor, Richard's sister, had been murdered by a French spy. He'd posed as an English cook and poisoned them, the officers they'd had to dinner, and the remainder of the local militia troop, all with a deadly variety of mushroom. Though the cook had been found dead, there had been two subsequent, though far less effectual, poisonings.

Richard had investigated them rigorously. The only link he'd found was that several of the officers in each troop had fought on the continent and were decorated for their service against the French. Not terribly unusual, as local militias were always looking for men to augment their rosters and some men, when they returned from fulfilling their duty abroad, found they missed military life. The militia was a less dangerous, less rigorous substitute. A means by which to ease back into civilian life, by Darcy's way of thinking.

Still, for three events scattered about England, service on the Continent was a tenuous connection. Even the mode of poisoning had not remained the same, the second two incidents far subtler than the first. Had they stood alone, everyone would have been fooled into believing they were, indeed, instances of food gone sour. But in view of the deadly mushrooms employed by the only apprehended, though deceased, member of the ring of French sympathizers, Richard saw the poisonings for what they were.

So he'd set traps, using his influence as a colonel and the son of an earl to arrange for several militia troops to be packed with men decorated for their service on the Continent. Richard had seen those troops assigned to various obscure towns throughout England. Once the towns were selected, Richard found assorted convoluted ways to get people he trusted as near as possible to those units. Thus, Darcy had been cajoled into befriending Bingley and manipulating him into selecting a country residence near one of Richard's chosen locations. Darcy was easily able to influence Bingley to lease Netherfield Park. It eased Darcy's conscience that the estate really was a good choice. Thus, Darcy was there with the Bingleys and Hursts before the handpicked militia troop had even been dispatched.

In each troop, only the leader, in Meryton's case Colonel Forster, knew the truth of Richard's plan going in. Each had discretion as to who in their troop they told. Insofar as overly convoluted plans went, Richard's seemed fairly sound. Still, Darcy had not expected the plan to work. He'd been mostly convinced that the first poisoning was an accident and the subsequent two simply, as Sir William Lucas had suggested, bad food.

And then the anonymous letter had arrived and Richard had involved Wickham, much to Darcy's dismay.

Somewhere above, Mrs. Bennet's voice rose in complaint, but was soon soothed, allowing Darcy to return to his thoughts.

It was not unusual for members of Darcy's family to seek assistance from Wickham. For most of his life, Wickham had been a favorite of Darcy's father and uncles, filling whatever roles they required. He was educated and charming enough to add enjoyment to any gathering. Trustworthy and astute enough to handle matters of delicacy. The son of Darcy's late father's steward, Wickham had always been happy to help wherever Mr. George Darcy, Sir Lewis, or the earl required. It made sense that Richard would call on Wickham to be the final piece of the trap.

And Wickham had readily agreed to come, much to Darcy's aggravation. Posing as a disgruntled militia member was not what Wickham should be doing with his days. Darcy had been so pleased, so proud, when Wickham was ordained. His true passion was the church, and he'd fulfilled that dream and been granted the living in Kympton by Darcy's father. Then George Darcy had felt obligated to take them aside and reveal the truth of Wickham's parentage.

Darcy's friend had been devastated. He'd reverted to his old ways of helping here and there. A shallow, flittering existence that Darcy knew wore on Wickham's soul.

But Wickham said he could not lead a flock, could not be responsible for their souls, when his very name was a lie. When he had no notion of who he truly was. So, he'd hired out the living, and now here he was, trying to help Richard capture a spy and comatose in a chair, struggling for his life.

Darcy looked over his shoulder to find Wickham's condition unchanged and the footman, Mathew, waiting. "Any word on Mr. Wickham's chamber?" Darcy asked.

The footman shook his head. "I am certain it will be ready soon, sir."

Nodding, Darcy turned back to the window, his mind returning to his Bingley problem.

The moment Meryton was selected as the location for one of Richard's traps, largely for the small market town's remote yet centralized location and the availability of Netherfield Park, Darcy had mentioned Bingley's lack of a country estate or experience managing one. Eager for the advancement friendship with Darcy could bring, Bingley had immediately seized on the suggestion that he should look for a manor to lease. It had been nothing to bring him around to Meryton.

Now, Bingley would surely reflect on Darcy's none too subtle suggestions regarding estates and Meryton and come to the realization of Darcy's duplicity. Darcy was not looking forward to the apology he would have to make.

He glanced over his shoulder at Wickham's white countenance again. How long did it take to make up a bed?

"Mr. Darcy, Mr. Wickham's room is ready," Miss Bennet said.

Darcy swiveled the other way to see her framed in the parlor doorway, her hands tightly twined, the first show of agitation he'd seen from her. Her gaze rested on Wickham, worry pulling at her features.

"Mathew, please assist Mr. Darcy in bringing up Mr. Wickham."

They got an even less sensible Wickham up from the chair, the act requiring them both this time, and Miss Bennet led the way up. With little fuss they had Wickham supine atop the coverlet, for Darcy wished to clean him up before settling him under the sheets. Miss Bennet also showed him which room would be his. She'd already had towels, basins, water, soap, and a small selection of victual brought up, including some broth for Wickham.

"I have had his things sent for from the barracks, but I do not know how quickly our man will meet with success," she added as they returned to

Wickham's room, where a chair had been placed beside the bed.

Darcy could not ask for more thoughtful hospitality. "I thank you, Miss Bennet, for your thoroughness and kindness."

"Mr. Wickham acted very bravely this evening and deserves every consideration," she said firmly.

"Thank you," Darcy repeated.

She left him then, closing the door softly behind her.

"Miss," Darcy heard the footman, Mathew, say in a low voice in the hall. "Will Mr. Wickham be well?"

"We must pray so, Mathew," Miss Bennet replied almost too softly to hear.

"What ails him? Only, the staff will worry, miss, and I'm sorry for asking."

"I already explained this to Hill, and you have every right to ask." There was a pause. Then, even quieter, she said, "Members of the militia were poisoned, and there is a chance the food eaten at Netherfield Park this evening was as well. Mr. Wickham, who has eaten some, came to warn us before he collapsed."

"Did you eat the food there, miss?" Mathew asked with clear alarm.

"A bit. I am afraid we all did."

"Then I will pray for you and your family as well, miss."

"Thank you."

Their footfalls moved away in opposite directions, and Darcy set to tending his friend. A short while later, he heard the commotion as the remainder of the family returned. He hoped the rest of their evening had been less eventful but did not leave Wickham's side to inquire. He also hoped that Wickham was wrong about the poison, for it was not only the Bennets, and Darcy, who had eaten at the ball. All of the guests had.

Chapter Eight

Darcy woke in a somewhat exhausted state. The only sleep he'd managed had been seated in the chair beside Wickham's bed, his head lolling at an uncomfortable angle. A long night of praying that Wickham would take each next, shallow breath had left Darcy's head pounding.

It had also given him more than enough time to pen a missive to Richard, detailing all that had occurred. Richard would want Wickham's account as well, but that would need to wait. Darcy refused to even consider that Wickham might decline further and be unable to provide it.

Feeling shaky and weak, more so than tension and lack of sleep could account for, Darcy retreated to the room allotted to him to make his ablutions. He suspected he, too, had consumed some of the poison, though far less than Wickham had. If so, Wickham's warning had likely saved Darcy and many others.

Before descending for breakfast, he quickly reread his letter to Richard. Satisfied, Darcy sealed the missive and took it down to place it on the salver in the entrance hall, where several outgoing letters from the Bennets also waited to be posted. He then entered the breakfast parlor to the sight of Mr. and Mrs. Bennet at the table, aware of an unsettling pang of disappointment and worry at the absence of Miss Elizabeth, for he'd assumed her an early riser.

Mr. and Mrs. Bennet both looked up when Darcy joined them.

He nodded in greeting and asked tentatively, "May I enquire as to how you both feel this morning?" Though his true wish was to ask after all in the household, especially the absent Miss Bennets.

"I woke early, feeling quite ill," Mrs. Bennet replied. "Do you believe it is the poison, Mr. Darcy? Mr. Bennet was ill as well." She cast her husband, who looked hale enough if a touch pale as he folded the paper he'd been reading, a watery-eyed look. "Is this to be it, then? Will Mr. Bennet perish and Mr. Collins be called back to take my home from me? Oh, if only he'd tendered his offer to Elizabeth before the ball, I would not be made to worry."

Mr. Collins had intended to offer for Miss Elizabeth? Darcy worked not to frown at the absurdity of the idea. She was far too intelligent and vivacious for that oaf. "I, too, feel not quite well," Darcy admitted. "Based on when Mr. Wickham consumed the poisoned porridge and when he fell ill, I believe those of us who dined but lightly, and heeded Mr. Wickham's call to eat no more, now suffer the beginnings of our ailment. We can only hope his warning came in time, for dinner had just begun." But Darcy had eaten the soup, as had everyone at the table, so if the soup was poisoned, they all were.

"Oh," Mrs. Bennet spoke with a catch in her throat. "I saw how unwell poor, brave Mr. Wickham looked last night. I pray that is not to be our fate, Mr. Bennet."

"As do I," Mr. Bennet said dryly, his gaze dropping to the paper waiting beside his plate.

That plate, Darcy noted, held only dry toast, and Mr. Bennet's cup only black coffee. That appealed to Darcy as well, the idea of attempting more making him queasy. Mrs. Bennet's plate, in contrast, held slices of meat and sweets. He raised his gaze from it to find she studied him shrewdly.

Catching him looking, she instantly replaced the cunning glint in her eyes with despair. "If this is the mere start of my woes, I do so wish to make calls after breakfast, while I am still up to doing so."

"To see your sister, among others?" Mr. Bennet asked.

"Yes." A look of perfect understanding passed between husband and wife before Mrs. Bennet turned back to Darcy. "Having not been considered an appropriate guest by the Bingleys, Mrs. Phillips will wish for a full report on last evening's events. She will have heard rumors and will be terribly worried about us all." Mrs. Bennet adopted a dismal expression. "Sadly, our carriage is not new. I am always saying that you should replace it, Mr. Bennet, am I not?" Not pausing for an answer she returned her full attention to Darcy. "I fear that in my weakened state, our carriage will not offer a smooth enough journey to permit calls. The jouncing and swaying will be too much while I am so ill with poison."

"That is a shame, my dear," Mr. Bennet murmured, taking up his paper.

Silence settled about them. Darcy reached for a slice of toast from the rack on the table.

"If only we had such a well-appointed carriage as yours, Mr. Darcy, I am certain I could make my calls," Mrs. Bennet said loudly.

Realizing what was required of him and not begrudging Mrs. Bennet the use of his carriage in light of the Bennets' hospitality, Darcy said, "If you would care to employ my carriage, Mrs. Bennet, it is at your disposal for the duration of my stay here." He turned to Mr. Bennet. "It is my hope that Mr. Wickham and I may remain until he is improved? I do not mean to impose, but I do not believe it would be good to move him. He is quite ill."

"You may remain for so long as you feel it is necessary," Mr. Bennet replied.

Speaking over her husband, Mrs. Bennet said, "Why, Mr. Darcy, what a kind offer. It would be so very useful if I could employ your conveyance. In, say, thirty minutes?"

Darcy raised his eyebrows but merely nodded.

Again, before anyone else could speak, Mrs. Bennet turned to one of the waiting footmen and ordered him to see Darcy's carriage readied. She then proceeded to eat very rapidly. Darcy hadn't even finished his coffee when she left, saying she planned to call on several people.

Mr. Bennet looked after her, bemused. "I do not believe she consumed much at Netherfield Park. It seems her endless loquaciousness has some advantage. She was too busy speaking to eat."

Darcy nodded, recalling quite well how Mrs. Bennet's over-loud voice had filled the dining room from the moment they were all seated. Curious, as it worried him not to have seen any of the young ladies yet this morning, he said, "Mrs. Bennet seems very keen to reassure her sister of the wellbeing of this household. May I take that to mean that your daughters *are* well?"

"Mrs. Hill has assured me they are well enough, though Kitty and Lydia are suffering. Not as keenly as Mr. Wickham."

Darcy digested that. He hoped the report was true and not simply Mr. Bennet ignoring the needs of his offspring. "If I may pry, is reassurance the only reason Mrs. Bennet wishes to visit her sister?" After all, a note could have easily been sent, especially if Mrs. Bennet was not feeling well.

Mr. Bennet shook his head. "Gossip is, to be certain, the real reason. By my estimation, the Phillips hire their servants based on their ability to find out what is going on in Meryton. By now, Mrs. Phillips will know all. Also, it is your carriage."

"My carriage?" Mr. Darcy repeated, though he suspected he knew why Mrs. Bennet wished to employ the conveyance.

Mr. Bennet shrugged. "It is newer and more luxurious, with four matched bays, not two unmatched farm horses that sometimes pull a carriage."

"I understand."

"In truth," Mr. Bennet continued, "I am glad she's going. I would like to know what is happening." He looked down at his half-eaten toast and half-drunk coffee. "If you will excuse me, I am not as loquacious as my wife. I believe I will lie down."

"Certainly." Darcy stood along with his host and did not retake his seat when Mr. Bennet left the room. Instead, he asked for a tray and began assembling toast and tea for Wickham, in case he'd woken.

Darcy brought the tray up to find Wickham asleep, his breath shallow but even. Setting the tray aside, Darcy switched out the cool compress on Wickham's brow, wishing he knew something, anything, more to do. He would summon the local apothecary, but he suspected the man, Jones, must be quite busy. Perhaps, if he hunted Jones down, Darcy could learn something useful.

Darcy made his way out to the stable to find, as he'd hoped, that his efficient staff had brought his riding mount even though he had not thought to specifically request the beast along with his possessions. In view of how matters stood, he was pleased with the persona he'd adopted for the journey; that of a somewhat snooty and entitled gentleman. That pretense had him traveling with more members of his staff than he normally would.

Darcy had not wanted to come to Meryton by such guile, or to use a false persona. In fact, such pretense sat very ill with him. But Richard had insisted. He wanted Darcy to have as many allies about him as possible on the chance that there would be a poisoning. It seemed more and more as if Richard had been right to insist on the subterfuge.

Darcy had brought not only his valet Stevens and his coachman, but two grooms, a footman, and five horses. Four for his carriage and one to ride. He knew that to be excessive, but he could afford excess. And Bingley could afford to feed Darcy's servants and horses.

Mr. Bennet, however, Darcy suspected, could not. Or at least, would notice the strain. Locating his grooms, Darcy said, "Ryan, please saddle my horse," before turning to the second. "Roger, I will need you to go into Meryton to buy grain." Darcy pulled out several bills. "While you are there, see what information you can get, be it fact or hyperbole." His groom would be able to speak easily with those Darcy could not. "I am afraid that even though I am going into town, you will need to walk. I will ride."

"Yes, sir," Roger said and accepted the bills.

Darcy's horse was ready in short order, and not long after that he rode into Meryton. There, he was unsurprised to find that the apothecary was out. Apparently, the man had been racing about all through the night, mostly calming what the residents considered to be hysteria, rather than treating true illnesses. Now, no one knew if he was at a private residence or the barracks. On top of being unable to locate Jones, no one Darcy spoke to could tell him of any successful remedies for what ailed Wickham and, presumably, the others who had eaten the poisoned food, Darcy among them.

A brief stop to speak with a harried Colonel Forster found similar information, or lack thereof, except for the worrying and lamentable report that several of the men who'd eaten the porridge, the same Wickham had, were dead. The others were all quite ill, including the cook. The officers Colonel Forster had removed from the ball were less so, though the colonel was gray about the mouth. Darcy also learned that Miss Bennet's efficiency had beaten him to claiming Wickham's possessions, which were on their way to Longbourn.

He returned there, hoping that Roger, or even Mrs. Bennet, had better luck learning something more useful than he had, only to find that his groom had yet to return with the grain and Mrs. Bennet was still out. Leaving his horse to his other groom, Ryan, Darcy slipped inside and up the staircase, eager to check on Wickham. As he climbed, he could hear Miss Elizabeth's voice in the front parlor but nothing to indicate to whom she spoke.

To his profound relief, Darcy found Wickham awake and half the toast eaten.

Wickham turned a face nearly the same color as the sheets to him, but his eyes were blessedly lucid. "Darcy. I'd hoped you were about. Tell me, for I've seen no one. Where am I?"

It spoke of how near to death Wickham had been the evening before that he didn't know, and Darcy swallowed down fear for his friend to say lightly, "We are in Longbourn. The Bennets kindly offered their hospitality."

Wickham's eyebrows rose. "That is kind, considering how you have behaved, and some of the things I have said about you."

"Which I do not deem to have been all that necessary," Darcy said a touch sourly.

Wickham gave him an innocent look. "We agreed, did we not, that you would act the boor and I would besmirch you, in the hope that any malcontent plotting a poisoning would seek me out as an ally."

"We did, but as that part of Richard's plan did not work, I regret it." He had not enjoyed being so high-handed and aloof, nor the insults he'd delivered. Particularly the one he'd issued, unprovoked and unwarranted, to Miss Elizabeth.

"As I said, it is very kind of them to shelter us." Wickham's face pinched. "Are all in the household well?"

"I believe they suffer mild symptoms, perhaps the younger sisters more so than the others, but none are overly ill."

"And you?" Wickham pressed, looking Darcy up and down.

"I admit to feeling slightly…off, I would label it. More tired than I should, and with little appetite. A dull throb in my head. Nothing overly concerning. If I'd made a late night of it, I would not be able to tell that I had not simply over indulged."

"As if you ever do," Wickham said with a weak smile. Tension drained from him, leaving him looking limp. "Thank heaven all here are well."

"In fact, it is thanks to you, and to Mr. Bennet's caution."

Wickham shrugged at that. He closed his eyes for a moment, then opened them to ask, "May I borrow Stevens? I believe I will require help to bathe and dress."

"Bathe and dress?" Darcy shook his head. "You are remaining abed. You are not well."

Wickham chuckled, the sound slightly ragged. "You think I do not know as much?"

"Then bed it is."

"It will do me no good. I am not ill. I am poisoned. And unable to sleep any longer. And bored quite out of my mind. It would do me good, I believe, to sit in quiet company."

Which Darcy supposed Wickham would have with Mrs. Bennet out and the younger sisters unwell, so after a moment's hesitation, Darcy nodded and summoned Stevens.

Wickham did not ask for broader news as Darcy and Stevens helped him get ready, and Darcy didn't offer any. No doubt Wickham would request the state of the troop and the partygoers when he felt up to learning their fates. Nor did Darcy have much news to tell.

Darcy led the way down to the parlor, going first out of fear that Wickham would stumble on the stairs. They entered to find Miss Bennet and Miss Elizabeth, who both greeted them with worried eyes for Wickham. Miss Elizabeth sat on a settee mending a tear in the gown she'd worn the evening before. Miss Bennet was at a table writing in what appeared to be a ledger.

"Mr. Darcy, Mr. Wickham," Miss Elizabeth greeted. "How pleasant to see you both. Do join us. Should I call for tea?"

Darcy glanced at Wickham, who nodded and said, "Tea would be pleasant, thank you, though I do not know if I can do justice to more than plain rolls."

Miss Elizabeth grimaced. "Yes, we have all been feeling a touch delicate today. I am certain Mrs. Hill will have something mild for us."

"If I may beg your pardon, I will join you in a moment," Miss Bennet said and returned to her ledger.

Inexplicably drawn to her, Darcy moved to the chair beside the settee Miss Elizabeth used. He assumed Wickham would follow, but he wandered to the window near Miss Bennet to look out. Hands clasped behind his back, Wickham stood in the weak November sunlight. After requesting tea, Miss Elizabeth watched him with worried eyes.

"Is he well enough to be up?" she asked Darcy in a low voice.

Her concern for Wickham both touched him and evoked a swirl of some dark, nameless worry. How fond of Wickham was Miss Elizabeth? "He insisted."

She pursed her lips, nodded, and returned to her mending.

After a time, Wickham turned from the window to Miss Bennet. "If it is not too presumptuous of me to enquire, Miss Bennet, what are you writing so diligently?"

She looked up with one of her pleasant smiles. The same one, insofar as Darcy could judge, that she offered everyone, be they a servant, family, or

Mr. Bingley. "My father has put me in charge of managing some of our charitable contributions and I am behind in making entries." She gestured to a pile of scraps of paper that rested beside her on the desk.

"Perhaps I can be of assistance?" Wickham asked. "I am keen to find occupation that taxes my mind without similarly burdening my form."

"I have just finished, but you could check my arithmetic."

Wickham bowed. "I would be happy to."

He drew up a chair and soon the two had their heads bent, both capped by light-colored curls, over the ledger.

Realizing he now, before tea arrived, had the perfect opportunity to tender one of what he was beginning to see would be many apologies brought on by Richard's ridiculous plan of subterfuge, Darcy turned to Miss Elizabeth. Awkwardness brought on by guilt and regret rendering his words clipped, he said, "Miss Elizabeth, I am sorry I insulted you at the assembly. Believe me, it had nothing to do with you."

She stared at him for long enough that he had to fight the urge to fidget. "Nothing to do with me? That I was not handsome enough to dance with has nothing to do with me?"

Her even tone and closed expression gave him little by which to gauge the depth of her feelings, so he ventured, "That is the case. It was my intention only to alienate the community. I selected you because you seemed sufficiently popular to do so, and attractive and confident enough not to be hurt by my words." With a wince at his own honesty, he added, "Also, Bingley provided me the opening."

Calm eyes contemplated him. "I recall Colonel Forster saying last night that Mr. Wickham was to be perceived as a victim. Why did that mean that you were forced to alienate the community?"

Darcy gestured in his friend's direction. "We planned for him to tell stories about me which would garner sympathy because I was so obnoxious. The deception was also meant to suggest that he, how shall I say it, was not in sympathy with those who are in power in England." Recalling her concern for Wickham moments ago, Darcy had never so regrated agreeing to Richard's plan.

She shook her head. "You are creating more questions than answers."

"Ask them." He very much wanted to put things right between them. It cut him every time disdain filled her lovely eyes when she looked at him. She did not regard him with such right now, which he hoped meant she was receptive to his words.

"The first question I have is, are you in power in England?"

"Only by dint of being wealthy and having the ear of a peer, who is my cousin. But I am aware that is considerable power compared to the average man."

She nodded, her expression contemplative.

"What else?" he urged.

"Why did you want Mr. Wickham to be sympathized with?"

"We wanted to create the appearance that he had a legitimate grievance. Last year, there were three possible poisonings among the militia." He paused, suddenly aware that they had not caught the poisoner. How much should he reveal of Richard's plan? Would the ploy of putting together groups of men known to have fought well against France work a second time? "Steps were taken to narrow down which militias might be targeted. We have similarly compelling targets set up in several towns, with other allies in place to monitor them and offer assistance. Wickham could have been called to any one of them."

"Then why was he called here?" she asked, frowning.

"An anonymous letter was sent to the Earl of Matlock, claiming that a poisoning would take place in Meryton."

Her eyes flew wide. "And the porridge was still left unattended?"

Darcy shook his head. "It was left attended. Rather, the cook was meant to be feigning sleep. He was part of the trap." Which had been Colonel Forster's addition to the plan.

Miss Elizabeth grew thoughtful again. "I read about the other poisonings in the paper." With an apologetic shrug she added, "I was in agreement with the opinion that at least the second two were accidental. They seemed too ineffectual to be true attempts to poison anyone."

"Two could have been due to bad food. We were not certain." Rather, Darcy and many others were not. Richard was certain a conspiracy was afoot and had taken his sister's life. "The first was definitely poison, and the poisoner was identified. Unfortunately, he killed himself before he could be questioned."

"Yes. I read that." She looked down at her mending, though she no longer stitched as they spoke. "I am still uncertain why you are involved. You are not in the regulars or the militia, I assume."

"I am not. We felt it would be too suspicious to have extra officers happen to be visiting friends near our traps." Darcy shrugged, trying to find words that didn't sound boastful as he continued, "I am not an officer or trained in any way, but I can bring considerable resources to bear when required."

That earned him another thoughtful look, but at least she still seemed receptive to his explanation. "So Mr. Wickham was waiting, as it were, for a reason to suspect one of your potential traps over the others?"

Darcy nodded. "Yes."

"And once one of the traps was sprung, he was sent in."

"Yes."

"But if you expected him, why did you seem angry when he arrived? And he seemed…ashamed? Guilty?" She cocked her head to the side, awaiting Darcy's answer with interest.

Recalling that day on the street in Meryton, Darcy was impressed with Miss Elizabeth's powers of observation. "I was angry because Wickham was meant to arrive several days earlier. He managed to convey to me later that he had a bad cold."

"A cold?"

"Yes. He lost his voice and was coughing constantly. There was no way for him to get in touch with me secretly, since my mail was put on a very public table at Netherfield Park."

"I wasn't very sick," Mr. Wickham said where he sat before Miss Bennet's ledger. "But I did not feel up to charming people in that state."

"And now you have been poisoned," Miss Bennet said, the expression she turned on Wickham sympathetic. "How awful to be ill twice in so short a time. Especially when what you were doing sounds dangerous."

Darcy hadn't realized they listened, but he turned to Miss Bennet and nodded. "It is not so dangerous a thing for me to be here ready to offer what assistance I can, and members of the militia agreed to put themselves in harm's way when they joined." He directed his next words to Wickham, some of the fear he'd felt throughout a night of watching his friend struggle not to succumb to poison leaking into his tone. "But you are a civilian, not trained for deception in any way, and it was wrong of Richard to involve you."

Wickham shrugged. "I had no other occupation and I do have a way with people, and catching whoever is behind these poisonings is important. To England and to your family."

Darcy had more to say to that but, acutely aware of the Miss Bennets watching them, simply frowned and pointed out, "But we did not catch the poisoner and now he knows that you are no friend to him."

"He obviously never thought I was," Wickham said lightly.

Miss Bennet turned her calm smile on him. "What you did was very brave. You saved lives."

Wickham flushed slightly, a splash of color in his overly pale cheeks. "I only did what was right." He raised a trembling hand to scrub a finger across the bridge of his nose, obviously embarrassed by her praise.

The maids chose that moment to arrive with the tea. Wickham and Miss Bennet joined them around the low table at the center of the parlor, Miss Bennet serving, and conversation shifted to less strenuous topics. Darcy watched Wickham, ready to remove him if he showed too much fatigue. He wasn't so preoccupied with that so as not to notice, however, that Miss Bennet cast Wickham several long, considering looks.

Chapter Nine

While Jane served tea with her usual calm competence, Elizabeth contemplated Mr. Darcy's apology. It was prettily and thoroughly done, but she was still angry. It occurred to her she may be less forgiving than usual because she did not feel entirely well, though certainly far better than Mr. Wickham must. Could she blame her lack of forgiveness on that, or was there more to her ire? Mr. Darcy had, after all, insulted her within her hearing, and before an entire assembly. How could he imagine she would not be troubled by that?

Yes, it was a compliment, the way he phrased his remorse, saying that he could tell she had the poise and confidence to endure his set down. But that did not take away from the pique and shame she'd endured. Would she feel better if she required Mr. Darcy to repeat his apology? Before her mother, for one, and perhaps before Lady Lucas.

Thoughts of her mother brought her gaze to the parlor doorway as she absently accepted a cup of tea from Jane. Mr. Wickham was obviously quite unwell. Elizabeth wondered that Mr. Darcy had supported him coming down to the parlor at all. Mr. Wickham would not be able to endure Mrs. Bennet. Elizabeth must make certain he was removed the moment her mother returned.

"Thank you for checking my arithmetic," Jane said to Mr. Wickham, and Elizabeth endeavored to rein in her wayward thoughts so she might participate in conversation.

"You must have known it required no checking." The smile he gave her was not the overly charming one he'd employed since arriving in Meryton, but rather less showy and, to Elizabeth's eye, more sincere.

"Jane likely wished to show off her efforts," Elizabeth said by way of teasing her sister.

"Well..." Jane flushed. "Perhaps a bit. No one ever takes an interest but you, Lizzy. Even Papa does not. So long as I do not overspend, he is indifferent to where I allocate the funds."

"Only because he has the utmost confidence in your choices," Elizabeth said quickly.

"Where do you focus your endeavors, Miss Bennet?" Mr. Darcy asked politely before taking a sip of tea.

Her expression warming, Jane launched into a softly spoken, but no less passionate for that, explanation to which both men seemed to listen with sincere interest.

Elizabeth looked from Mr. Darcy to Mr. Wickham and back, aware of an aggravation that could not entirely be explained away by her fatigue and overall lack of feeling well, which she knew Jane suffered and suspected Mr. Darcy did as well. Perhaps she was angry with Mr. Darcy, and Mr. Wickham for that matter, not because of any insult but because they had fooled her so thoroughly.

So well, in truth, that a part of her still did not believe they were friends. But the rapport between Mr. Wickham and Mr. Darcy supported their claim, and the deception had been undertaken for a laudable cause. Elizabeth would simply have to forgive them, she supposed, but it would take her a while to readjust her opinions of these two men.

And to overcome the sting of being so easily duped.

A knock sounded and she swiveled to look out the large front window. She had been so wrapped in her thoughts so as not to notice the arrival of a carriage. Without, she saw the Lucases' conveyance depart. A moment later, Charlotte was shown in. Elizabeth did not miss the quick, assessing look Mr. Darcy gave Mr. Wickham as both men rose in greeting. She, too, wondered whether Mr. Wickham seemed to be growing too tired for more company.

But Charlotte was an easy companion and Mr. Wickham appeared no more shaky or pale than when he'd first come down, so Elizabeth pressed that worry aside to greet her friend. Once they were all seated again and Charlotte was served tea, Elizabeth asked, "Why did you come by carriage?" Generally, she and Charlotte walked when visiting one another.

Worry in her eyes, Charlotte replied, "I was returning containers to Miss Bingley. When I left, Mother and Father were not feeling well. They insist they simply overindulged, but I want the carriage there should they require it."

"Returning containers?" Mr. Wickham repeated sharply. "Of…food?"

"Empty of food now." Charlotte sighed, shaking her head. She, too, looked paler than usual, and the tightness about her eyes could as easily be from pain as worry. "I went home in the first carriage with my father and Maria, while John, Arthur, and my mother returned later. Miss Bingley, apparently, was quite distraught about the amount of food that remained." Charlotte looked from face to face in open fear. "My mother persuaded Miss Bingley to give her the leftovers."

"And they were all eaten?" Mr. Wickham exchanged a worried look with Mr. Darcy.

"I am afraid so," Charlotte said quietly. "I argued against it, but Mother and Father continued the celebratory atmosphere into the night. There was so much food, they even shared some with the servants." In her lap, her fingers twisted tight. "I do not feel entirely myself this morning. At Netherfield, I spoke only to a few members of the staff. They said the family was still abed." Pleadingly, Charlotte said, "Please tell me that my lack of wellness is simply my mind fooling me."

Elizabeth exchanged a look with her sister. As gently as she could, she said, "Jane and I do not feel well, and Mary, Kitty, and Lydia are all abed they feel so poorly."

"Oh." Charlotte squeezed her eyes closed for a moment.

"Why would your parents take such a risk?" Mr. Darcy asked, his expression incredulous.

Charlotte opened her eyes. "They have never fully recovered from the early days of their marriage, when they were shopkeepers and every penny had to be saved to grow my father's business."

"But so far, only you and your parents are unwell?" Mr. Darcy asked with an intensity that surprised Elizabeth.

Charlotte nodded. "When I left, that was the case, but Maria, John, and Arthur were not yet awake when I went to Netherfield Park. I admit, I called there earlier than is polite, seeking information. I could wait and wonder no longer."

"And what time was the additional food consumed?" Mr. Wickham asked, as intent as Mr. Darcy.

"Several hours past midnight."

Elizabeth could practically see the calculations being done in both men's heads.

Footfalls sounded on the staircase and Elizabeth turned to see her younger sisters, none looking fully well, come down. They piled into the parlor. Mary, who preferred eating over speaking when at a formal dinner, looked nearly as unwell as Mr. Wickham.

"Ugh," Lydia said, throwing herself into a chair as everyone retook their seats after greetings were given. "I drank far too much wine. I feel terrible."

Out of the corner of her eye, Elizabeth saw Mr. Wickham and Mr. Darcy exchange worried looks.

"Then you do not believe it to be the food?" Charlotte asked hopefully. She looked about. "Everyone did drink more than they typically might. Fresh bottles of wine and Mrs. Hurst's boiled eggs were all that were deemed safe by many."

"All I know is that I feel awful." Despite her words, Lydia turned a coquettish smile on Mr. Wickham. "Your silliness about poison certainly made for an exciting evening, and more of a ruckus than a party, what with all the imbibing."

"You really did interrupt everything," Kitty added more sullenly, rubbing her temples.

"But I just could not endure anyone else dancing with such lovely ladies when I wasn't there," Mr. Wickham claimed.

Lydia giggled. "You do not look fit to dance with anyone."

"I do not feel well," Mary muttered. Rising from the chair she'd claimed, she hurried back out of the room.

Charlotte looked after her in worry. "I had best return home. I—I want to see how everyone is faring."

They all stood yet again, the men bowing. Impulsively, Elizabeth embraced Charlotte, who was very pale and anxious. As Jane stepped forward to do the same, a movement caught Elizabeth's eye.

Mr. Darcy made a strange, subtle gesture, to which Mr. Wickham nodded slightly and gestured back. Their gazes met and understanding passed between them. Elizabeth walked Charlotte out, wondering what had been communicated.

When she reentered the room, Mr. Darcy said, "Miss Elizabeth, I feel the need to stretch my legs. It is my understanding that you are the precise person to apply to. Will you walk with me?"

Elizabeth raised her eyebrows at that. How convoluted the man was. Still, she nodded. It would soothe her to be out of doors.

"They abandon me," Mr. Wickham said dramatically. "Anyone can see I am not up to a walk. My only solace will be if the remainder of you lovely young ladies will keep me company."

Lydia and Jane both offered smiles and assurance they would stay. Kitty merely muttered, "I am not walking anywhere," and sank back in her chair, eyes closed.

Mr. Darcy turned to Elizabeth. "I will fetch my hat."

She joined him in ascending the staircase, a sudden, odd shyness washing over her. It felt overly intimate to be walking up to the various bedrooms beside this man, whose broad shoulders and height seemed to take up more than his fair share of the stairwell.

She shook off that feeling as she collected her outerwear and soon, they stepped from the house and into the drive. Rather than setting out, Mr. Darcy looked about, appearing hesitant, so Elizabeth ventured, "Did you have a particular destination in mind? Only, you seemed to communicate something to Mr. Wickham, so it occurs to me that you may have a goal for this walk."

Belatedly, she wondered if that goal was simply to spend time with her. A flighty sort of panic bubbled up at that idea. Not the sour dismay she'd felt when she realized that Mr. Collins might propose to her, but something indefinably different.

Mr. Darcy's smile was grateful. "You are observant and yes, I do have a goal. Lucas Lodge. I want you with me because they may not permit me entrance."

"Not permit you entrance?" Despite how he'd behaved, no one in Meryton had denied Mr. Darcy access to their homes, least of all the Lucases.

"By my calculations, if any at Lucas Lodge have been poisoned, they will have grown considerably more ill while Miss Lucas was out. If they are all as unwell as Wickham was yesterday evening, I am afraid of what sort of chaos she may be walking into and how the household will view a visitor. You know them well and will be allowed in regardless."

"Then we should go this way." Elizabeth gestured. "I do not believe we will overtake Charlotte, but we will not be far behind her."

They set out through the crisp November air, Elizabeth's mind awhirl with worry. Mr. Darcy and Mr. Wickham clearly suspected poison. Elizabeth could not deny that she did not feel entirely well, and she had only eaten half a bowl of soup. How much soup would make someone as ill as Mr. Wickham? Had only the soup been poisoned?

"There must have been poison in the soup," she said as they crested a low dale.

"How do you deduce that?" Mr. Darcy asked with genuine interest…if Elizabeth could credit her interpretation of his tone, which she was now uncertain she could after he had fooled her so thoroughly.

"I ate only soup."

"How much?"

"About half of a bowl."

He nodded sharply. "I am pleased it was only half."

"You can thank Mr. Collins. He had my soup cleared away before I could eat more." At the time, Elizabeth had been annoyed.

Mr. Darcy cast her an inscrutable look. "I will thank him when next we meet at Rosings."

Elizabeth fell into her thoughts once more. Curious, she asked, "What were the hand gestures you and Mr. Wickham used? Are they some sort of spy language you learned for this undertaking?"

Mr. Darcy shook his head. "No. They are from when Wickham assisted my uncle, when my aunt was ill. A sort of shorthand we developed."

"Maybe you are wrong about Mr. Wickham's suitability as a spy," Elizabeth suggested lightly, earning a sharp look before they fell once more into silence.

Not long thereafter they descended a low rise, Lucas Lodge spread out before them, still rendered miniscule by distance. There was no sign of Charlotte, who had likely hurried due to her fears.

Elizabeth had fears as well. "Everyone will have eaten the soup. If everyone who was at the ball is ill, what will we do? Meryton has only Mr. Jones."

"Without Mr. Collins to spare me, I ate an entire bowl. I do not feel well, but I am not overly ill. If only the porridge and the soup were poisoned, and people at the ball had but a single serving of soup, it is my hope that we will need to worry only about those who are particularly vulnerable. Those who already suffer an ailment or are aged."

Elizabeth nodded as Lucas Lodge grew larger before them. She was pleased now that the Phillips were not considered good enough company by Miss Bingley. Her aunt loved white soup and always managed to secure a second helping. "But you fear it was not simply the soup," she ventured.

"When I spoke with Colonel Forster this morning, he informed me that several in the militia have died," Mr. Darcy said, his voice quiet even though they were alone on the path. "Wickham came very near to doing so last night as well. I cannot fathom that the poisoner would be so competent in dosing the porridge yet so incompetent in poisoning what the officers were meant to eat, so I can only assume the second dose of poison was divided."

Sorrow went through her at the thought of the dead militia members, and fear. Elizabeth hoped Mr. Darcy was wrong about more than one dish at Netherfield Park being poisoned. After all, the poisoners had been fairly ineffectual on two of their three attempts thus far, or so the papers said. After the first horrible poisoning, only a few people had died during the second, and no one during the third.

Even while she sought the comfort of that thought, Elizabeth increased her pace, Mr. Darcy easily matching her stride.

They arrived at Lucas Lodge and Elizabeth tried to believe that all seemed well despite an odd stillness and already having observed that smoke rose from fewer chimneys than usual. Mr. Darcy knocked, the sound echoing behind the door.

They waited. He pulled out a pocket watch. They waited longer.

He put the watch away and knocked again, louder.

After several long moments, the watch came out again. Shoving it away, he tried the door.

It was locked.

Mr. Darcy turned to Elizabeth. "Do you know where the servants' entrance is?"

"I do, but will that not be locked as well?" Elizabeth asked as she turned to lead the way.

"If it is, we will attempt a window."

Chapter Ten

When Elizabeth and Mr. Darcy reached it, the servants' entrance of Lucas Lodge wasn't locked, but the small room into which they stepped was dark and empty.

"At least you have good fortune today," Elizabeth observed, looking about the dingy little room where servants changed their shoes and left their outerwear. Not much of that was in evidence. "You found us an unlocked door, so we need not attempt entering via a window."

Mr. Darcy shrugged. "I believe it is more a question of good insight than good fortune. If there is illness here, panicked servants might flee, fearing infection even if someone had the wherewithal to reassure them that poison is the culprit. Panicked people do not lock up behind them."

Mr. Darcy's insight about fleeing servants turned out to be tragically correct. The farther into the house they went, the more chaos they found. It seemed the entire family, and many of the staff, were quite ill. Half of the servants who could, ill or not, had left. Some were too sick to leave, and a scant few were well enough to help Charlotte, who was rushing from room to room assisting her kin.

After speaking to Charlotte, Mr. Darcy sent to Longbourn for his servants. He then, to Elizabeth's surprise, gave himself the task of bringing in wood and lighting fireplaces, for the house was quite cold. For her part, Elizabeth set to assisting Charlotte with her ill relations and staff. When Mr. Darcy's people arrived to help, Jane came with them.

"Lydia and Kitty aren't feeling well," she told Elizabeth when they met in the kitchen. "I do not know if that is because of the food or having too much wine, because Mary says she is beginning to feel a bit better. She did not partake of wine."

"Or perhaps they simply did not care to come here," Elizabeth returned.

Jane's eyes widened slightly. Then she frowned.

Elizabeth gestured to a large pot on the stove, being stirred by one of the few remaining maids, a younger girl who only came in the day, and so hadn't had any of the food brought in the night before. "Will you take broth to Maria?"

Jane nodded and took a bowl.

Elizabeth took two others and went to check on Charlotte's youngest siblings and their nanny, who regarded Elizabeth with stricken eyes set in a white face and whispered, "We were given food from the ball as a special treat."

Returning from the distressing scene of very ill children being tended by a woman who could hardly remain on her feet, having done all she could for them at the moment, Elizabeth found Mr. Darcy and her Uncle Phillips coming down the hall. "Uncle Phillips," she greeted, then cast Mr. Darcy a questioning look. Had he summoned the attorney?

"Elizabeth. Mr. Darcy mentioned that you and Jane are here offering assistance. Which room is Sir William's?"

Pivoting, Elizabeth led the way. She pushed open the door and stepped back. Worried they might require something and knowing no servants would answer their call, Elizabeth lingered in the hallway. The gentlemen did not close the door behind them.

"Sir William," Uncle Phillips greeted. "I came as soon as I heard how dire the situation is."

"Why?" Sir William sounded querulous and weak. "I have a will."

"I know, sir, but it is possible, given the situation…that is, it is possible that if Miss Lucas is the only survivor, she will have problems. There will be vultures claiming to be executors of your survivors' estates even if they survive you only by minutes. I wrote your will. It was not designed for this situ—"

"Say no more," Sir William cut in, his voice firmer now. "What do you recommend?"

Elizabeth had never heard him sound like that before. For the first time in her memory, she saw signs of the successful businessman who had earned enough to support his wife and seven children without working anymore. Enough so that his sons expected to live on their income after their father died.

"There are several choices. The quickest is a codicil to your current will stating that none of your family can inherit unless they outlive you by at least thirty days."

"Let's do that." A long sigh sounded. When he spoke again, Sir William's voice was once again weaker. "More can be done later when I'm up to it."

"Ah, yes, sir." There was a pause and Uncle Phillips added, "I can work out something more comprehensive for you to sign later. This will merely be a, ah, well, in case the worst happens."

Grimly, Sir William muttered, "Let us hope it does not."

"Yes, sir."

Mr. Darcy came out then, closing the door softly behind him. He raised his eyebrows and Elizabeth flushed, aware he knew she'd been listening. "I had best bring Sir William some broth," she murmured and hurried away.

She and Jane continued to help anywhere they could, as did Mr. Darcy, though more than once hours passed without Elizabeth seeing him. At one point, she learned from Charlotte that one of the maids who remained knew how to bake bread, and so found the girl and went to the kitchen with her to be what help she could. Mr. Darcy brought them firewood, for which Elizabeth was grateful. She felt weak and a bit lightheaded and didn't fancy carrying in armloads of wood.

Jane discovered that two of the servants who had remained had collapsed in their rooms, both quite ill and nearly insensible, and did her best to help them. Elizabeth went hours without seeing her as well, or Charlotte, who was clearly torn as to which of her family members she should be assisting. Two more times, Elizabeth went to care for the nanny and the youngest children. She did not know if any in the nursery would live. Mr. Jones arrived and went from room to room checking each victim but had little to offer by way of assistance or solace.

Elizabeth was helping Maria get into a clean nightgown when she heard a carriage pull up. Visitors? Mr. Jones returning? The knocker sounded. She heard quick steps go down the hall, too heavy to be Charlotte or Jane. Mr. Darcy's footfalls, she assumed. Everyone else was either too sick or too exhausted to move so quickly. Elizabeth had seen him an hour or so ago and he looked tired, but not as drained as she felt.

She finished helping Maria and went out into the hall to discover what the voices she heard meant. Mr. Darcy was greeting two women and two men. They were dressed as servants, yet better dressed than most servants. Too tired to wonder from whence they'd come or why, Elizabeth moved on to her next task, checking on Lady Lucas. As she neared Lady Lucas's room, Jane stepped out. She placed a finger to her lips, indicating silence, and closed the door softly.

"She's finally asleep," Jane whispered, then led the way down the hall to the stairwell.

Looking up, Mr. Darcy gestured to them. They came down and he introduced the four servants who had arrived, then said, "Miss Bennet, Miss Elizabeth, can you show Hannah and Betsy what needs to be done? I will instruct Archie and Marcus."

"Yes. Certainly," Elizabeth said, wondering where Mr. Darcy had called them in from. Based on the darkness outside the window and the gnawing in her gut, for she'd managed only a single slice of bread since arriving, they could have come all the way from London if he'd sent for them immediately.

Elizabeth and Jane quickly showed the women around, starting with the kitchen and moving up to the sickrooms. Betsy, the younger of the two, ended up staying with the nanny and children, her face grave. Back in the hallway, Hannah said, "I believe our most urgent need is clean nightclothes and linen. Can you show me the facilities to do laundry?"

Elizabeth started to shake her head, uncertain where the Lucases did their wash, even as Jane said, "I can."

They were halfway back down the staircase when the knocker sounded again. "I'll answer," Elizabeth said, moving to do so while Jane took Hannah to the laundry.

Outside, she found Mary, who looked well rested. "Lizzy. Good. I've come to help, and you, Jane, and Mr. Darcy are to go back. Food has been left out for you."

"I thought you were unwell," Elizabeth said. Staring out into the darkness again she felt weak and disoriented. For how many hours had she been in this house, ministering to the ill? Since well before noon, but what time was it now?

"I was, but I spent the day resting once I heard where you and Jane were and why."

"And Kitty and Lydia?"

Mary shrugged. "They say they are very ill but I've heard them giggling together in their room." She lifted her gaze, looking past Elizabeth. "Mr. Darcy. Papa says you, Lizzy, and Jane are to return and eat and rest. I will help Charlotte now."

"I could use a meal, and rest," he admitted.

With as tired as she was, Elizabeth saw no point in arguing. Instead, she said, "Do not overtire yourself," to Mary, by way of acceptance.

Elizabeth and Mr. Darcy introduced Mary to Hannah and Betsy, collected Jane, and returned to Longbourn. They arrived to find the house silent and nearly dark, and Elizabeth realized it must be late indeed. Everyone had retired save Mr. Wickham, who claimed to have slept for most of the day. He looked better but not well.

The four of them sat down to a cold meal and Elizabeth could only give thanks that none of their staff had been brought any food from Netherfield Park. She concentrated on her plate, trying not to think of the servants Jane had found, one of whom had been quite delirious.

"You all look exhausted," Mr. Wickham said. He'd put a roll on his plate and a single slice of cold meat. Elizabeth didn't know if he had already eaten or was still too unwell to consume much. "I feel like an utter cad for lying about all day."

"Nonsense," Jane said immediately. "You are far more ill than any of us. You needed to rest."

Elizabeth nodded, too tired to voice her agreement.

"Miss Bennet is correct," Mr. Darcy said quietly. "You would simply have become another in need of help."

"Perhaps tomorrow, then." Mr. Wickham tore off a small piece of bread. "If I am as much improved tomorrow as today, I will be nearly well." He popped the bit of bread in his mouth.

"Any new news from Forster?" Mr. Darcy asked.

Mr. Wickham's face settled into grave lines. "More of the men have died."

Mr. Darcy stilled in cutting his meat, his eyes closing for a moment. "That is unfortunate."

"We were meant to prevent that outcome," Mr. Wickham murmured, looking down at his plate.

On their behalf, anger sparked in Elizabeth. "It is not your fault that the man Colonel Forster selected to be the sleep-feigning cook proved to be as ineffectual at guarding the food as he'd been ordered to pretend."

"No." Mr. Darcy started cutting his food again. "I suppose it is not."

"We should ask Forster why that man was selected," Wickham said slowly.

"I am certain Richard will," Mr. Darcy replied. "I already wrote to him."

"As did I." Mr. Wickham tore his roll in half. "In great detail. It seemed the least I could do while here resting while you worked. I would imagine Forster wrote to him as well, and to his superiors."

"Wrote to whom?" Elizabeth asked, starting to feel a bit better now that she'd managed to eat a bit.

"Colonel Richard Fitzwilliam." Mr. Darcy clarified. "I mentioned that he is behind the investigation and this plan to lay a trap."

Their earlier conversation returned to Elizabeth at the gentleman's full name. "Yes. I remember now. He is coming here, then?"

Mr. Darcy nodded. "I imagine he will. He will want to investigate this matter personally."

"I wish him godspeed, then," Jane said. "And success in discovering who has done this terrible thing."

Elizabeth frowned, something catching at her mind. Letters to superiors? What thought had nearly come to her?

"Have you any other news, Mr. Wickham?" Jane was asking. "Of the village? Are there other homes as beset as the Lucases'?"

"I have no official news but I do have your mother's gossip, which has apparently been gleaned in large part from your Aunt Phillips."

"I would have it," Mr. Darcy stated.

Elizabeth turned to him, surprised. "You want gossip, Mr. Darcy?"

"Normally, no, but if it is to be all the news we have, then yes. I, too, am concerned for those in the community who attended the ball."

Mr. Wickham obligingly repeated Mrs. Bennet's report on what seemed to Elizabeth to be just about everyone in Meryton. Fortunately, though others were ill, no other household was as hard hit as the Lucases. Elizabeth could not help but glance in the direction of the lodge, worried for Charlotte and her family.

"And at Netherfield Park?" Darcy asked when Mr. Wickham finished.

Jane's head came up, her interest clear.

Mr. Wickham grimaced. "Mrs. Bennet had some especially interesting gossip about that." He slanted a look at Jane. "Apparently, Miss Bingley and Mr. Hurst are both quite unwell, but illness has not stopped Miss Bingley from making demands of her brother's household."

Elizabeth fancied illness would make Miss Bingley more demanding than ever, but she still hoped the other woman, and Mr. Hurst, would be well soon.

"It appears that quite a number of the staff fell ill," Mr. Wickham continued. "When she learned of that, Miss Bingley decreed that everyone who was sick should be let go. She said they had stolen food and that theft would not be tolerated. Mr. Bingley, by all reports, then pointed out that the cook was obliged to taste what he was cooking. Miss Bingley said the chef, and only he, could remain of those who were ill."

Jane gasped, her expression stricken. "But that is awful. I tended some of the staff at the Lucases today. They were in no state to be cast out."

"Surely Mr. Bingley overruled letting them go?" Elizabeth protested.

"No," Mr. Wickham replied gravely. "Mrs. Hurst also supported letting go what she described as 'disloyal servants,' and Mr. Hurst, apparently, is too ill to have any opinion on the matter. Rumor has it, though, that Mr. Bingley did pay them for the full quarter. For those he'd hired in from London, he also paid their way back."

Her expression troubled, Jane looked down at her plate. "I cannot condone casting out the ill."

"Nor can I. A quarter's wages will hardly pay for their care." Mr. Wickham's tone held condemnation. He and Mr. Darcy exchanged a look.

Mr. Darcy nodded.

"It is worse than that." Elizabeth spoke slowly as the thought came to her. "That was reprehensible, even cruel, but even from a selfish standpoint, casting them out was foolish. It truly does seem as if the food was poisoned, which means that someone working at Netherfield Park may be the poisoner. That person would not have eaten the food, one imagines."

Mr. Darcy concluded grimly, "Meaning that not only did the Bingleys cast out ill staff in need of aid, they cast out the members of their household who are less likely to have poisoned them, and kept the ones who are more likely to have done so."

"We do not have any reason to suspect that anyone at Netherfield Park is the poisoner," Mr. Wickham said firmly. "It is more likely someone hiding in Meryton. Even walking, someone could easily poison the porridge early in the day and reach Netherfield Park in time to poison dinner. In fact, they could do so at least ten times over."

Mr. Darcy set down his utensils, his food only half eaten. "True enough."

Elizabeth wondered if he did not have much of an appetite because his stomach still ached, as hers did, or because of the talk of poisoning and cast out servants. She no longer felt much like eating, either.

Chapter Eleven

Colonel Richard Fitzwilliam sat at his desk in the Matlock London house, rereading Darcy's missive, then Colonel Forster's, comparing both with the notes he'd composed on previous readings. Between their reports and Wickham's, Richard had narrowed his suspects down to four men: Pratt, Denny, Chamberlayne, and Carter.

All four had been sighted in or around the camp kitchen on the morning of the day that half of Forster's troop fell ill. Of course, so had most every member of the militia stationed in Meryton. None of the four had become very ill after the ball, but that could also be said for several of the other officers. What made these four stand out was that they had also visited the kitchen at Netherfield Park on the night the poisoned food was served.

Unfortunately, none could be placed near any of the other three poisonings. Moreover, not a one had obvious ties to the French. But Richard knew full well that men could be bought. Especially desperate men. He need only discover if any of the four were such.

He would begin, he decided, with Lieutenant Pratt, for the simple reason that Pratt's family lived the closest, not because Pratt was his prime suspect. That honor belonged jointly to Mr. Denny and Mr. Carter. The first for having been in London. Denny had befriended Wickham on his way back to Meryton, happening to take the same coach as Wickham had, and had then, according to Wickham's report, introduced him as a comrade.

All of which begged the question of if Mr. Denny was simply an amiable fellow who had, truly by chance, happened upon Wickham on his journey to Meryton, or was an astute agent of the French?

Then there was Carter. Not overly suspicious, except that Forster had stood near enough to his men to overhear Carter urging a Miss Lydia Bennet to suggest a tour of the kitchen. If this Captain Carter had wanted to see the kitchen, why not make the suggestion himself? Why badger a young lady to do so if not to allay later suspicion?

Those two anomalies, Denny's visit to London and too-coincidental befriending of Wickham, and Carter's apparent goal of investigating dinner preparations, made them Richard's top two suspects over Pratt and Chamberlayne.

Soft hands settled on Richard's shoulders and he tipped his head back to smile up at his wife, Vivian. She lightly kissed his forehead. "Will you join me for dinner or is your work too pressing?"

He shook his head. "It is not pressing. Rather, there is no more to be done now, though I hope to leave early tomorrow."

"So you will dine with me?"

"I will." Neatening his notes, Richard stood, then turned to take Vivian in his arms. "I am sorry I will be traveling."

A fierceness entered her eyes. "There is nothing to be sorry for. You must discover who killed them."

Richard hugged her to him, nodding. The loss of his sister and brother-by-marriage still hurt, and it hurt Vivian as well, who had been very close with Richard's sister. Girlhood friends, they'd been overjoyed when he'd fallen for Vivian and she for him. Vivian and his sister had plans, he knew, to raise their children together. Send them to the same schools. Have them share their coming out. All the great milestones of motherhood.

Now, Richard's sister Elinor was dead and none of that would happen.

"I will," Richard said softly. "I will set things right." As right as they could be.

Vivian leaned back to look up at him. "I know you will," she said and, coming up on her toes, kissed him in a way that made him not only want to skip dinner, but not to leave on the morrow.

Yet leave he did, taking only his batman, Boyle, with him, and little in the way of trappings. Richard hoped that by appearing unthreatening and unimposing, he would be better able to draw out the information he required. No one would want to say much to Colonel Richard Fitzwilliam, wealthy son of a peer and spare to the Earl of Matlock, but Mr. Fitzwilliam, a careworn officer in the regulars, should have better luck.

The first thing Richard did on his way to interrogate Pratt's relations, was buy a ham. He'd found that such a gift made people both more amiable and created in them a feeling of debt. Both would work in his favor.

He also, talking ideas over with Boyle, concocted a ruse. They could not know how much the men's families would have heard about what had taken place in Meryton, so they settled on the idea that Richard was investigating every officer in the regiment because they had a tip that one was secretly a Frenchman who'd grown up with an English nanny, allowing him to speak English without an accent. This would give Richard an excuse to ask about his suspects' backgrounds and should not raise the hackles of anyone he made inquiries of. That was, unless by some strange chance one of the four truly was a Frenchman with an English nanny.

Richard doubted the case would be solved that easily, though.

Officers in the militia received their ranks from owning property or being the heir to property. As he had records of the property each man had claimed when taking his commission, Richard was surprised by how difficult locating Pratt's relations proved. Finally, he was directed to the home of a Mr. and Mrs. Manner.

Standing beside his horse in their dusty drive, Boyle at his side, Richard made introductions and went over his ruse for being there, then concluded with, "So, in my quest for Lieutenant Pratt's parentage, I have been directed here to your land, Mr. and Mrs. Manner. Can either of you clarify Mr. Pratt's parentage for me?"

The Manners exchanged a look, Mr. Manner standing with his arms crossed over his chest. Richard could see the occasional twitch of the curtains as someone peeked out of the house but they had yet to invite him and Boyle in.

Grudgingly, Mrs. Manner said, "Lieutenant Pratt's my brother. He owned half this land when he signed up. My husband bought out his share. We delayed the sale until after he received his signing bonus for the militia. That's not against the law."

"Certainly not," Richard replied amiably. Pretending sudden inspiration, he turned to Boyle and asked for the ham. "I say, while I have you here, could you take this ham off my hands? The family of the last officer I interviewed insisted I take it, but I don't want my superiors to think I've been bribed."

Mrs. Manner exchanged another look with her man, who shrugged. She held out her hands.

Richard placed the ham into them and added, "We wouldn't mind a bite, though."

She went still, then shrugged and pulled in the ham.

In short order, everyone in the Manner family was gathered to eat ham and bread.

After spending most of the meal getting the family to talk about things that were obviously not of interest to any investigation, Richard, with Boyle's help, skillfully led the conversation back to Pratt. As he anticipated, he ended up with more information than a formal interview would give. Much of it pointed to Pratt being a less than perfect example of a gentleman, but none to desperation or any sympathy with the French.

Richard's next stop was at a farm run by Mr. Aaron Chamberlayne, Lieutenant Benjamin Chamberlayne's older brother. Aaron Chamberlayne was a large, nasally voiced, grim man, but a second ham went a long way to thawing him as well. When pressed about Mr. Chamberlayne's standing, his brother said, "Yeah, Ben's my heir. For now."

"Why only for now?" Richard asked.

"Going to marry, aren't I?" Aaron Chamberlayne shoved some ham into his mouth. Around it, he continued, "Miss Margarette Haddington. I reckon she'll want to be heir then and, of course, I expect to have sons."

"Many happy returns." Richard exchanged a look with Boyle. Was no longer being his brother's heir enough to push a man to take money to poison his fellows for the French? "When is the happy occasion?"

"I reckon two more months."

"Why the wait?" Richard asked.

Chamberlayne took another bite of ham, seeming to prefer to speak with his mouth full. "Her father passed and she wants to mourn for a full year. Says she has to be proper respectful." More ham in hand, he gestured behind him. "She owns the farm next to mine. It'll be convenient to run both."

"Are you farming it now?" Boyle put in.

"No." Chamberlayne inserted the ham in his mouth so he could use his fingers to scratch at the side of his head. "I don't understand it. When her father got sick, he hired someone to run the place. She's insisting on keeping him. Waste of money if you ask me. Soon as we marry, he's gone, I can tell you that."

Not overly interested in Miss Haddington or her farm, Richard brought the conversation back to Chamberlayne's brother. The man was happy to talk about his younger brother's ineptitude as a farmer in his youth and how happy his parents were to get rid of him when he joined the militia at sixteen, which gave Richard the opportunity to ask, "Will you take him back when his five years are up, then? You will by then, I assume, have two farms to run."

Chamberlayne shook his head. "I will not, and they're up soon, too. I have no idea what he'll do and no intention of giving him anything. He's had more than enough. When our pa died, I got the farm, but Ben inherited most of the money that should have come with it."

"That must have caused you some hardship," Boyle said, sympathy in his voice.

"Indeed it did." Chamberlayne reached for more ham.

Richard waited until the ham found Chamberlayne's mouth and asked, "How much did he inherit?" He knew the question to be impolite, but a mouth full of ham seemed to soften Aaron Chamberlayne.

"Too much to give to a younger son, but not enough for him to live on," Chamberlayne said around the ham. "He visits me twice a year during the harvest and planting seasons. The amount of work he does covers the food he eats, but he doesn't put in a full day's work. He says he's a guest, not a worker, so he takes time off. I just think he wants free room and board away from the militia. He's small, you see, and everyone teases him about his size."

Somehow, Richard suspected it was Chamberlayne who teased his brother about being small, rather than 'everyone.' The look he exchanged with Boyle suggested his batman agreed.

"Anyways, I have work that needs doing." Chamberlayne took one more slice of ham, then wrapped up the rest, not bothering to check if Richard and Boyle were through.

Neither had eaten much. It was difficult to enjoy food while watching Chamberlayne eat. Richard could only hope Miss Haddington knew what she was marrying.

Taking the hint of the removed ham, Richard and Boyle departed. Richard doubted they would have learned anything more of use, even had Chamberlayne been more convivial.

Two hams later found Richard and Boyle on their way to Meryton. Sadly, even using the ham ploy, they hadn't learned anything of interest about either of Richard's top suspects, Denny and Carter. Denny, by all accounts, truly was an amiable young gentleman, loved by his family and the community. Carter, in contrast, was viewed with far less favor, with hints that he'd joined the militia to extract himself from a situation involving a local miss, but nothing Richard could discover about either man spoke of desperation or ties to France.

Chapter Twelve

A few days after the ball found a very worried Elizabeth walking slowly back to Longbourn from Lucas Lodge, where she had gone daily to help Charlotte. Jane had not joined Elizabeth today as she had on previous days, there being far less to do now. Alongside Charlotte, the oft-summoned Mr. Jones, and the servants Mr. Darcy had brought in, who indeed turned out to be from London, Elizabeth and Jane had done all they could. Alas, of Charlotte's family, only her youngest sister, a child, still lived now, and little Susan was quite ill. Charlotte was in a state of misery and Elizabeth knew no way to assist her.

Mary had not returned to Lucas Lodge, for it turned out she was far more ill than she'd pretended. Kitty and Lydia, too, were unwell, and for one fearful day, Mr. Bennet had taken to his bed. Only Jane, too mortified to eat more than a few bites of anything at the ball, Elizabeth, thanks to Mr. Collins' ridiculousness, and Mrs. Bennet, who had talked too much to eat, were relatively unaffected. Mr. Darcy, Elizabeth felt, was more ill than he allowed, but he was also a man both larger than Mary, Kitty and Lydia, and younger and fitter than Mr. Bennet. So, perhaps he did not feel as ill as they. However he felt, he worked diligently to assist the Lucas household and Mr. Wickham.

Elizabeth entered on the heels of the mail and took the stack of letters into the parlor, dismissing the servant who'd collected them. There, she found her parents, Jane, and both Mr. Darcy and Mr. Wickham. Mr. Wickham, for all he'd been very ill indeed and was not fully recovered, insisted on being dressed and out of bed every day. Kitty and Lydia were still taking their meals in bed, but Mary would manage dinner, Elizabeth hoped.

"How does Miss Lucas fare?" Mr. Darcy asked as he retook his seat after greeting her.

"Both John and Arthur succumbed last night," Elizabeth replied softly. "Only little Susan remains." She dropped her gaze to the stack of letters she held, knowing she must sort them, her mind numb on Charlotte's behalf.

"Oh," Mrs. Bennet cried. "Poor dear Charlotte." She swiveled to face Elizabeth's father. "That could have been you, Mr. Bennet, and where would that leave us?" She pulled out her handkerchief and snuffled loudly.

"Is Lady Catherine de Bourgh not your aunt, Mr. Darcy?" Elizabeth said, speaking a touch loudly to curtail whatever sarcasm her father might contemplate for his reply. "Papa, she has written to you."

She crossed to hand him the letter, then set two more on the table beside him, gave one to her mother, and two to Mr. Wickham.

"She is indeed my aunt," Mr. Darcy agreed as, lastly, Elizabeth handed him his mail.

She took the empty space beside him on the settee, pleased he did not add anything about Mr. Collins. That would only keep her mother contemplating Mr. Bennet's demise.

"Why is Lady Catherine de Bourgh writing to you?" Elizabeth's mother demanded of her father.

"Let us find out, shall we?" He cracked the seal on the letter, skimmed it, then read aloud,

> *Dear Mr. Bennet,*
>
> *I regret to inform you that your cousin, Mr. William Collins, is dead. He claims by poison administered prior to his departure from your home, though I cannot confirm this.*
>
> *I can confirm that, upon the realization of the extent of his illness, I demanded he write a will and provided the assistance of my solicitor. In said document, of which he made me executor, he names what he calls your 'fair daughters.' They are listed as Jane, Elizabeth, Mary, Catherine (known as Kitty), and Lydia. Each is to receive one pound. You and Mrs. Bennet are each to receive two pounds.*
>
> *He brought three servants with him when he moved into the Hunsford parsonage. They received fifty pounds each. The residual of the estate is to be divided equally between his three aunts. This includes his personal property. I have written to said aunts pertaining to this.*
>
> *I will personally ensure that your legacies reach you and your family within a month.*
>
> *Lady Catherine de Bourgh*

During the reading Mrs. Bennet had recovered enough from her earlier worry over her husband's near demise to lower her handkerchief. "That is outrageous. Two pounds?" She glared at Mr. Bennet. "He is your nearest relation. He should have left you more. If you had died, he would have all of Longbourn."

"He may be my nearest relation, but I am not his," Mr. Bennet temporized.

"I am certain there is an error," Mrs. Bennet rejoindered. "How can we trust this Lady Catherine? She is likely keeping our portion for herself. She—"

"Mama," Elizabeth cut in. "You speak of Mr. Darcy's aunt."

Mrs. Bennet kept talking, ignoring Elizabeth. "—undoubtedly feels she has a right to any money she likes."

Elizabeth's father raised a staying hand and asked Mr. Darcy, "May I assume you know your aunt well?"

"We both do," Mr. Darcy said, gesturing to Mr. Wickham.

"Is she honest?"

"Yes," Mr. Darcy said firmly.

"Exceedingly," Mr. Wickham agreed.

"There you have it, my dear," Mr. Bennet said. While Mrs. Bennet continued to glare at him, he folded the letter and set it aside, reaching for the next.

"I simply cannot believe he would leave us so little," Mrs. Bennet declared. She looked around, searching for support.

Mustering a soothing tone, Elizabeth said, "Mama, we'd only just met him, and you cannot say we got on with him terribly well."

"He was going to marry you, Lizzy. Surely you, of all of us, must feel keenly that one pound is insufficient."

"I would feel wrong accepting anything more," Elizabeth said firmly, well aware that she would never have accepted Mr. Collins' proposal. She was also quite keenly aware of Mr. Darcy seated on the other end of the settee, listening. For some reason it troubled her to have him hear that she'd been meant to marry her cousin, even though she knew she would not have done so.

"Receiving one pound will be quite nice," Jane said. "I will give mine to Mrs. Rylie."

Mrs. Bennet huffed.

Before she could speak, Mr. Wickham turned to Jane. "Am I correct in recalling that name from your ledger?"

"Yes." Jane smiled at him. "She is one of our tenants and recently widowed. I am certain she requires the funds."

"That is very good of you, Jane." Elizabeth approved of Jane's behavior though she wasn't certain she could bring herself to emulate it. She usually saved her coin for books.

Jane turned her smile on Elizabeth. "You should give yours to the Wilsons."

"And the Wilsons are?" Mr. Darcy asked.

"A family that lives along the shortcut between Meryton and Netherfield

Park, near a cottage I believe is home to a Miss Hervey," Mr. Wickham said and, though his tone and expression remained quite neutral, Elizabeth had the sudden suspicion that half the reason he spoke was to regain Jane's attention. "Mr. Wilson recently broke his leg and so cannot work at the moment. That is in Miss Bennet's ledger as well."

If his goal was to secure Jane's smile, he succeeded.

"Indeed?" Mr. Darcy asked of no one in particular.

Mr. Wickham glanced at him. Mr. Darcy cocked an eyebrow. Mr. Wickham offered the slightest nod, another of those looks of understanding passing between them. A new suspicion came to Elizabeth. Namely, that neither Mrs. Rylie nor the Wilsons would require her or Jane's generosity. The two gentlemen would ensure they were provided for.

Mrs. Bennet sniffed again. "Mr. Collins left us so little, it does not matter what you choose to do with your portion and I daresay you are foolish to squander it on charity."

Elizabeth looked away, hiding her amusement at how easily Mrs. Bennet could contradict herself.

A knock sounded. With a lack of preamble born of familiarity, Mrs. Phillips soon appeared in the doorway of the parlor. She handed off her outerwear as she entered, saying, "Sally, tea please." The gentlemen stood in greeting but she ignored them, turning to her sister to declare, "Mr. Hurst is dead, Miss Bingley is improving, and something must be done about Charlotte Lucas."

"Mr. Hurst is dead?" Jane repeated. "How awful."

"Done about Charlotte how?" Elizabeth asked with concern for her friend. Charlotte had been anguished of heart but was in all other ways well when Elizabeth had seen her not an hour ago.

"She is alone at Lucas Lodge without a chaperone," Mrs. Phillips clarified. "I went to inform her of as much but she refused to see me."

Pain on behalf of her friend welled in Elizabeth's chest. She had not thought of Charlotte's terrible loss in those terms. Indeed, she had neither a male relation nor an older female to shelter her reputation.

"She must be removed to somewhere more suitable," Mrs. Phillips continued.

"I believe Miss Lucas wishes to remain with Miss Susan," Mr. Wickham said. "And she is too ill to move."

"Well, Miss Lucas cannot remain there alone with servants and her young sister, as if she is the lady of the household," Mrs. Phillips said insistently. "It is simply not safe. Meryton is rife with rumors and each one I hear doubles Miss Lucas's worth."

Elizabeth had not thought of that, either. "Not safe?" she reiterated. "From…gentlemen?"

Mrs. Phillips sniffed. "Not true gentlemen, no, but men to be certain. I will not have the poor girl set upon in her grief."

"Mrs. Phillips, my servants will permit you in if I ask them to," Mr. Darcy said. "Would you be willing to stay with her until arrangements can be made? It would be charitable for you to do so."

Mrs. Phillips took a step back, nearly colliding with Sally, who had returned with a tray for her, and squawked, "Stay? In a house of death?"

"You cannot ask poor Mrs. Phillips to stay in so terrible a place," Mrs. Bennet declared. "She will not be able to find a moment's rest surrounded by such ill fortune."

Elizabeth fought not to pull a face. If she offered to stay with Charlotte, would they consider that a help or merely point out that she was no chaperon, still requiring one of her own?

"Your desire not to assist Miss Lucas in this way is very understandable," Mr. Bennet drawled. "Perhaps we should ask Mrs. Long."

Mrs. Phillips and Mrs. Bennet simultaneously exclaimed, "I'll go."

Elizabeth had to look away again, her amusement this time for how adroitly her father could handle her mother when he wished to. As she turned her head, she caught Mr. Darcy watching her. She looked away, uncertainty fluttering in her stomach. Why was he looking at her, rather than at the people speaking?

"I see Miss Lucas has gone from a dearth of assistance to an abundance," Mr. Bennet said dryly.

"Assisting her would be less of an imposition if turns were taken," Jane said to no one in particular.

"You take your tea, sister, and I will go make ready to depart for Lucas Lodge." Mrs. Bennet stood. "That is, if I may borrow your carriage, Mr. Darcy? So that your staff will readily see that I have your blessing to enter."

Her eyes held such a mixture of triumph and challenge that Elizabeth fought yet again not to chuckle.

Mr. Darcy smiled slightly. "You may certainly take my carriage, Mrs. Bennet. Consider it at your disposal."

"And my turn will begin this evening," Mrs. Phillips declared. "That is, if your conveyance can be spared to bring me from Meryton, Mr. Darcy? I will, after I finish my tea, need to return home to make ready and to inform Mr. Phillips."

"Mr. Darcy put his carriage at my disposal," Mrs. Bennet protested.

"You will not require it any longer once you return to Longbourn for the evening, sister," Mrs. Phillips pointed out.

"I am certain my driver can accommodate you both." Mr. Darcy stood. "I will go convey my instructions." He cast one of his looks of communication at Mr. Wickham.

He rose as well. "If you will excuse me, all, I believe a touch of fresh air is called for, to aid my recovery."

Mr. Darcy's expression turned questioning. Mr. Wickham offered a slight shrug. Together, the two left the room, followed by Mrs. Bennet.

Jane sighed.

"Whatever is the matter, dear?" Mrs. Phillips asked as she fixed her tea.

"Mr. Wickham had said he would consider my notes on charitable opportunities. Being new to the region, he sees the people here with fresh eyes, and I admit that he is also more astute than I am. He has already pointed out one family that has been taking advantage of my generosity, and helped me find a more worthy recipient."

"Has he?" Mr. Bennet asked, looking up from another of his letters.

Jane nodded. "Hopefully I have not been boring him with my inquiries for his opinions, but I am finding his insights valuable. I believe him to be a very good judge of people."

Unlike me, Elizabeth thought glumly, still stung at being so thoroughly fooled by the two gentlemen who currently resided at Longbourn with them.

"I am certain he will find time for further discussions with you, dear," Aunt Phillips said. "Any gentleman would be pleased to discuss most any topic with you, you being so lovely."

Jane blushed at that, but rather than drop her gaze as she normally would have, she asked, "Aunt, is it true that Mr. Bingley dismissed most of his staff while they were ill?"

Aunt Phillips pursed her lips. "It is. And a right ungentlemanly thing to do if you ask me."

"Mr. Morris would have a list of them, would he not?" Jane pressed. "I believe he is the land agent for Netherfield Park."

Aunt Phillips blinked a few times, thinking. "I imagine he would."

"Might Uncle Phillips inquire for their names?"

"Why?" Elizabeth asked her sister, curious.

"I would like to locate those I can, to learn if they are well." Jane swiveled to look at their father, who watched her over the top of the missive he held. "I have some of the charitable funds for the quarter left. I know Netherfield Park is not Longbourn, but some of them may be in dire need."

"Those funds are for you to allocate as you feel best, my dear," their father replied. "Do so."

Jane nodded, looking pleased, and their aunt turned the conversation to gossip about the village. Mrs. Phillips reported the latest tally of how many of the militia members had died, revisited the fate of the occupants of Netherfield Park, and reported on those others ill in the village and Mr. Jones' apparent collapse from lack of sleep. All of which Elizabeth fervently hoped was as exaggerated as Charlotte's monetary worth was coming to be.

Chapter Thirteen

Darcy went into the hall with Wickham and Mrs. Bennet, the latter immediately going up to ready for her outing. With the chatter of the Miss Bennets and Mrs. Phillips murmuring in the room they'd left, Darcy turned to regard his friend.

"I will accompany you to Lucas Lodge, if I may," Wickham said softly.

It didn't surprise Darcy that Wickham had guessed he wished to speak with Miss Lucas before Mrs. Bennet's arrival. "I plan to ride."

"I am certain Mr. Bennet has a mount I may borrow. We can ask in the stable."

Darcy shook his head, though he was certain of that as well. "I meant, are you up to riding?" To his eye, Wickham still looked wilted and pale. That, coupled with all the death at Lucas Lodge, had Darcy worried anew for his friend.

"In fact, I believe it will do me good." He met Darcy's gaze squarely. "I do not believe I am in danger any longer. It is time to rebuild my strength."

"Very well, but I will retrieve your outerwear." Not brooking any argument, Darcy went up the steps which he knew Wickham still took slowly.

He came back down moments later to the sight of Wickham leaning against the wall outside the parlor, a strange, wistful smile on his face. Darcy raised an eyebrow in question. Sighting him, Wickham shrugged and pushed away from the wall, holding out a hand to take his coat.

In the stable, Darcy ordered his carriage made ready for Mrs. Bennet, as well as his horse and a borrowed mount saddled. Darcy insisted they take the roadway, not wanting Wickham to ride an unfamiliar mount across uneven terrain. Wickham suffered his coddling good-naturedly.

The ride to Lucas Lodge was short and the air not overly cold for November. As they neared, they sighted a man at the door, gesticulating and speaking loud enough that they could hear his voice from the lane, if not his words. Two of Darcy's staff blocked his way, and the door slammed closed before him. In unspoken accord, Darcy and Wickham did not turn up the drive. A few moments later, the man pelted by, whipping his horse as he raced up the lane. Once he was out of sight, they turned their mounts and went back.

Darcy's knock was met by a twitch of a nearby curtain, then the door opened to Hannah, who appeared relieved. "Mr. Darcy. Mr. Wickham. Am I pleased to see you," she said, ushering them inside. After calling for one of Darcy's men to go see to their mounts, Hannah led the way into the front parlor.

"We saw your recent guest from the lane," Darcy said by way of inquiry.

Hannah shook her head. "He was no guest here. He is not on the list of people Miss Lucas is willing to see." She cast a quick look about and added, "The ones she lets in are bad enough."

"What do you mean?" Darcy asked.

"We had to bodily eject a man who pretended to be a cousin of Miss Lucas and wasn't. Then there are the neighbors and acquaintances who stay too long and try to sit too near. We didn't let in a fellow who insisted Sir William owed him money he'd come to collect." She raised her gaze heavenward. "He showed me paperwork that spelled 'Lucas' incorrectly."

"It is fortunate you are here to assist her," Wickham said.

"Do you believe she is up to speaking with us?" Darcy asked. Would Miss Lucas welcome the joint chaperoning of Mrs. Bennet and Mrs. Phillips? His staff were obviously doing their best, and a fine job, but true chaperoning would satisfy society more fully.

Hannah looked down for a moment. "We lost Miss Susan a short while ago, so I am not certain. I will ask Miss Lucas if she is indisposed."

Sorrow for this woman he hardly knew settled more fully on Darcy. Miss Lucas was now the only member of her family left.

Hannah slipped from the room.

Darcy remained standing but Wickham sat, though he rose again a short time later when Miss Lucas entered. They both bowed to her, murmuring their sympathy.

Her features were pinched, her eyes dark circles. Never a beauty, she looked haggard beyond her years. Darcy wished there was something he could do to ease her pain, but imagined only time would do that.

"Please, sit," she said softly, dropping into a chair. "Would you care for tea?"

Darcy shook his head. "We came to see if we can offer any assistance."

"You have already done so much." She turned to include Wickham in her remark. "Both of you, even if my family did not heed your warning, Mr. Wickham, it was still nobly given, and Mr. Darcy, your staff have been a godsend."

"They will remain for as long as they are needed," he promised.

"Thank you." She dropped her gaze to hands that rested limp in her lap. "I believe, what I would truly like, is to be less alone."

"With that, I think we can help you."

Miss Lucas looked up, questioning.

"Mrs. Bennet is on her way here this very moment, to offer to stay with you for the remainder of the day, and Mrs. Phillips has already pledged to spend the night. They plan that one or the other of them will be with you at all times."

The gratitude on Miss Lucas's face spoke of the depth of her desire for a companion for, uncharitably, Darcy presumed that normally the constant attendance of one or the other of the two sisters would be an imposition. "Thank you."

"It is rather a joint effort of the Bennets and Mrs. Phillips," Wickham said. "We are merely messengers."

"And here to divert Mrs. Bennet if I refuse her company?" Miss Lucas said with a spark of her usual wit, then sighed, dropping her gaze once more.

Past her, out the front window, Darcy took in his carriage coming up the drive. "She is here."

Mrs. Bennet was shown in, all three rising to greet her. She halted in the doorway, studying Miss Lucas, then asked, "Susan?"

"Gone," Miss Lucas whispered, her voice shattering.

"Oh, you dear girl." Arms wide, Mrs. Bennet came forward and enveloped Miss Lucas in an embrace. "Now, now," she murmured, patting Miss Lucas's back. "You go ahead and cry. That's right. Cry yourself out for a bit and we'll go collect your things. You will come back to Longbourn with me, dear."

Miss Lucas sniffed, raising her head from Mrs. Bennet's plump shoulder. "May I? Please? It is so empty here."

"Certainly you may. Such a dear friend as you. We will make room. Mr. Darcy can bunk in with Mr. Wickham. Mr. Darcy hardly touches his bed anyways. Always up late writing letters. Up early seeing to his affairs. Up at night watching over that one." Mrs. Bennet nodded her head at Wickham.

Wickham cleared his throat. "It occurs to me, Miss Lucas, that if you will be at Longbourn, it may be best if Darcy and I remain here."

Did Darcy detect a note of regret in Wickham's voice? Oddly, that emotion stirred in Darcy's chest as well.

Turning from Mrs. Bennet, Miss Lucas retrieved an abused looking handkerchief from her sleeve and dabbed at her eyes. "Truly?" Her gaze shifted to Darcy.

"I agree with Mr. Wickham," he assured her. "Not only will there then be enough room at Longbourn for that household to return to a semblance of normalcy, but you will not need to fret over your home in your absence."

"Thank you both," she whispered.

"But you must continue to take dinner at Longbourn," Mrs. Bennet said firmly, looking past Charlotte to Darcy and Wickham. "It will be simpler for the servants if Lucas Lodge is not required to make meals."

The staff would still need to prepare food for themselves, and Darcy desired to take other meals aside from dinner, but as he had no objection to dining at Longbourn, he merely nodded.

That agreed upon, they arranged for Darcy's carriage to take Mrs. Bennet and Miss Lucas to Longbourn, where a message would be dispatched to Mrs. Phillips, and then return with his and Wickham's luggage.

After Miss Lucas was packed and the ladies ensconced in Darcy's conveyance and on their way, he and Wickham took stock of the house and staff. They arranged for several of the lower windows and doors to be reinforced and set up shifts for Darcy's two men and the few loyal servants who remained to walk the halls at night, then returned to the parlor.

"I believe the time has come for me to call on Bingley, and for you to rest," Darcy said firmly. With how many had died and how ill Wickham had been the night after eating the porridge, Darcy was not taking any chances with his friend.

Not objecting, Wickham sank into a chair. "If you ride, it will be no trouble for you to look at the Wilsons' farm."

Darcy nodded. "I will certainly assess the place, but I trust both your word and Miss Bennet's. I will arrange something anonymous for the Wilsons, and for Mrs. Rylie. Is there anyone else from Miss Bennet's ledger you would like to assist?"

Wickham smiled slightly. "I will let you know. How goes the hunt for Bingley's ejected staff?"

Darcy pulled free the letters Miss Elizabeth had handed him. "I have not had time to find out." He passed them to Wickham, one from his man of business, one from his housekeeper at Pemberley, Mrs. Reynolds, and one from his sister Georgiana. "Feel free to discover what you may."

"I should not read Georgie's letter, surely."

Darcy shrugged. "That is up to you. She would not say anything to me that she would not to you, for you are every bit as much a brother to her." In fact, at some points, Darcy had been a touch jealous of how well his little sister loved Wickham. Now that they were all older, he could only consider it a boon that she felt she had two brothers, especially with the loss of both parents, an uncle, and, most recently, their cousin Elinor and her husband.

"We will see," Wickham said with his usual forbearance of active disagreement. "I have a letter from her too, which will likely content me. Also, you should know that Miss Bennet plans to seek out Bingley's ejected staff as well, to offer assistance." Expression a bit sheepish, Wickham added, "I overheard her saying as much while I waited for you to fetch my coat."

"Should we tell her we are already looking into it?"

"And admit I eavesdropped?" Wickham shook his head. "Besides, who can say her method will not prove better for locating and assisting them?"

Darcy nodded. "Very well, then. I am off to Netherfield Park."

His expression sympathetic, Wickham said, "Good luck with Bingley."

"Thank you. I will need it."

Collecting his mount, Darcy set out for Netherfield Park. On the way, he took in the Wilsons' tidy farm, the wife and children all out working. The husband worked as well, though he was seated with his broken leg out at an awkward angle, mending tack. Something he would normally have done in the evening, not in the afternoon with more pressing work to be done.

Darcy reached Netherfield and was pleased that enough staff remained, at least, for someone to take his horse. He marched up the steps, took a girding breath, and knocked.

A footman let him in and went to seek audience with Bingley, causing Darcy to wonder about the fate of the butler. The young man returned shortly and led the way to the same drawing room in which they had spent their days when Darcy was Bingley's guest. The room seemed over large and empty with only Bingley there, rising from his seat in the center to offer a stiff greeting.

Darcy returned the bow. "News has traveled about Mr. Hurst. I offer my condolences."

Bingley nodded in acknowledgement. "Thank you. I will pass them along to my sister."

Silence drew out and Bingley remained standing, not asking Darcy to sit.

"I hear, as well, that Miss Bingley is feeling improved?" Darcy ventured.

"She is. Louisa nurses her diligently. Despite her grief, she will permit no one else to take on the task. She spends her waking hours with our sister. We are hopeful that Caroline will recover."

"And you and Mrs. Hurst were unaffected?" Darcy asked. "By the poison, that is. Not by grief."

"If you must know, I was somewhat ill, though never in danger." Bingley stood with his back rigid, his shoulders straight under the fabric of his dark coat. "Louisa complained a bit at first, but she didn't let it interfere with the nursing of her husband and sister. It was a period of…some turmoil."

"I imagine it was." Darcy forwent pointing out that Bingley had added to the chaos by dismissing so much of the staff. "Do you require any assistance? Servants from London?"

"We are short-staffed, but as we are not entertaining, we are managing."

Seeking to make amends for his abuse of Bingley's friendship, Darcy pressed, "Still, if you—"

"We do not need anything. Thank you for the offer, Mr. Darcy," Bingley said with a touch of asperity.

So, he was 'Mr. Darcy,' rather than 'Darcy.' Bingley, and perhaps Darcy should think of him as 'Mr. Bingley,' must be very angry with him. Darcy had best tender his apology and hope for mercy. "I am sorry I deceived you as to my reason for suggesting you take this estate. I required an excuse to be here." Darcy did not want to defend himself by saying that the estate was a good choice for Bingley.

Bingley's features pinched. "And when you *happened* to meet me at the Earl of Matlock's party, may I now assume that was not coincidence?"

"Correct. The whole party was planned for me to meet you." As well as for a few others of their confidants to meet men similar to Bingley, for Meryton had not been the only trap Richard laid. "Mr. Hurst was in the same club as the Earl of Matlock and his heir, and a frequent visitor to his London house."

"So, you deigned to associate with me because you needed some poor fool you could push into leasing an estate and then inviting you to visit." Bingley looked away, his hands balled and his profile tight. "Here I thought you actually liked me. That my trade background could be overlooked. Instead, your attention was all for your scheme, not done out of real friendship."

That stung. "I judge people by who they are, not their ancestors."

"And you associate with the Earl of Matlock because?"

"You know he is my uncle. Along with him and an aunt, I have no brothers, one sister, and three cousins. My association with them is based on family ties and frequent contact while growing up."

"Excuse my skepticism, but I don't know anyone in your circle of friends who isn't a member of the *ton*."

"Mr. Wickham."

"The son of your father's steward?" Bingley turned back to eye him. "And how did that friendship come about?"

"We were raised almost as brothers."

Bingley's gaze was cold. "I suppose that explains Wickham."

Darcy didn't think the absence of the honorific was a sign of Bingley's close relationship with the man he should call *Mr.* Wickham.

"But can you name anyone else?" Bingley said harshly.

Darcy named three men, one of whom Bingley, no Mr. Bingley, had met. The one Mr. Bingley had met was somewhat like Mr. Bingley. He had a father in trade but was raised almost as a gentleman. Another of the three was a clergyman. The third was in trade, but his sister had married someone Darcy knew from Cambridge. He concluded by saying, "I judge people by who they are, not what their parents are."

After a long silence, Mr. Bingley asked, "And my status with you?"

"Is unknown. You do not truly know me, which is my fault. I pretended to be someone I am not. I imposed upon you. That is not a good start to a friendship."

"Then I must now consider you an acquaintance who may someday become a friend." Mr. Bingley extended his hand.

Darcy shook it, feeling more like a fraud than when he'd pretended to be someone he wasn't.

"I thank you for your condolence and your offer of assistance, Mr. Darcy. I believe you know your way out."

Darcy nodded, uncertain still where he stood with Mr. Bingley, or if he even wished to be friends with the man at this time. There was too much awkwardness, and Darcy soundly disapproved of how Mr. Bingley had handled both Wickham's warning about the food, and his ill staff. As he rode away, Darcy wondered if he would ever visit Netherfield Park, or see Mr. Bingley, again.

Chapter Fourteen

Darcy then, after a bit of thought, turned his mount in the direction of Meryton. By his estimation, Mrs. Phillips already knew that she was not needed at Lucas Lodge for the evening, but he could use the excuse of making certain as an opportunity to seek more gossip. Something was not sitting right with him about the poisoning. He needed as much information as he could gather to discover what that might be.

He was readily welcomed and found himself seated for tea with no effort on his part. After ensuring that Mrs. Phillips knew she did not need to attend Miss Lucas at Lucas Lodge, Darcy was subjected to a babble of information about the tea service. Apparently, the rather ornate cups had been left to Mrs. Phillips by Mr. Phillips' late mother.

Finally, while the tea brewed, Mrs. Phillips asked, "And how do you take your tea, Mr. Darcy?"

"Cream, no sugar." Darcy rushed on, this being his first opening, to say, "I have just come from Netherfield Park," hoping to turn the conversation away from Mrs. Phillips' long gone relations to more recent news.

"Oh, yes, so sad about Mr. Hurst. How terrible." Mrs. Phillips handed him his tea. "And him such an amiable fellow, while that sour Miss Bingley improves. Not that bad things don't happen to good people."

"Yes, that is—"

"Not that Mrs. Hurst won't be relieved, I imagine, once the shock is passed. Many times, as he played cards, I saw the look she cast him. Spent too freely, that man did, mark my word."

Darcy knew Hurst played with Darcy's cousin Henry, who played for high stakes. Henry usually lost money, although less so with Hurst. "Yes, well, some gentlemen—"

"And that poor woman, mourning her husband yet needed to care for her ill sister," Mrs. Phillips said while Darcy mused that he must ask Elizabeth what technique she used for getting a word in edgewise with her aunt. Sagely, Mrs. Phillips continued, "That is what happens when you let go your staff, though, to be certain. More work for the lady of the house."

"I did note that they seemed short—"

"But they still have Mrs. Nicholls, bless her, who was only a touch ill and is recovered now. I heard that from the butcher just this morning, though I daresay she never let on to the Bingleys that she was unwell, what with how they were behaving. Yes, Mrs. Nicholls is up and well and will have Netherfield Park back in order."

"I agree, she must not have permitted them to—"

"And a blessing, as well, that their cook recovered." Mrs. Phillips continued over Darcy. "Can you imagine, all those ill people, and only the cook being allowed to stay?" She waggled her teaspoon at Darcy. "What Mr. Bingley and his sisters didn't know, nor trouble to discover, was that Mrs. Nicholls had twice as much soup made so the staff could have some. If anyone, I reckon, it's Mrs. Nicholls who should have been let go, not that Mr. Bingley will hear it from me."

Darcy had not known that, either. If the staff only had soup and only had small bowls of that, they should all recover. Still, he hoped his man had found them and ensured they were well. Darcy could not pardon the irresponsibleness of sending them away as Mr. Bingley had. It was the duty of a gentleman to look after those in his employ.

"Not that every cook recovered from that awful day," Mrs. Phillips said in morose tones. "The militia's cook, he died this morning, didn't he? Poor man. Likely ate far more, checking to see what was done and what wasn't."

"The militia's cook died?" Darcy asked sharply. That rather eliminated the man as the killer or a co-conspirator.

"Oh yes. It's all around the village. I heard it from the milkman, and the butcher, and when I passed by the inn, and all."

"And how is the village?" Darcy asked, still trying to digest the death of the militia's cook. "How do the other families who were at the ball fare?"

That diverted Mrs. Phillips down another list of who was ill and who was not, and who had died and who deserved their fate, or didn't. Darcy remained for nearly an hour and learned much, although he had no idea if any of it would be useful.

Dinner that evening at Longbourn was somber, though Darcy could see that it pleased Miss Elizabeth that Miss Mary attended. For her part, Miss Mary seemed thin and worn, and said little, but Darcy judged her to be on the mend. Of the youngest two sisters, nothing was seen, and while he hoped they were well, Darcy could not precisely mind their absence. Especially with Miss Lucas in such a deep state of mourning.

The following day, after a peaceful if somber night at Lucas Lodge, Wickham insisted he was fit enough for walking, and in desperate need of doing so after his enforced rest. They walked first to Longbourn, seeking companions to join them. Despite the cold, both Miss Bennet and Miss Elizabeth agreed. Miss Mary, who seemed even more improved over the evening before, still did not want to risk the crisp December breeze. The youngest two Miss Bennets, it turned out, were already on their way to Meryton. Now that there was no chance they would be pressed into assisting at Lucas Lodge, they seemed suddenly well-recovered from the poisoning and had declared themselves quite bored.

As the four of them set out, they paired off into two groups, by what Darcy suspected to be design on the part of Wickham. Since that left Miss Elizabeth by his side, Darcy supposed he did not mind Wickham's desire to discuss charitable works with Miss Bennet. For his part, Darcy wished to satisfy himself that Miss Lucas was getting on well. She required peace, and he was uncertain how easy that was to come by in the Bennet household, especially as more of the sisters recovered.

Darcy knew that Miss Lucas's care was not his concern, yet he could not shake his guilt at not doing more to prevent the deaths in her family. If he had sent Wickham away and remained, he felt certain he could have stopped the Lucases from taking home so much food. In his worry for his friend, he hadn't considered what more damage could be done to the community. No other household had suffered as the Lucases had, but how many of the other deaths, such as Mr. Hurst's, could he have prevented if only he had been more adamant? Had remained to argue against consuming the food?

"You seem very glum, Mr. Darcy," Miss Elizabeth said softly. "Is something amiss?"

A glance took in the worry on her face. A glance took in the worry on her face. Seeing her lovely features take on that emotion on his behalf warmed Darcy. "I was simply recounting the events of the ball in my mind and wishing I had done more."

"Mr. Wickham warned everyone, and you and Colonel Forster added your influence to his words. Other than attempt to destroy the food, I fail to see what more you could have done," she said firmly. "It was not your household, after all."

He shrugged, feeling little exonerated. "How is Miss Lucas faring?"

"As well as can be hoped, I believe. We put her in the guest room, but my mother has also given her use of her room during the day. It is larger, with a comfortable chair and a dressing table that Charlotte can use as a desk. Mother said that, except when she changes for dinner, she has no need of the room, and that Charlotte should have a space to retreat."

Darcy schooled any surprise at such consideration from his features. He realized this was the second time Mrs. Bennet had impressed him, the first being her invitation for Miss Lucas to reside at Longbourn. "That is very considerate of your mother."

Miss Elizabeth smiled. "It is, but not as selfless as it seems."

"Oh?" Darcy asked, aware that Miss Bennet and Wickham were walking faster than they were, the distance between them growing.

"Charlotte had been turning away most visitors to Lucas Lodge. When people call on her at Longbourn, she is not at home to them, either. But if they call on *us* when they really want to see Charlotte, good manners make it so they must stay for at least a quarter of an hour. Mama loves visitors."

"I thought your mother was too straightforward to be so cleverly devious," Darcy said.

"She has never been subtle," Miss Elizabeth admitted. "I doubt anyone is fooled, but they endure her chatter in the hope of an audience with Charlotte."

"Is Miss Lucas still too distraught, then, even to accept condolences?"

"On the contrary. She said this morning that she will allot four hours a day to doing so, though I recommended fewer."

"Fewer?" he repeated with a frown. "With the extent of her loss and the popularity of her family, there must be many who wish to call."

"And when they do, she welcomes their sympathy." Tartness crept into Miss Elizabeth's tone. "Have you not had reports from your staff of what she has been enduring?"

Darcy thought back to Hannah's words about a man being escorted out and another who'd claimed Sir William owed him money. "Some."

"So far, Charlotte has endured three distant relatives claiming to be her guardian or trustee. She has been set upon by six collectors of imaginary debts. She has been proposed to twice." Outright anger made Miss Elizabeth's words brittle. "We have allocated a maid and a footman to sit with her when she has company. At Lucas Lodge, your staff were already forced to remove more than one person bodily. In one case, two footmen were required to drag a so-called gentleman out."

"That seems extreme." Darcy wondered if Hannah had not elaborated because she'd felt the situation controlled, or because she'd worried he would disapprove.

"Extreme measures were used for extreme behavior," Miss Elizabeth said crisply. "Neither I, nor my family, have patience for such atrocious treatment of a dear friend who is in the deepest mourning."

"I am glad Miss Lucas has such protection," Darcy assured Miss Elizabeth, realizing that her defensiveness was aimed at him. "I cannot imagine what her life would be like if she had to handle each visitor by herself. Is she planning to set up a household? Hire a chaperone?"

"I do not know. She has yet to speak about it." Miss Elizabeth drew in a calming breath, then let it out in a cloud of steam in the cold air. "I am sorry for my tone. I know you also want what is best for Charlotte."

"Think nothing of it. It speaks well of you that you are so vehement on behalf of your friend when she is at her most vulnerable. She is lucky to have you to worry for her."

When Miss Elizabeth did not reply, Darcy glanced at her. She had a slight flush on her cheeks.

Darting a look at him, she said, "That is not the only apology I owe you."

"It is not?" He thought back, but could recall no slight on her part.

"I decided that you were a terrible person on very little evidence. I was wrong."

A fresh stab of guilt went through him. "You believed what I pretended to be and what Mr. Wickham said about me. We were trying to deceive people. If anything, I owe you an apology. I am not even certain how Richard convinced me to be a part of this scheme. I abhor pretense."

She mulled that over for a moment, then asked, "Did Mr. Bingley know?"

"No. I thought that was obvious from the way he behaved after Mr. Wickham announced that the food might be poisoned."

"That did support the notion that Mr. Bingley, too, was fooled, but in view of his tolerance of your behavior at the assembly, I was uncertain. At the time, he seemed surprised, yet he did not reprimand you. I thought, perhaps, that meant he knew of the deception."

That drew a wry smile. "Publicly he offered me no censure for the insult I gave you, no, but he did urge me to dance at the assembly. He also suggested that I could stay in my room for the duration of the ball. My behavior decidedly embarrassed him." Perhaps he should have offered Bingley more of an apology.

"As it should have."

"I agree," Darcy said.

"Why did he not insist you behave? You were his guest, and your behavior a reflection upon him."

"He did not want me to leave. Mr. Bingley may not act like a snob, but in a way he is. He liked the idea of being the most important person in the neighborhood. Part of that was bringing London friends to show off."

Miss Elizabeth chuckled. "And you are quite showy, with your splendid carriage, your impeccably made suits, and your ten thousand a year. Or was that part of the fabrication?"

Heat raced up the back of Darcy's neck. He muttered, "It is actually a touch more."

They walked on in silence for a time while Darcy wondered why Miss Elizabeth found that so humorous, which she did, given her expression. Or was it his embarrassment at his wealth that amused her?

"Were the Hursts not showy enough?" she asked after a time.

"Mr. Hurst is…was, that is, a second son. He owned a nice house in a fashionable neighborhood but needed his wife's dowry to maintain it." Darcy shrugged. "Mostly, he preferred to live off Bingley's greater wealth and allocate his own funds to gambling."

"Poor Mrs. Hurst," Miss Elizabeth murmured. "I hope he left her with enough on which to live. I know one cannot compare it to Charlotte's loss, but losing a husband must be terrible."

"I do not know what her situation is. We can hope her sister recovers."

"I do hope so, for their sakes." Miss Elizabeth raised her gaze to seek Miss Bennet and Wickham where they walked ahead along the narrow trail they followed between two fallow fields. "Though I do not care to be in their company again, if I am honest."

"Because of the treatment of their staff?"

Miss Elizabeth nodded. "Jane feels even more strongly about it than I do. I have rarely seen her so displeased with anyone." Miss Elizabeth cast him a quick look. "She even procured a list of the staff and sent it to our uncle in London, asking him to track them down and ensure they are all well. She offered to send the money our father gives her for charitable work and her pin money."

Darcy was impressed with Miss Bennet's dedication. Ahead, Wickham turned to her with a laugh.

Because he had not heard his friend laugh like that in years, not since learning of his true parentage, or the lack of information as to it, Darcy felt compelled to ask, "Is that because your sister wants to ensure that Mr. Bingley has done right by the staff?"

Surprise widened Miss Elizabeth's eyes. "You believe Jane aided them on Mr. Bingley's behalf?" She shook her head. "She did so to help people who require help, not for Mr. Bingley. He is included in her disapproval." Miss Elizabeth clamped her bowlike mouth closed then, turning troubled eyes on her sister.

Her worry brought fresh concern to Darcy. Had his question prompted Miss Elizabeth to realize that her sister may have aided the staff out of continued affection for Mr. Bingley?

Before he could frame that question without giving offence, Miss Elizabeth murmured, "I hope speaking with Mr. Wickham is cheering Jane."

"She requires cheering?" Darcy asked before realizing that to be certain she did, with so many neighbors dead.

"We all do."

They walked on, Darcy once again struggling to find the right words to somehow politely ask if Miss Bennet was in love with Mr. Bingley.

"But in addition to the departed," Miss Elizabeth murmured, "I believe Jane mourns the loss of the man she thought Mr. Bingley was."

"That is a sad thing to mourn," he replied, though relief eased worry from his heart. Not that one chuckle meant there was anything between Wickham and Miss Bennet, but he did not want to see his friend finally reach for happiness, only to discover the lady's heart otherwise engaged.

Ahead of them, Wickham and Miss Bennet reached their destination, a high bluff overlooking the winter countryside. Joining them, Miss Elizabeth pointed out various landmarks, her easy cheer such that no one would guess the weighty nature of their conversation on the walk there. But Darcy noticed that she, too, leveled several assessing looks on Wickham and her sister.

When they returned to Longbourn, Miss Lucas came out to greet them, hurrying down the drive. Miss Elizabeth immediately rushed forward, but Miss Lucas gestured her back. Reaching them, she said, "I hoped for a word with Mr. Darcy. I don't want unknown listeners, but I want someone to be with me when I speak to him."

Her brow creased with confusion, Miss Elizabeth asked, "Do you mean you would like us all to stay, or would you prefer us to stand a bit away?"

"You may all stay, and I apologize for keeping you outside longer." Miss Lucas twisted her fingers tight.

"What has happened?" Miss Elizabeth asked with clear worry.

Miss Lucas looked about the empty yard before the house. "You know I have had several proposals, both by mail and in person. Three of the officers have proposed, as has Mr. Goulding and his son, who is only twenty, and Mr. Robinson, among others. His wife died of the poison. He should be in deep mourning, not proposing to me while I am." Miss Lucas's hands untwined to come up and cover her face for a moment.

Miss Elizabeth put an arm about her while Miss Bennet went to her other side, murmuring soothingly.

"I can assure you, Miss Lucas, that neither Darcy nor I will propose to you," Wickham said solemnly.

Miss Lucas lowered her hands, her smile shaky. "Thank you. That is more reassuring than you know, but it is not the crux of my troubles. Today, Mr. Denny called. He, too, proposed. When I refused him, he did not seem overly upset. He said, 'You cannot blame a fellow for trying.' Then he rose to leave, but he turned back, all worried, and added, 'You should know, though, Miss Lucas, that there's been talk about kidnapping.'"

Miss Bennet gasped. Miss Elizabeth's arm tightened about Miss Lucas's shoulders.

"Was he making a threat?" Wickham asked, his eyes flinty.

Miss Lucas shook her head. "I do not believe so. He said, 'I thought you should know so you can take precautions,' and he seemed sincere." She turned to Darcy. "Is that…would someone truly kidnap me?"

Darcy should have considered it himself. "It is unlikely, but not impossible. If you are careful, I doubt anyone will try."

"Careful?" Miss Lucas repeated, the word trembling. "What does that mean? What must I do?"

"You are safer with people around you. You can hire servants and a companion so that you can live comfortably without fear," Darcy said.

"How can I trust anyone? Many of the staff who have been with my family for years fled, abandoned them, when they grew ill, fearing sickness. Perhaps the few who remained loyal cannot be bought, but new ones?" She shook her head, her face stricken.

"Did your father truly leave you so much?" Miss Bennet asked tentatively.

"It does not matter what he left me." Miss Lucas's words were laced with bitterness. "Rumor gives me far more, and even if anyone believed the truth, I daresay it is enough."

"What are your plans?" Wickham asked.

Taking in her confused look, Darcy clarified, "Do you plan to stay in Meryton? You could sell Lucas Lodge, live in it, or rent it out. Your father's income supported nine people. Even without knowing how much you inherited, it is safe to say that you could live very well on that money."

"I do not want to live in Lucas Lodge," Miss Lucas said quickly. She gave Miss Elizabeth a watery smile. "I am very grateful to the Bennets for inviting me to stay with them. Lucas Lodge is too full of death. Everywhere I look, I see those I have lost. Not only my family. The two servants who died had been with us since I was a child." She shook her head, tears leaking down her cheeks. "I would like to get away. But as an orphaned spinster, I have no place in society."

"Marriage would alleviate many of your troubles."

"Mr. Darcy," Miss Elizabeth exclaimed.

"No, he is correct," Miss Lucas said. "And I have always hoped to marry. I would have married anyone who could offer me a decent life." She dropped her gaze, swiping at her cheeks with a handkerchief. "I was trying to get Mr. Collins to propose to me."

"Mr. Collins?" Miss Elizabeth echoed incredulously.

Miss Lucas looked back up, her red-rimmed eyes defiant. "Yes. You were not going to accept his offer of marriage, so why not me? He came to Hertfordshire seeking a wife, after all."

Miss Elizabeth shook her head, still appearing stunned. "Charlotte, I am astonished."

"Because you would have accepted him?" Darcy did not realize he said the words aloud until Miss Elizabeth turned to him in surprise.

"Because Charlotte deserves so much better," she said. "She is correct that I would never have accepted my cousin's offer."

Miss Lucas let out a forlorn sigh that coalesced before her in the frosty air. "I would have been delighted to fall in love with a man who loved me and could have supported me, but I have never been pretty, and I no longer have the advantage of youth. Before, all I could hope for was a man who wanted a wife, almost any wife, who could keep house and bear him children. Now my choice will be limited to fortune hunters."

"I ask again," Wickham said softly. "What will you do?"

"I thought at first that I would take a year to grieve. With eight family members dead, it almost seems as if I should take eight years to come to terms with their deaths. I want nothing more than to withdraw from the world, but the world is intruding. And it will never stop until I am safely married."

Chapter Fifteen

From Darcy's last missive to reach him in his travels, Richard knew his cousin and Wickham had taken up residence at a place called Longbourn, located near both the village of Meryton and Netherfield Park. Because that knowledge did not suit Richard's plans, he ignored it as he and Boyle made their way to speak with Mr. Bingley as December ushered in even cooler weather than November had held. Richard wanted to see firsthand where each of the poisonings took place, and to give himself and Boyle the opportunity to ask questions and nose about.

Richard was shown into a large drawing room, Boyle disappearing, undoubtedly already subtly quizzing the staff. Mr. Bingley, whom Richard had met at his father's, rose to greet him.

"I am afraid Mr. Darcy is no longer in residence," Mr. Bingley said a touch stiffly.

Richard feigned surprise. "Did he return to London?"

Mr. Bingley shook his head, crossing to stand before a large window. "He went to Longbourn with Wickham."

The sour note in Mr. Bingley's voice spoke volumes.

He glanced over his shoulder at Richard. "I assume you are a part of this conspiracy to use me as an excuse for Mr. Darcy to be near Meryton?"

Richard winced. "I am afraid, in fact, that it was all my idea. Darcy did not care for it, or for involving Mr. Wickham, but I insisted." Richard did not elaborate on his other traps. Knowing he was not the only man to be duped would be no salve to Mr. Bingley.

"I assume, under normal circumstances, I would not have been invited to the earl's home. Nor would your brother, you, or your cousin have deigned to interact with me."

"Then you assume wrong," Richard said firmly. "We all find you a genuinely affable fellow and an asset to social occasions."

Mr. Bingley continued to stare out the window at the gray December landscape.

Richard cleared his throat. "As you know my purpose in being here, may I interview you and your relations? It would help me uncover the culprit behind these poisonings."

"You cannot interview Mr. Hurst. He died."

"I am sorry to hear that. My brother will be as well."

"And my sister Caroline is abed, though she has been feeling somewhat improved," Mr. Bingley continued without turning from the window. "Mrs. Hurst is with her, but I will summon her if you like."

"If I may, I will begin with you."

Mr. Bingley shrugged.

With a grimace for the other man's misery, Richard said, "My report stated that four officers went into the kitchen. Did anyone else, aside from the staff, visit there?"

Mr. Bingley cast him an incredulous look. "How would I possibly know that?"

"True. Do you have a list of your staff, then? I would, if I may, like to interview them as well."

Mr. Bingley returned his gaze to the garden. "Very few are left."

"That many died?" Richard asked, stunned. The reports Richard had received from Darcy, Wickham, and Forster hadn't made things sound as bad as that.

But Mr. Bingley was shaking his head. "They were dismissed. Some were local but many had been brought in from London, and so were sent back."

Richard suspected there was more to that, but Mr. Bingley's closed tone indicated no more information would be forthcoming on the topic, so Richard attempted another tack. "Have you any notion which dishes were poisoned?"

"I believe the soup was. Nearly everyone ate that before the warning was brought, and everyone I have heard of was at least a touch ill. Aside from that, I am not certain. Hurst ate a great deal of the duck. It is a favorite of his. I ate little of it, though it is a favorite of mine as well, and was far less ill."

"And Mrs. Hurst? Miss Bingley?"

Mr. Bingley shook his head. "I did not see Caroline take much of the duck, but I was not watching. Louisa does not care for duck and she was hardly ill at all."

"So, the duck is suspect. Any other dishes?"

Mr. Bingley rubbed at his temples. "I can hardly recall what else was served. There were vegetables, I imagine, and fresh salmon and a beef dish. Caroline would know. She made the menu, though I recall Louisa went to the kitchen to make certain there would be duck for Hurst. Caroline was displeased, saying she did not need her older sister checking her menu."

"The last report I received listed quite a few members of the community as ill."

"I do not know anything about that. We have not been receiving many callers."

Richard wondered if that was because of the death and illness in the house, or if no one wished to call on the home where so many in the community had been poisoned. "May I have your permission to speak with what staff remain?"

"Do as you like. You may even stay the night if you wish. There is plenty of room, though I cannot say what sort of hospitality we can offer."

"Thank you," Richard said pleasantly, though he did not look forward to remaining in such a dismal place. "That would be helpful. The afternoon wanes."

Bingley nodded and went to yank a bell pull. Silence descended as they waited. A maid came and Bingley asked for a room to be made up for Richard and his batman. The girl promised to return when Richard's accommodations were ready.

Mr. Bingley remained by the window, so Richard stood where he was, not willing to sit when his host did not. After a time, footfalls sounded. A woman gowned in mourning and obviously not a member of the staff entered. Sighting Richard she halted, then resumed her way across the room.

"Charles, one of the maids is readying accommodations." The woman glanced again at Richard. "She said we have a guest."

Mr. Bingley turned from the window. "Colonel Fitzwilliam, my sister, Mrs. Hurst. Louisa, this is Colonel Fitzwilliam, son to the Earl of Matlock."

The reason he was permitted to stay, Richard realized.

Mrs. Hurst's features, already pinched, squeezed tighter. She dipped a curtsy, greeting Richard with, "Colonel," before turning back to her brother. "Is a guest appropriate, Charles?"

Mr. Bingley shrugged. "Does it matter?"

Mrs. Hurst scowled.

"Mrs. Hurst, if I may," Richard began, uncertain if he would have another opportunity to speak with her, even though he would stay the night. "May I ask if you saw anyone strange in the kitchen the day of the ball?"

"Me?" She shook her head. "I did not enter the kitchen on the day of the ball."

"Did you not?" Richard slanted a look at Mr. Bingley. "I must be mistaken. I was under the impression that you checked on a dish. A favorite of your late husband's."

She stared at him, her face motionless for a long moment. Sudden tears filled her eyes. "That is right. I had forgotten." She pulled out her handkerchief and turned away, starting from the room with rapid steps.

"Mrs. Hurst," Richard called after. "Did you or your sister eat the duck?"

She paused, swinging back to look at him with anger clear beneath her tears. "I do not care for duck and I have no notion what Caroline ate."

"Do you imagine I will be able to ask her tonight or tomorrow?"

"All I know is that I must attend her." With that, Mrs. Hurst hurried away.

"I know it is early but I believe I will retire for the evening," Mr. Bingley said. "I am certain someone will show you to your chambers soon. I will see you at breakfast, Colonel."

Richard stared after him, wishing his plan had worked better, or that Wickham's warning had come sooner so that this family, and the others who attended the ball, could have been saved. Tamping down his guilt and remorse, he went to seek the kitchen so he could begin questioning the staff. He hoped Boyle was having better luck uncovering information.

The following morning the house felt oddly still, but when Richard came down to take breakfast, Mr. Bingley was in the parlor. His plate was bare, but he had coffee at his elbow. He did not look as if he'd slept well.

"Good morning, Mr. Bingley."

He dipped his head. "Colonel."

Richard took cheese and a roll from the limited selection on the sideboard. A footman, the only member of the staff visible, came forward to offer coffee. Richard gladly accepted.

"You will be off to Longbourn today, I assume?" Mr. Bingley asked, his tone more one of command than question.

"Indeed, and I thank you for your hospitality last night."

"You are always welcome under my roof. My side of our acquaintance was unfeigned."

Richard cocked an eyebrow at that. Apparently, Mr. Bingley had spent the night nursing his grievances, as if he had not joined Hurst at the earl's for social gain. "I thank you for that."

Mr. Bingley nodded sharply.

Richard turned at the sound of footfalls in the corridor, able to identify them as Mrs. Hurst's after her approach the day before.

She rushed into the parlor, face white. With a glare at Richard, she announced, "Caroline is dead." Whirling, she stormed back out of the room.

Richard stared after her, shocked.

"But…she'd been improving," Mr. Bingley whispered. He stood, his chair scraping back.

Richard rose as well. "Mr. Bingley. You have my sincerest condolences. Is there anything—"

"You can find out who did this thing," Mr. Bingley interrupted, his words accompanied by a scowl. "Find them, and bring them to justice." With that, he hurried after his sister.

Richard looked down at his roll and coffee, then went to collect Boyle.

Rather than seek Longbourn directly, Richard and Boyle rode into

Meryton to find Colonel Forster.

Both before and after being directed to Colonel Forster's headquarters, they passed enough people garbed in mourning black to sear Richard's conscience. He'd been a fool to think he could lay such a trap without harming the local citizenry. They had been caught unaware, and had suffered, and he was to blame.

Yet, would not the poisoner have selected a regiment to attack regardless of Richard's scheme? One even less prepared? For if Wickham had not been here seeking the poisoner, no warning would have interrupted the meal at Mr. Bingley's Ball.

One thing Richard knew for certain was, he was going to court-martial Forster's cook. The man had been told quite specifically to guard the porridge. To only feign sleep. If the cook had done his duty, the poisoner would have been caught in the act and none of the food at the ball would have been tainted.

Forster looked worn, his face pinched, as he and Richard sat in his office.

"We don't know anything," Forster said bitterly. "The cook admitted to having fallen asleep."

"I'll have a few choice words to say to him about that," Richard muttered grimly.

"Not in this life, you won't." Forster's tone was dry.

Richard stared at him, nonplussed.

"You did not receive my latest missive then." Forster tapped one of his lists. "The cook died."

Richard let out an oath. "At least that eliminates him." He felt a pang of guilt for his ire with the man. Yes, Richard had been angry with such negligence, but he would not have pressed for the cook to lose his life for his sin of sleeping on duty.

"Aside from not catching the poisoner, he did his job well," Forster said. "Weeks of feigning sleep saw word of his slothfulness spread, as we'd intended. Everyone knew of the habit. Anyone could have come in and poisoned the porridge."

"But not everyone had access to the kitchen at Netherfield Park," Richard said encouragingly.

Forster scrubbed at his face. "True. Did you find anything on the four officers who went into the kitchen?"

"Nothing on Carter or Denny. They are what they claim to be. Pratt got his rank somewhat dubiously, and Chamberlayne has nothing to go home to. That makes him a possible candidate for resenting England." That was thin and Richard knew it.

"Any of them could have been paid," Forster said.

"I'd thought that as well," Richard said slowly. "But the more I consider it, the less certain I am."

Forster looked up hopefully. "How so?"

Richard shrugged. "Pay in advance, and the man you pay takes the money and does nothing. Or he takes the money and tells the authorities. Pay him afterward? Once the deed is done, he has no way of collecting, as I doubt whoever might pay him would also give an address. Also, he is subject to blackmail." Richard shrugged again. "I can see someone supplying poison, but paying? No."

Colonel Forster sat back in his chair. "I wish we had a simple answer. Chamberlayne would be simple, but I wouldn't like it. He works harder than most. There is no one I can cross off the list."

"If the food the soldiers ate was easily poisoned, then the important part is at Netherfield Park," Richard pointed out. "That crosses nearly everyone off the list. At least, as far as the regiment is concerned. I imagine it adds a great deal of others. Apparently, many of the staff were brought in from London. That means they could be anyone."

"I have a list of everyone who was in the kitchen, but it's a long list." Forster shuffled through his papers. "To make matters worse, Mr. Bingley dismissed most of them back to London the morning after the ball."

"Yes. We will need to track them down."

"So the poisoner might not even be in Meryton still," Forster said glumly. "He could be off to seek another target already."

"May I see your list?"

Nodding, Forster handed Richard a document. "You may keep this copy."

"All of these people had access to the kitchen?" Richard had to admit, it was a rather long list indeed.

"The only person I am certain was not in the kitchen is Mr. Bingley, because he would have been noticed and remarked on by those we interviewed. Even the stable help brought boxes in, because of the ball. And the only dish we know was not poisoned was the salmon. All of those only mildly affected had eaten soup and then nothing, or the salmon." Forster paused and then added, "I have to say, your Mr. Wickham is very good at gathering and ordering information. I had my doubts when you suggested him. A priest has no business posing as a militia member, but he has proved invaluable."

"He generally does," Richard acknowledged, his attention on the list. "I think we can eliminate anyone who died. And that eliminates Miss Bingley."

"She died?"

"Yes."

Forster took out another list, to which he added Miss Bingley's name.

"That is everyone who died?" Even from across the desk, Richard could see the list was long.

Forster shook his head. "Because Mr. Bingley dismissed so much of his staff, we do not yet have a complete list of those who died." He tapped a section of the page where all the names held one surname: Lucas. "The hardest hit is the Lucas household. Not only did they ignore Mr. Wickham's warning, and mine, and Mr. Darcy's, they took home much of the extra food. Sir William and Lady Lucas died, as well as six of their seven children and several of the staff. The daughter who lives is being besieged by fortune hunters."

"Already?" Richard was aware of a sharp annoyance with his gender.

"She is rumored to be worth a hundred thousand pounds. Even if that is exaggerated, with her father's estate alone she is indisputably an heiress."

"That is quite the temptation," Richard allowed.

His expression thoughtful, Forster murmured, "It certainly is." Refocusing on Richard he continued, "I wish I had more to tell you."

Richard stood, bringing Forster to his feet. "I will go discover what Darcy and Wickham know. Longbourn, I've been told?"

"Not any longer."

Chapter Sixteen

After promising to arrange time for Richard to interview the officers and the troop, starting with the four men who had entered the kitchen, Forster directed Richard to a location called Lucas Lodge, not to Longbourn. Richard could not help but wonder why Darcy and Wickham were apparently residing with the aforementioned heiress.

He and Boyle arrived to be greeted by a woman Richard recognized as a member of Darcy's London staff, adding to his bemusement. While Boyle went around to the servants' entrance, Richard was shown into a pleasant drawing room, where Darcy and Wickham waited.

After greetings were exchanged, Richard said, "This is a new way to increase your holdings, Darcy. Taking over the estate of an orphaned young woman."

"Though technically an orphan, Miss Lucas is seven and twenty, and we are residing here to safeguard her estate," Darcy said as they took their seats. "Hannah, may we have tea? Whatever is available will do."

The woman who'd shown Richard in nodded and left.

"So." Leaning forward, Richard braced his elbows on his knees and steepled his fingers. "Tell me what you know."

They did, at length, while absently consuming tea and rolls. Then Richard went over all he had learned thus far. When he concluded, they sat in silence for a long moment.

"It is a shame Miss Bingley passed," Wickham said quietly. "Rumor had her recovering."

"The youngest three Bennet daughters were ill in waves," Darcy countered. "Perhaps Miss Bingley did not rest as she should have, much as Miss Mary did not."

Recalling his two brief interactions with Mrs. Hurst, Richard shook his head. "Mrs. Hurst seemed rather domineering and dedicated to her sister's care. I do not imagine Miss Bingley was permitted to strain herself."

"I highly suspect that Miss Kitty's and Miss Lydia's first bouts of illness were the result of too much wine," Wickham added.

Richard sighed, slumping in his chair. "But what conclusions can be drawn from any of it?"

"Perhaps it was indeed one of the staff who returned to London," Darcy said slowly.

"But they all ate the soup, the one dish everyone seems certain was poisoned, and became ill," Richard protested.

Darcy nodded. "Yes, but we know with as much certainty as we can that a single bowl of soup would not kill a grown, healthy man. Why poison two dishes? Why not put as much poison in the soup as was put in the porridge, which killed several members of the troop?"

"So that you could be seen eating the soup and would become ill," Wickham said. "It makes sense."

"Which now makes the dismissed staff our primary suspects," Richard nearly growled. "And Mr. Bingley sent them away."

"My man in London has been tracking them down," Darcy said. "Some of them died, so we may as well eliminate them. The poisoner would not have more than one bowl of that soup."

"Unless he was suicidal, like the man who poisoned my sister," Richard said quietly.

Darcy cast him a sympathetic look. "Let us not further complicate the matter by considering the dead as suspects. It was generally agreed that the poisoner did not end his life until his hideout was surrounded. It was an act of desperation, likely to ensure he would not reveal his co-conspirators."

Richard shrugged, not entirely convinced.

"Miss Bennet also has her uncle in London tracking down the staff Bingley dismissed," Wickham said lightly. "If Darcy's man cannot find them all, we can apply to him. A Mr. Gardiner, I believe."

"Miss Bennet?" Richard asked, noting how the lines of tension about Wickham's eyes and mouth eased as he spoke of her.

"The Bennets of Longbourn," Darcy clarified. "I am certain I mentioned them in my letter. They are one of the families who heeded Wickham's warning."

"Ah, yes." Richard had, in fact, recalled the name. His interest was more in Wickham's mention of the woman. "Five daughters, I believe you said, all unmarried." He managed a tight grin. "Is that the real reason you are both hiding here?"

"We are residing here because Miss Lucas is residing with them for her safety, and wishes her home protected," Darcy said stiffly.

Richard exchanged an amused look with Wickham. Darcy was never one to be teased.

"And that protection is needed," Darcy continued. "We have had two break-in attempts here. Moreover, Miss Lucas is better off in a crowded household. Several attempts have been made to bribe the Bennets' staff into revealing which window is hers."

Richard raised his eyebrows. "How do you handle that?"

"I pay a pound to any servant who takes the offered bribe and reveals the secret that Miss Lucas is, in fact, still living here. They then give the briber directions to my window."

"That must lead to some entertaining nights."

"Two so far," Darcy said dryly.

"Darcy has all the fun," Wickham grumbled in mock annoyance.

"I have not told the Bennets or Miss Lucas," Darcy added. "I do not want to further alarm her. The agreement is between me and their staff."

"I would like to meet Miss Lucas and these Bennets," Richard mused.

Darcy nodded. "In fact, we dine with them every evening. Assuming you mean to remain here, I will send a note asking if you may join us. I am certain that, upon meeting you, Miss Lucas will be amenable to having you reside in Lucas Lodge with us."

Humor leaving him, Richard looked around the well-appointed drawing room again. "You would say, then, that it is widely known that Miss Lucas is too distraught to reside in her own home?"

"In this community?" Wickham nodded. "Yes."

Richard's frown deepened. What if…he hated to address the thought, but before his trap had been sprung, he'd feared… "Stationing 'traps' in the form of veteran-rich troops about the country was the final attempt to catch the poisoner."

"It was?" Darcy frowned, obviously not following Richard's logic.

"My superiors had decided that the first attack was isolated, possibly even an honest mistake on the part of a man who was not raised in England and, therefore, did not know that the mushrooms he cooked into several dishes were poisonous."

"And the other two?" Wickham asked.

"Spoiled food, just as the papers hypothesized." Richard pushed a hand through his hair. "This elaborate trap of mine was my last opportunity to prove otherwise. When that letter arrived at my father's saying a poisoning would take place here, I was…I am ashamed to say I was elated. I could not dispatch you quickly enough," he added to Wickham. "All I could think was that now, finally, I would avenge Elinor and Christian. But what if…" Richard looked about at the fine furnishings again. "Would you say that Miss Lucas cared for her family? A woman of seven and twenty still living at home may have felt some resentment. A woman who publicly puts on a show of such extreme grief as to drive her from her home, well, that could be a woman who is trying hard not to be suspected."

Darcy and Wickham both stared at him.

Richard shrugged. "It would not be the first time someone copied a crime."

Darcy sat back, his expression thoughtful.

Wickham shook his head. "I cannot see Miss Lucas poisoning a regiment and an entire ballroom to kill her family. Or imagine her killing them at all."

"We are getting too far afield," Darcy said in that firm tone that meant his mind was made up. "First, you suggest considering the dead. Now, you suggest considering everyone in Meryton, no matter their connection to the French or the poisoning of the porridge, which your theory would render a mere distraction." Darcy threw up his hands. "We would have to consider everyone who gained in any small way, from Miss Lucas to whoever now receives Miss Bingley's dowry, to Mr. Robinson, whose wife died, to—" He swiveled to Wickham. "What is the name of that woman whose husband and son died?"

"It is in our notes, but I agree with you." Wickham turned back to Richard. "Firstly, Miss Lucas was never near the kitchen. Secondly, we quizzed the staff here and she did not go out on the morning the porridge was poisoned. As we've had no inkling of a confederate—"

"But you would not, would you?" Richard pointed out quickly. "He or she would stay hidden for some time."

"Thirdly," Wickham carried on with a quelling look, then gentled his tone with sympathy, continuing, "You are overcomplicating the issue. We all want to find out who was behind Elinor and Newcomb's deaths. Let us focus on that."

Richard rubbed at his temples. "Perhaps you are right."

Still, as they rode over to Longbourn later, on horseback rather than taking Darcy's carriage, as apparently the Bennets were making use of that, Richard could not forget how close he'd come to deeming his sister and her husband's deaths a tragic accident. Only hours before the anonymous letter arrived, he'd been nearly certain of it.

Fortunately, the good cheer they met with at Longbourn, despite Miss Lucas's clear state of mourning, went a long way to pressing such unhappy musings from Richard's mind. Still, he found Miss Lucas both sad and quick of wit, and neither assuaged his misgivings. The eldest Miss Bennet, who Wickham gravitated to like a moth to a flame, was lovely and soft spoken. Her next younger sister, Miss Elizabeth, proved sharp tongued but amiable, and seemed to hold a fascination for Darcy, though Richard could not ascertain if her interest was born of like or dislike. The younger three sisters, two of whom attached themselves to him like barnacles, were vapid, though not all in the same way, and their mother a touch vulgar but obviously kind.

Of the Bennet lot, only Mr. Bennet showed the combination of both intelligence and cynicism Richard would associate with a murderer, and he had obviously gained nothing from any of the deaths. Unless one counted an additional woman in his already full household as a boon, which the gentleman obviously did not.

Later, when Richard claimed his bed in Lucas Lodge that evening, it was with the chatter of Miss Kitty and Miss Lydia filling his mind against the backdrop of Miss Lucas's bereaved face. He suspected none of them, and yet everyone, and felt no closer to solving the mystery of the poisoner than before.

Chapter Seventeen

Darcy stepped out into the crisp air of early morning the day following his cousin's arrival at Lucas Lodge, his breath forming plumes before him. With the limited staff, he'd taken the duty of feeding and watering the hens, letting them out of the coop each morning and ushering them back in at night. Early on, he'd lost one to a fox due to a poor head count but was rather proud to have lost no others. He'd never tended chickens before. They clucked and chortled to see him, following him about endearingly as he scattered their food.

"Hannah said I would find you back here, but this is a sight I never thought I would see," Miss Elizabeth's amused voice said.

He turned to find her striding down the path from the house, her smile luminous in the morning light. Sunlight gilded her smooth skin, glinting off her dark locks. Darcy could not help but wonder if a woman had ever looked as lovely as Miss Elizabeth did in that moment.

A chicken pecked at his boot.

He looked down to a sea of demanding eyes and returned to scattering grain. Increasingly, he'd been aware of Miss Elizabeth's allure, uncertain how he'd missed it initially. Oh, he'd found her handsome enough. As he'd told her, that and her obvious confidence were why he'd selected her for his public disparagement.

But this was something more. She invaded his thoughts. He often wondered at her opinion, or looked forward to conveying something to her.

It was…troubling. They were in the midst of a murder investigation.

"You do not speak or cluck at them while you feed them?" she asked, reaching his side.

Scattering the last of the food he turned to her, dusting his hands together. "Should I?"

"Most people talk to their chickens."

"They are not my chickens," he pointed out.

She chuckled. "Fair enough."

"You are here, then, to check on my chicken tending skills?"

That earned him another smile. "I doubt that is necessary. I am here because I am concerned about how much my mother is using your carriage.

I know you have not complained, but it seems an imposition."

"It is no imposition. My horses get gentle exercise, and your mother is pleased."

Miss Elizabeth's expression was skeptical. "But yesterday she went to Ashworth. That is ten miles away. It must have taken her more than an hour to reach it."

"Almost two hours," Darcy said. "Your mother does not care to be jostled, so the horses go slowly."

"Four hours for what must have been a half an hour visit?" Miss Elizabeth's eyebrows winged upward. "Surely, that is beyond what is reasonable."

"My men brought grain," Darcy said. "The horses were fed and watered. There was little wear on the carriage at that speed." He shrugged.

Miss Elizabeth studied his face for a long moment. Darcy had to work to breathe as normal, wondering what she deduced. What she saw in his features.

And if she liked what she saw.

Finally, she said, "It is very kind of you to permit her to so liberally employ your conveyance."

In concession to her acceptance he asked, "Would you be reassured if I admit that the act is not entirely selfless?"

New amusement brightened her eyes. "I would. Pray tell, how so?"

He lowered his voice, conspiratorial, to say, "I suspect the carriage is the real reason your mother feeds us every evening. Your cook is very good."

He was rewarded by Miss Elizabeth leaning closer to hear, and then her playful rejoinder of, "And I am certain you could not possibly find anyone else to cook as well."

With mock seriousness, Darcy replied, "Indeed not. Your mother's cook is the best cook in Longbourn."

Elizabeth laughed again, as he'd meant her to. Longbourn was a tiny village which contained the Bennets, the Lucases, and several cottages.

"A more serious but honest compliment is that the dishes your mother serves are as good as similar dishes I had at Netherfield Park. Admittedly, they brought in such luxuries as hot-house fruit, but when the same food is served, your mother's cook does as well or better than the Bingleys' cook."

"I will have to repeat that to her."

"I have already told her."

Pleasure further warmed Miss Elizabeth's eyes. "Thank you. Not everyone is as kind to my mother as they might be."

"It never hurts to pay a deserved compliment." He hesitated. The truth was, he would not be as kind to Mrs. Bennet, despite her fine cook, if not for his growing appreciation of Miss Elizabeth's company. He longed to confess as much, but that would change their relationship. She was relaxed with him. Easy. He did not want to lose that.

And yet he could not go on forever this way, as he'd begun to want more.

"I have another issue I would like to bring up," Miss Elizabeth said, looking out across the yard, apparently oblivious to his inner tumult. "I am concerned about Charlotte. She did sew, at least at first, but now that she has two mourning dresses, she does nothing. She receives visitors, writes thank you letters, and sits. Sometimes she cries in her room. She used to be active. She helped in the kitchen, did mending." Elizabeth gestured to the pecking hens. "Raised chickens."

"She is grieving," Darcy said quietly. "People do so in different ways." His mind went to when first his mother, then his father, died. Especially after his father's passing, for a time he, too, had done nothing. Not even read.

"I know." Miss Elizabeth turned troubled eyes to him. "But I still worry for her. I know she does not sleep well. I would like her to get some exercise, but she is concerned about leaving the protection of the house."

That Darcy could assist with, and Miss Elizabeth was correct. Even in the depths of his grief, he had walked. He'd found solace in Pemberley's grounds. "I could send servants with her."

"I do not believe she would be comfortable walking with strangers." Her expression beseeching, she said, "I realize my friends and relations are already imposing on you, but do you believe, perhaps, you, Mr. Wickham, and Colonel Fitzwilliam if you like, could come by before tea and offer to escort us on a walk? I do not mean to ask more of you, but I truly believe it would help Charlotte."

Looking into Miss Elizabeth's hopeful gaze, Darcy wondered if she sought his presence only on behalf of her friend. "We would be delighted to call on your household and offer our service as walking companions."

"Thank you, Mr. Darcy." She glanced upward, into the sky, checking the height of the sun. "I had best return before breakfast is cleared. I have yet to eat."

Darcy bowed. "Until this afternoon, then."

She offered a final smile and retreated back along the path she'd come down. Just before turning the corner that would take her out of sight around the house, she looked back, giving a final wave. Darcy returned the gesture.

That afternoon, Darcy, Wickham, and Richard rode over to Longbourn and issued a general invitation to walk. All five Bennet sisters agreed readily, but Miss Lucas remained silent as she studied her slippers where they peeked from beneath the hem of her black gown.

"Charlotte?" Miss Elizabeth asked. "You will walk with us, I hope?"

Miss Lucas raised her pale visage. "Where do you plan to walk?"

"I want to go into Meryton," Miss Lydia declared loudly. "I haven't had a new ribbon since before that dreadful ball."

"Oh, yes, I want a ribbon," Miss Kitty echoed.

"I believe there is new sheet music in," Miss Mary said to no one in particular.

Miss Lucas returned her gaze to her shoes.

Darcy cast Wickham, nearest to Miss Lydia, a quick look. She was the ringleader. Wickham needed to persuade her that town was not her goal.

With a slight nod, Wickham turned to her. "But Miss Lydia, I have a deep longing to take the view from Oakham Mount this afternoon." He made a dramatic, sweeping gesture that encompassed the parlor windows. "Can you not see the glory of this fine December day? Why squander it on town?"

Miss Lydia glanced out the window. Indeed, the sun shone brightly, which it had not of late. "But views are so boring, and Aunt Phillips will have all the latest news, and I want a ribbon."

"As do I," Miss Kitty said staunchly.

Miss Mary, in contrast, studied Miss Lucas, a line of thought marring her brow.

"I, too, would prefer a bucolic trek," Miss Bennet said. "I will lend you my blue ribbons if you forsake the idea of town, Lydia."

Miss Lydia's eyes narrowed. "You will give me your blue ribbons to keep, and we will go to Oakham Mount."

"Very well," Miss Bennet said with the ease of someone who values kindness over possessions. "I will give you my blue ribbons. Now, let us all go gather our outerwear before these kind gentlemen grow weary of sisterly bickering and depart."

"No gentleman could ever grow weary of your presence, Miss Bennet," Wickham declared.

She blinked at him, a slight stain of pink creeping into her cheeks as her gaze searched his.

"What about my ribbons?" Miss Kitty asked. "I wanted ribbons as well."

"It is settled," Miss Elizabeth said brightly, ignoring Miss Kitty. "Come, Charlotte, let us make ready." She looped her arm through Miss Lucas's and all but dragged her from the room, the other ladies following.

Miss Elizabeth led the way, keeping Miss Lucas with her. Darcy hoped out of care for her friend, not a desire to be away from him, for they customarily walked together. The route Miss Elizabeth took them on proved circuitous. Not once did they come near enough others to exchange greetings beyond a friendly wave, though they did see, in the distance, women hanging clothes, farmers feeding stock, and someone trying to take out a stump.

The weather remained fine and they returned glad of the hot tea Mrs. Bennet had ready, though they were not overly cold. Mrs. Bennet regaled them with gossip from her calls. She also informed them that no fewer than four people had tried to call on Miss Lucas. By Darcy's estimate, she did not appear sorry to have missed them.

All in all, Darcy reflected, a satisfying afternoon. Not as much so as if he had walked arm in arm with Miss Elizabeth, but he could not begrudge Miss Lucas her friend's care. By the end of their walk, her eyes were a touch brighter and her face less pale. Miss Elizabeth's plan had obviously been a success.

Tea was nearly over when Mr. Phillips was shown in. Rather than greet them, he went to Mr. Bennet's library, where that gentleman could habitually be found. A moment later, a footman appeared, asking for Darcy, Wickham, and Miss Lucas.

"Whyever does Mr. Bennet want the three of you?" Mrs. Bennet asked. "He will leave us with only the colonel for company." She swiveled to face Richard. "And fine company you are indeed, sir."

Darcy noted Elizabeth's amusement. He, too, found Mrs. Bennet's ability to give insult, at the same moment as praise, entertaining.

"Mr. Bennet said Mr. Phillips has come about Sir William's will, mum," the footman said.

"And he requires two of our three gentlemen guests for that?" Mrs. Bennet's face pinched for a moment, then she shrugged. "You had best go to him, then, Mr. Darcy, Mr. Wickham. Surely it cannot be a matter that will keep you for long."

Darcy could not help exchanging a bemused look with Wickham as they stood. Neither of them required Mrs. Bennet's permission to leave the parlor.

"Elizabeth, I want you to come too," Miss Lucas said, sounding almost desperate. "Please."

"Certainly." Miss Elizabeth spoke calmly, offering her friend a reassuring look. "Only, do tell me if at any time you require me to step out."

Her visage grateful, Miss Lucas nodded.

In the hall outside the parlor, Darcy and Wickham stepped aside, permitting Miss Elizabeth and Miss Lucas to lead the way. The four joined Mr. Bennet and Mr. Phillips, the latter of whom sat behind Mr. Bennet's desk with a sheaf of papers before him. He neatened them as everyone settled into the crowd of extra chairs carried into the room.

"Miss Lucas," Mr. Phillips began. "With your permission, I would like to explain to you about your father's will. I have asked Mr. Darcy and Mr. Wickham to join us because they are mentioned."

Darcy looked questioningly to Wickham, who shrugged his ignorance.

"Elizabeth is not mentioned," Mr. Phillips added.

Miss Lucas, seated beside her friend, reached to take Miss Elizabeth's hand. "I want Elizabeth with me."

Darcy took in Miss Lucas's red-rimmed eyes. Her pallor. Though he had lost both parents, he knew he could not fully comprehend what Miss Lucas suffered. Her life had been fully and suddenly uprooted in a tragedy that defied understanding.

"Certainly," Mr. Phillips said. He looked around. "By rights, Mr. Goulding should be here as well. I sent around a note."

"Mr. Goulding?" Charlotte repeated with a frown.

Mr. Phillips nodded. "Your father named three trustees. Me, Mr. Bennet, and Mr. Goulding."

"Is there any way to remove Mr. Goulding?" Charlotte asked, her grip tight on Miss Elizabeth's hand. "He proposed marriage to me."

Miss Elizabeth cast her a commiserative look.

"He can be removed if he is deemed unfit." Mr. Phillips shuffled the papers again. "Any two of us three, with the written approval of either Mr. Darcy or Mr. Wickham, may oust any one of the others."

Darcy exchanged another look with Wickham.

"Why them?" Miss Lucas asked.

"Your father wanted an outsider to be able to veto any two of us taking over."

"Can we, then?" Miss Lucas looked about the room. "Remove Mr. Goulding, that is?"

Darcy would certainly agree to it.

"As I am only now calling this meeting, he will not have known that he is one of your trustees when he asked for your hand," Mr. Phillips pointed out. "Your father trusted him for his business sense." He cleared his throat and added, "Not to disparage anyone present, but that may be an area where Goulding's expertise is valuable."

Which Darcy took to mean that Mr. Bennet was not as savvy.

"And he is magistrate," Mr. Phillips added. "There is no reason to aggravate him unduly. I would advise waiting before removing him."

Miss Lucas pressed her lips tight together, frowning. "Do I need his permission to marry?"

"No." Mr. Phillips moved a different page to the top of the stack. "We have control of your money, but not of your actions. Your servants will be paid by your trustees, wherever you live. Your budget is the same as what your family lived on."

"What do the trustees gain for their efforts?" Darcy asked, eyeing the two brothers-by-marriage. He trusted Mr. Bennet, but people could do unexpected things when money became involved, and he hardly knew Mr. Phillips.

As if reading his thoughts, Mr. Bennet cast him an amused look.

"Each trustee receives payment for their service," Mr. Phillips replied, then hastened to add, "But the amount is fixed. We cannot raid the trust.

However, the amount is generous enough to be worth the time we spend."

Mr. Bennet raised his eyebrows at that, leaning forward to peer at the page before Mr. Phillips.

"Will you be trustees indefinitely?" Miss Elizabeth asked. "It is, after all, Charlotte's money and she is of age."

Mr. Phillips shook his head. "Technically, yes, but it will become a burden on us, you see. We will be compensated generously at first, but after two years, we are to be paid considerably less. If the trust is wound up by then, meaning if you marry, Miss Lucas, we receive a bonus. Sir William was an astute businessman." Mr. Phillips took off his spectacles to wipe them with his handkerchief and then added, "What is not in the trust is the money you inherit from those who died after Sir William. You are the only heir."

Darcy had not taken time to note which of Miss Lucas's relations had died precisely when, during the tumult of work and tragedy in the wake of the poisoning. He did not suppose it truly mattered.

Mr. Phillips returned his spectacles to his nose. "Do you plan to live in Lucas Lodge?"

"I would like to lease it and invest the money that brings in," Miss Lucas said firmly and quickly enough that Darcy knew she had already thought the idea through. "I do not wish to live there."

That earned another sympathetic look from Miss Elizabeth.

"Are you certain?" Mr. Phillips asked. "Even a short lease would see you removed from your home. You may be letting grief cloud your judgment."

Miss Lucas squared her shoulders. "I am not fanciful enough to claim there are ghosts there, but there are memories. I am not ready to move on, but I hope to be someday. The house will tether me to my family. I want to go somewhere else where I can keep busy and not think about..." Releasing Miss Elizabeth, Miss Lucas buried her face in her hands.

Miss Elizabeth drew her into an embrace, which proved awkward seated as they were, and stroked her friend's back as Miss Lucas clung to her.

The room fell uncomfortably silent, except for Miss Lucas's sobs. Mr. Phillips removed his spectacles again and recleaned them.

Finally, Miss Lucas quieted, releasing Miss Elizabeth. Mr. Bennet proffered a handkerchief.

Taking it to dab at her eyes, Miss Lucas said, "I am sorry. I am not at my best."

"That is understandable," Mr. Bennet said kindly.

"If you will not live in Lucas Lodge, where will you go?" Miss Elizabeth asked.

"Somewhere I can get away from suitors." Miss Lucas continued to blot her eyes.

"All of them?" Miss Elizabeth caught her friend's free hand. "You always said you wanted to marry. Has that changed?"

Miss Lucas let out a sigh. "No. It has not. I would prefer the respectability of being a married woman. I want reasonable comfort, which my inheritance should guarantee. I would like to marry someone with whom I share mutual respect. Preferably, we would like each other. I long ago gave up on the idea of marrying for love, but I do not want to be married simply for money."

"Unfortunately, there is a general sentiment that you owe it to Meryton to marry someone local," Mr. Phillips said tentatively.

Miss Elizabeth turned a fierce look on her uncle. "That is Charlotte's choice."

"Agreed," Mr. Bennet said with surprising firmness. "As much as we would all like to see Sir William's money remain here and his estate in your family, Miss Lucas, it is your choice."

"Yes, well." Mr. Phillips looked about.

Darcy wondered if he wished he had done more to track down Mr. Goulding, who would likely back the idea of keeping Miss Lucas, and her wealth, in their community.

"May I ask, how much have I been left?" Miss Lucas said tentatively.

Mr. Phillips shuffled his papers, though he must know, before saying, "Not including Lucas Lodge, you have about fifty thousand pounds." He looked up from the page before him. "You must understand that you will be courted for your wealth."

"I do," Miss Lucas said in a tired voice. Her whole body seemed to sag, sinking into the chair she occupied. "Are we finished? I…I believe I would like to rest before dinner."

Everyone looked to Mr. Phillips who said, "Ah, yes. Certainly. I will inform Goulding of what I have told you. You, ah, need not be present."

"Thank you," Miss Lucas murmured, rising.

They all stood. En masse, they returned to the front hall.

Miss Lucas waved off Miss Elizabeth's assistance as she climbed the staircase, saying, "I need a few moments alone."

Mr. Phillips departed, Mr. Bennet retreating to his library. Wickham glanced from Darcy to Miss Elizabeth and slipped back into the parlor.

Darcy turned to study Miss Elizabeth's profile, suffused with worry as she gazed up the staircase after her friend. "She will be well, in time." A great deal of time, he imagined.

"I wish there was something to do for her," Miss Elizabeth murmured. "I cannot even comprehend the depths of her sorrow."

"Nor, hopefully, will you ever."

She turned to him, her expression grave. "I do believe Mr. Goulding should be removed as a trustee. His pursuit of her is not helping."

"Then you do not concur that he should be granted amnesty for not yet knowing his position?"

Miss Elizabeth shook her head, her features set. She cast another look up the staircase. "Charlotte will now never know for certain if the man she marries would have courted her without her wealth." She shook her head again. "I always knew that my lack of a dowry would make it difficult for me to marry and bemoaned that. I never realized it is also an advantage. Were a man to choose me, I could have some assurance of his genuine affection."

With a sigh, she turned from the staircase and went into the parlor to rejoin the others.

"Yes," Darcy murmured, alone in the entrance hall. "You will have every assurance that the man who asks for your hand deeply loves you."

Chapter Eighteen

The day following their outing with the Bennet ladies and Miss Lucas, Richard rode into town to begin interviewing the officers and men, starting with his four primary suspects. Forster had organized them into fifteen-minute slots, and provided Richard with a small, windowless room that boasted only one door. Two guards were stationed without, one at each end of the hallway, out of hearing.

He sat down with Captain Carter first.

Carter glared at Richard sullenly and, before Richard could speak, blurted, "I know I'm a suspect. All four of us, Denny, Pratt, Chamberlayne, and me, we all know. Frankly, we are looking at each other and wondering." Carter leaned forward. "All I can do is claim that I didn't poison anyone. All of us deny seeing anyone else put in poison." He threw up his hands. "That's all any of us can do. We all deny it. What good is it to question us?"

"It would be negligent not to," Richard replied calmly. "I already have Colonel Forster's report from when he questioned you about your foray into the Netherfield Park kitchen, but I would like to know why you encouraged Miss Lydia to make the suggestion."

Carter dropped his gaze. "I do not recall."

Richard cocked an eyebrow. "You cannot expect me to believe that."

Looking back up, Carter grimaced. "It does not put me in a good light."

"Tell me anyhow."

"Very well." Carter stared over Richard's shoulder for a moment, then met his gaze with sullen defiance. "I thought if I could get Miss Lydia to announce the plan, she would accompany us."

"And you wanted her to do that because?"

"Because she's always good for a bit of fun if you can get her alone."

"A bit of fun?" Richard repeated coldly.

"Not that," Carter said defensively. "Just a snog or two is all. Maybe a bit of a squeeze. I'm not after ruining young women who have no dowries."

"How noble of you," Richard said dryly. "I take that to mean that your prospects are not favorable for you once your five years are up?"

Carter's eyes narrowed. "You are thinking that a poisoner isn't someone who is looking forward to a happy future."

For all Richard did not care for the man, he had to credit Carter's intelligence. "Indeed."

"Then do not look at me," Carter said quickly. "I own a nice property that generates enough income to have bought me the rank of captain. And I have plenty of pocket money. Ask anyone."

Richard studied the other man until he started to squirm in his seat.

"It's true," Carter insisted. "And it's no crime that I would also like to find a wife with a bit of a dowry. Who wouldn't? But I'd take looks over a small dowry any day. I did propose to Miss Lucas, though. I would marry her in an instant. She's a hard-working, sensible woman. If she had accepted me, it would be quite a motive, but she did not, and I can't see how I could have anticipated her inheritance."

"A fair point," Richard said, letting his words agree while his voice remained full of skepticism.

Carter leaned forward again. "Look, I did not poison anybody, let alone half the regiment and half the town. I'm not a monster."

"Hm." Richard dipped his pen into the ink Forster had provided and started making notes, not looking up as he said, "Dismissed."

Carter tramped out, his footfalls somehow sullen.

Richard's interview with Pratt followed a similar line, with an addition of a litany of complaints.

"That poisoning ruined everything," Pratt grumbled. "We were sought after and entertained. Now no one invites us anywhere. We are ready to risk our lives to defend England, and no one wants us in their homes. I'm spending money I meant to save, just to have a few meals each week in the tavern. A man cannot live on what they're serving in the barracks."

Normally, Richard would have assumed that complaint was specious, but Forster had yet to get in a new cook. Richard had no idea who was preparing the troop's meals at the moment, but he suspected they were being careful, and he knew they were being watched.

Richard interviewed Denny next, keeping his mien as bland as he had at the start of both previous interviews, though a touch more excitement filled him. Denny had been to London, and had befriended Wickham on his way here to insinuate himself into the troop. Richard found both suspicious.

"Good afternoon, Colonel," Denny greeted as he entered. "Colonel Forster said you would be interviewing everyone. How can I be of assistance?"

Richard looked into that open, amiable face and saw no fear, guilt, or guile. Denny was either innocent or a very fine actor. "Please, take a seat. I have a few questions is all."

With apparent good cheer, Denny took the chair opposite Richard. "I will answer as best I can, sir."

"Good." Richard studied the other man for a moment longer, seeking any sign he was not as he presented himself and finding none. "I understand you took leave to visit London a short while back."

"Yes, sir. A great-aunt of mine is giving my sister a proper come out." Denny smiled happily. "We'd never be able to afford a real London come out, but Great Aunt Nilly can. I went to see my little sis in all her glory. She was capturing hearts left and right, I do not mind saying. It would be a fine thing if she could win a wealthy husband."

"Is that because there is not enough money for her?"

Denny scratched his head. "Well, there is enough for her to marry in the community, but it would be a fine thing if she could better herself, as it were. She's a right pretty girl. Always Great Aunt Nilly's favorite. It's a fine opportunity to be offered, certainly."

Richard tried to find some flaw in that. Not seeing one, he asked, "And you happened to meet Mr. Wickham on your way back here?"

If anything, Denny's smile grew. "What a grand coincidence that was. Him, on his way here to join our troop." Some of his cheer dimmed. "Although, I gather now that he was never in the militia. That you were using him as some sort of spy. Too bad, that. He's a fine fellow."

"You do not resent him for deceiving you?"

"He was doing his part, is all." Denny shrugged. "I doubt he had much more choice than I do when Colonel Forster orders me to lead the men on a run. Made Wickham lead plenty of those, too, he did. Runs well for a civvy."

"Hm." Richard made a few notes, letting Denny wait. When the other man started fidgeting, Richard lifted his gaze to ask, "So you have no complaints?"

"I would not say that."

"Oh?"

"Well, this poisoning business has soured things, hasn't it? And men I know, good men, died. I wasn't too close with any of those that did, but those who were are right unhappy. On top of that, us in the militia, we're pariahs now." Denny let out a sigh. "I'd say things were much better before the poisoning, to be certain."

"Yes. I imagine they were."

"And Miss Lucas refused me," Denny added glumly. "The only heiress I've ever met, or am likely to meet, and she turned me down." He stared glumly at the tabletop for a moment, then brightened. "Still, maybe my sis will meet some flush fellow and elevate us all a little."

"One can only hope," Richard replied. "Why did you go into the kitchen?"

"It seemed like a lark," Denny said with another shrug. "It was too bad Miss Lydia did not come with us, but it was still entertaining. That kitchen is half the size of my family's house. Maybe bigger. It was quite something to see, and everyone rushing about because fresh salmon had just arrived, and Mrs. Hurst coming through, spitting vitriol about the funds wasted on fish that had not even arrived in time. She even tried to convince the cook to leave the salmon in the cold room since it was causing such a ruckus, but the cook said he could manage. Then she gave us lot a glare that could have kept the fish cold all on its own, so we hurried out of there and back to the ball."

Richard pondered that for a moment before asking, "Why was it too bad that Miss Lydia did not join you in the kitchen?"

"A lot of fun, Miss Lydia is. She livens up a place. If she were a bit older, or had a little larger dowry, or didn't prefer Carter over me, I might ask her to marry me. A man would lead a happy life with someone as lively as she is as his bride."

Being married himself, Richard had not assessed the Bennet sisters in those terms but even his short, uninterested acquaintance told him that any reasonable man would want one of the two eldest for his bride, not their wild, uncouth, exceedingly young sister. Perhaps in five or six years Miss Lydia would develop into the sort of woman a man would care to marry, but he did not see that transformation taking place any time sooner.

"Does Miss Lydia have something to do with the poisoning, then, sir?"

Richard refocused on Denny. "She does not. Do you?"

Denny blinked once, clearly taken aback. "Ah, no sir. On my honor. That is not what you think, is it? Colonel Forster said these interviews are perfunctory."

"I am not yet certain what I think, Mr. Denny, but I have taken up enough of your time for the present. Thank you. You are dismissed."

"Right." Denny stood. "Sir, I didn't poison anyone. You know that, right?"

"You are dismissed," Richard repeated more firmly.

"Yes, sir." His expression worried, Denny hurried out.

Richard worked on his notes until Chamberlayne was shown in.

Once he was seated, Chamberlayne, much like Carter, began on his own, saying, "I imagine you want to know if I poisoned anyone."

Richard very much did, but doubted he could trust anything Chamberlayne said if he had. "Did you?"

Chamberlayne shook his head. "No."

"And you should be believed because?"

"My term is up in three weeks, and I'm happy about that. Why would I go and poison anyone now?"

Richard studied him. "An obvious answer would be money. A less obvious one, French sympathies you are running out of time to express."

Chamberlayne snorted. "I don't have any French sympathies."

"So you say." To aggravate the other man, because anger clouded judgment, Richard took up the pen and made some notes. The inked nub scratched over the page before him, loud in the silent room.

"Anyone who thinks one of the four of us is the poisoner isn't thinking," Chamberlayne said flatly.

Richard looked up. "Why? You had the opportunity."

"There is no way we could predict we would go into the kitchen."

"Captain Carter could have, as he suggested the activity."

"And it's unlikely any of us would carry poison to the ball on the chance that we could use it," Chamberlayne continued as if Richard hadn't spoken. "Aside from that, how could we get poison? I mean, Meryton has a few shops, but I doubt they carry much in the way of poison. Maybe they sell something to kill rats, but the shopkeepers would remember that."

"Mr. Denny was in London recently," Richard reminded Chamberlayne, wondering, as he did, if the man did not know that the symptoms were the same as those of the mushrooms used in the first poisoning, or did know and was trying to appear as if he didn't. Mushrooms which, though rare, did not necessarily need to come from London.

"Well, yes, Denny's been to London," Chamberlayne conceded. "But the other three of us haven't left the area since we came here. Are you suggesting that one of us hid the poison since we arrived? We don't really have so much privacy. It would be taking a big risk."

That was assuming the amount of poison required was large, but Richard forwent pointing that out. "You seem to have given this a great deal of thought, Mr. Chamberlayne."

"Little else to think on of late, is there?"

"You said you are happy that your five years are nearly up." From his visit to Chamberlayne's brother, Richard could not fathom why the man would be happy to return there. That made him suspicious.

"I am. In three weeks, I'm putting this all behind me."

"Three weeks?"

Chamberlayne nodded firmly.

"You are aware that if the poisoner is not uncovered before then, you may not be permitted to leave?"

"What?" Worry flashed across Chamberlayne's features. "No, I have to get back. You cannot keep me here. I'm not the poisoner."

"I am afraid Colonel Forster and I can, indeed, keep you here. Preferably not in the brig, but definitely by whatever means necessary. Quite a few people are dead, both military and civilian."

Chamberlayne stared at him, somewhere between disbelief and horror. He opened his mouth, closed it, then opened it again to mutter, "Well, then, I hope you find the poisoner."

"You may rest assured that I will," Richard said firmly.

After he dismissed Chamberlayne, Richard started his interviews with the other officers. By tomorrow, he hoped to be on to the enlisted men, and then, if he still had nothing, he could re-interview the staff at Netherfield. He had Forster's notes, but if needed, Richard would speak to everyone in Meryton, and anyone who'd been in Meryton at the time of the poisoning, until he uncovered the killer.

Chapter Nineteen

As she jostled along in the carriage with her parents and older sister, Elizabeth wished they were going almost anywhere other than Netherfield Park. From the tense, set look on Jane's face, she did as well. A few short weeks ago, Jane would have struggled to contain her joy at the idea of seeing Mr. Bingley.

That, however, was before his uncharitable treatment of an obviously unwell Mr. Wickham at the ball and his subsequent ejection of ill servants from his home. Worse, Jane had a letter from their Uncle Gardiner in London only yesterday, revealing that some of the cast out staff had perished. As they shared a room, Elizabeth knew her sister had been crying. Not, Elizabeth suspected, for the unknown staff, though Jane felt harm to others keenly, but over the last remnants of her affection for Mr. Bingley.

"We should have called sooner," Mrs. Bennet said into the stillness of the carriage. "We are the only family who has yet to call. Even Mrs. Long called, and even though she is expecting company and must make ready."

"Company?" Elizabeth repeated, for once thinking it might be better to have talk inside the carriage than silence.

"Yes. From far off. She will not say where. Because Mrs. Long is being so secretive, Mrs. Phillips has concocted outlandish explanations for why it may be an eligible gentleman for our community." Mrs. Bennet made a dismissive sound. "I am certain it will turn out to be one of Mrs. Long's many nieces."

"Assuredly you are correct, my dear," Mr. Bennet said, earning a smile from his wife and plunging them back into silence.

Upon their arrival they were shown into a parlor draped for mourning, the profusion of black sucking all cheer from the room. Both Mr. Bingley and Mrs. Hurst were similarly grim. Mr. Bingley, in particular, appeared white of face with so much black about him.

As they sat after greetings were exchanged, Mrs. Hurst offered, "Would you care for tea?"

"No, thank you," Mr. Bennet said quickly, even as Elizabeth's mother opened her mouth undoubtedly to accept.

Mrs. Hurst's features pinched tighter. She waved the hovering maid away.

"We are very sorry for your losses," Elizabeth's father said quietly. "It is terrible to have lost two so near to you in such short order."

"Caroline's death came as a great shock." Mr. Bingley raised a trembling hand, pressing his fingers to his temple. "We had truly thought she was over the worst and on the mend."

"Are you certain you are well, Mr. Bingley?" Jane asked, watching him with concern.

He dropped his hand, the look he turned on her hopeful.

Jane stared back with concern, but nothing Elizabeth could construe as affection.

Mr. Bingley must have thought the same, for his eagerness turned searching, then his features sagged with regret. "In truth, I have not been feeling myself these several days."

"Our losses weigh heavily upon Charles," Mrs. Hurst cast her brother a look that, though sympathetic, was brittle about the edges. "It was the same when our parents left us. Charles became quite ill in his grief. I feared we would lose him."

He cast her an annoyed look and sat straighter in his chair. "I was not that ill. You will leave the Bennets believing me sickly." He slanted a quick look Jane's way.

"No, certainly, you were not that ill." Mrs. Hurst's worried, pitying look belied her words. "And you are a grown man now. Far stronger than you were as a lad."

Studying Mr. Bingley, he did not appear very strong. Elizabeth had not expected him to be quite so affected by his losses. Did her surprise at the obvious depth of his grief make her a less good person?

Turning from watching her brother, Mrs. Hurst said, "I am sorry I did not believe Mr. Wickham. If only I had, I would have ordered the food thrown out. But it seemed so farfetched. Now I've lost my husband and sister, and when we leave here, I do not know what I will do."

"You will be taken care of, Louisa," Mr. Bingley said, marshaling a touch of vigor into his voice. "You have the house in London and, though there is nothing good about Caroline's passing, her dowry will be divided between us."

Mrs. Hurst looked down at her hands.

Mrs. Bennet opened her mouth to speak.

"Yes, well," Mr. Bennet said quickly. "We simply wished to express our deepest condolences." He stood, causing everyone to rise. "We will leave you to your grief."

"Thank you, Mr. Bennet, Mrs. Bennet," Mr. Bingley said. He turned another searching look on Jane, then dipped his head before raising it to add,

"Miss Bennet, Miss Elizabeth."

He'd lost weight, Elizabeth noted as she, along with Jane, curtsied.

They finished their farewells and returned to their carriage. Elizabeth stared out the window at Netherfield Park's lovely grounds as they rolled down the drive. Mr. Bingley certainly looked like a man wasting away from sorrow and yet, when he spoke of Miss Bingley's dowry, he did not sound like a desperately grieving man. But then, grief took many forms.

The following day, Mr. Bingley and Mrs. Hurst called on Charlotte to express their condolences for her many losses. As always, Charlotte went through the proper motions, but Elizabeth could tell her friend was not consoled by Mr. Bingley's and Mrs. Hurst's expressions of concern. Mrs. Bennet offered refreshments in a bid to extend their guests' visit, but they were refused. With another pining, wistful look for Jane, a diminished-seeming Mr. Bingley rose and departed, his black-clad sister by his side.

Later that afternoon, Mr. Darcy, Mr. Wickham, and Colonel Fitzwilliam called to ask if anyone would care for a walk. Predictably, Elizabeth's younger sisters were uninterested in exerting themselves in the cold December air if no ribbons or sheet music were to be had, but Elizabeth, Jane, and, to Elizabeth's pleased surprise, Charlotte, all agreed to go.

They gathered in the drive, and Mr. Wickham, after speaking quietly to Jane, offered her his arm. Together they took the lead, and Mr. Darcy offered Elizabeth his arm to follow. Colonel Fitzwilliam, taking a break from what Elizabeth gathered to be both tedious and unfruitful interviews, walked with Charlotte.

"It is a blustery day," Mr. Darcy commented as they followed the other two couples.

Elizabeth cast him a quick grin. "Do not worry. I will not permit the wind to take you."

"Thank you."

Out of the corner of her eye, she studied him, finding him so different from before. He was not so grim as she'd once imagined, nor so aloof and cold. Certainly, he'd been dedicated in his assistance to Charlotte. He'd shown an easy willingness to engage in even menial tasks such as feeding chickens and displayed admirable solicitousness for his friend when Mr. Wickham was ill.

"You are analyzing me," he murmured without looking.

Heat touched Elizabeth's cheeks, but she raised her chin. "And if I am?"

"If you are, I wonder what you conclude."

Elizabeth darted a look ahead, but the couples had separated as they walked, and Charlotte and Colonel Fitzwilliam seemed to be engaged in a conversation of their own. "For one, I am gratified for your dedication to assisting Charlotte."

"Residing in Miss Lucas's home for her is no imposition." Mr. Darcy's profile pinched in a grimace. "And I am not all nobility. The plan to station one of his carefully crafted militias designed to lure out the poisoner here was Richard's idea, but I was part of it. I cannot help but assume some guilt for what took place here and try to make amends."

"I believe we agreed that you are not to blame for the evil of a poisoner, or for people not heeding Mr. Wickham's timely warning."

"I should have done more."

"And yet, there was nothing more you could have done, with Mr. Wickham needing your care, and Netherfield Park not your household. You could hardly rush about taking up and destroying food. Mr. Bingley would have ordered you restrained and ejected."

Mr. Darcy pressed his lips together, not responding.

Which would not do. Elizabeth wished him neither unhappy nor silent. "On our last walk, you were telling me of your last ball at Pemberley. It sounded lovely."

As she hoped, that line of conversation allowed her to draw him into tales of his estate. Of the home, fields, and people he so obviously cherished. Elizabeth enjoyed hearing Mr. Darcy speak of Pemberley. By his words, she could picture his home so well, she felt almost as if she'd been there, and she loved the animation, the joy that overtook his features.

Rather, she corrected, she enjoyed those things. Was entertained by them. Love was a very strong and very daunting word.

Jane and Mr. Wickham turned up a path Elizabeth had not expected them to take, and she frowned, looking about her. "Where are we going?" she asked into a lull in Mr. Darcy's discourse.

"I believe Wickham has a specific goal for this outing."

"Does he?" Elizabeth looked past Charlotte and Colonel Fitzwilliam to where her sister walked arm in arm with Mr. Wickham. "To where does he lead us?"

"He wishes to visit a Miss Hervey."

Elizabeth frowned. "I do not believe I know her."

"Nor do I, but Wickham believes she may be in need of help."

In a short time, they approached a small cottage. There were three goats, two nanny and a kid, in a pasture easily large enough for them. There were also scrawny chickens wandering the yard and the winter remnants of a vegetable garden. A mixed sheepdog set to barking when they halted, but fell silent as a woman in her fifties and a boy of perhaps ten came out to greet them.

While Charlotte and Colonel Fitzwilliam hung back, Mr. Wickham and Jane approached. Elizabeth, where she paused on the dirt track with Mr. Darcy, was too far away to hear what was being said, but soon Mr. Wickham turned and gestured them all forward.

The six of them gathered around the woman and the boy, and Mr. Wickham said, "May I introduce Miss Hervey and her nephew's son, Oliver. Miss Hervey, this is Colonel Fitzwilliam, Mr. Darcy, Miss Lucas, and Miss Elizabeth Bennet."

"Pleased to meet you all, sirs, misses." Miss Hervey dipped a curtsy. At her side, Oliver made an unpracticed bow.

"As we are to meet you," Elizabeth said. "What a lovely nephew you have. Is he visiting?"

Miss Hervey shook her head. "He lives here with me, miss. He was raised in London, but his parents passed."

Oliver looked down, scuffing a boot in the half-frozen dirt at his feet.

"Miss Hervey was a lady's maid," Jane said.

"Aye." Miss Hervey nodded. "To Mrs. Griffiths. When she died, I was given lifetime use of this cottage and a pension."

"Griffiths?" Elizabeth repeated, knowing she knew the name but unable to place it.

"The Griffiths once owned Netherfield Park."

Elizabeth cast her sister a quick smile, grateful for the reminder.

"Netherfield Park has good hunting," Oliver said in a high, young voice, speaking for the first time.

"Aye, but you cannot be hunting there," Miss Hervey said firmly.

"I can. I brought down a pheasant last week with my slingshot. I got him good."

Miss Hervey cast the boy an alarmed look. "And I told you not to do it again and not to tell a soul. We aren't allowed to hunt that land. It isn't ours, boy."

"But you still cooked it," Oliver said sullenly.

Miss Hervey turned sheepish. "Aye, well, 'twas already dead."

Mr. Darcy exchanged a look with Mr. Wickham and Colonel Fitzwilliam. "How about you show us your slingshot?" Mr. Wickham said affably.

Oliver perked up at that.

As he got out his slingshot and displayed the draw, the three men converged on Oliver, Mr. Darcy speaking in low, even tones. Elizabeth didn't hear what Mr. Darcy said, but she did hear Oliver say, "But no one from Netherfield Park even hunts."

"Would you care to come in?" Miss Hervey asked, directing her question to Elizabeth, Jane, and Charlotte.

With a smile, Jane replied, "Thank you," and Miss Hervey led them in.

Elizabeth had been in many cottages for charitable reasons, but this was tiny by any standards, consisting of one room for nearly all purposes. Yet it was neat and clean, even the cubby near the fireplace where it looked as if

Oliver's bedding and possessions were stowed during waking hours.

Taking the few steps required, Charlotte walked into the kitchen area of the cottage, looking around. "I know you do not have much space, but I believe I have some items I can part with that you could use."

Elizabeth realized Charlotte meant items from Lucas Lodge, and wondered if she should protest her friend giving up her possessions while in such a dire stage of grief.

"I would be grateful for anything," Miss Hervey replied, sounding hopeful.

Charlotte turned from scrutinizing what passed as a kitchen. "Does Oliver read and write?"

"A little, miss."

"I have some books meant for children. If you can teach him, you are welcome to them. Can you teach him?"

Miss Hervey stood a bit taller. "Mrs. Griffiths would not have a personal maid who couldn't read and write. I would like to teach him, because when I die, he will have no one and no place to go. With the life he's living now, his only recourse will be to become a farm laborer."

"What life was he living before his parents died?" Jane asked.

"He was informally apprenticed to a cooper but lived in his family home. Once his folks were gone, the cooper didn't keep him on. He couldn't afford to take Oliver in, you see."

Jane nodded, her expression suffused with sympathy.

Mr. Wickham, Elizabeth reflected, had been right to bring them here. Miss Hervey and Oliver were good people, despite the boy's poaching, doing the best they knew how. A little help would go far in their lives, especially Oliver's.

A masculine cheer sounded without and Elizabeth raised her eyebrows, wondering what the gentlemen were up to. In silent accord, she and the other women filed back out of the little cottage.

They were, it turned out, in the midst of a slingshot competition. As she watched, Mr. Wickham shot one in a row of what appeared to be suspiciously like pheasant feathers, wedged into a fence rail, fortunately far from the three goats. By what Elizabeth could gather, Mr. Darcy had been eliminated easily, and then Colonel Fitzwilliam had fallen to Oliver's superior skills. It came down to the lad and Mr. Wickham, who was shortly proven to be outmatched.

Everyone gathered around Oliver, praising his success. Mr. Darcy produced a one-pound note and solemnly declared it to be the prize money. He handed it to a wide-eyed Oliver.

"I congratulate you on your win," Mr. Wickham said cheerfully. "But do not think for a moment that I won't return for a rematch."

"For another pound?" Oliver asked excitedly.

"That depends." Mr. Darcy's voice was grave. "This competition is only for amateurs, not for hunting professionals, if you take my meaning."

Oliver's face scrunched in serious thought. "You mean, you'll only come back for another contest if I promise to stop poaching?"

"Ah ha," Colonel Fitzwilliam exclaimed. "You admit, then, that it is poaching to hunt without permission on another man's land, be he a hunter or not?"

Oliver sighed. "Yeah. I suppose."

"Good lad." Mr. Wickham gestured to the makeshift targets. "I expect you to practice, and make certain you don't hit any goats."

"Yes, sir."

"We're going to be off, but you'd best reset the targets and keep working on your shot."

With a nod, Oliver skipped away in the direction of the fence.

"Thank you," Miss Hervey said quietly. "He is at that age where he wants to be a man and I am afraid my words on the matter of poaching were doomed to be ignored."

"He's a good lad," Mr. Wickham said with a shrug.

Mr. Darcy turned from watching the boy to Miss Hervey. "If you do not mind, I will arrange for some apple trees to be planted here. It will be a few years before they produce any fruit, but once they do, they should give you some variety."

"That would be very kind, Mr. Darcy. Thank you."

With that, Miss Hervey bid them farewell and they retraced their steps down the narrow trek.

They were about halfway back when they reached a fork in the trail they'd taken and Charlotte halted them. "I would like to go select items to give to Miss Hervey and Oliver." She looked about at the five of them, adding with sudden nervousness, "That is, if you will join me?"

"I am happy to," Elizabeth said immediately.

"Lucas Lodge is where Darcy and I will end up, regardless," Mr. Wickham added.

"I am afraid I must return to my work." Colonel Fitzwilliam sounded honestly regretful. "I will continue to Longbourn to collect my horse. I will see if yours can be returned to Lucas Lodge for you," he added to Mr. Darcy and Mr. Wickham.

With that sorted, and Charlotte now walking with Elizabeth and Mr. Darcy, they parted ways with the colonel and took the path to Lucas Lodge.

Charlotte was very quiet as they walked, and as much as she enjoyed speaking with Mr. Darcy, Elizabeth did not want to intrude on her friend's grief. Mr. Darcy must have agreed, for he made no effort at conversation either. Ahead of them, Mr. Wickham and Jane spoke softly.

Charlotte's expression was unreadable as she went to the kitchen while the gentlemen excused themselves to check on Colonel Fitzwilliam's success in seeing their mounts returned. She selected a few items, none of which Elizabeth felt held too much sentiment, before moving on to the nursery.

There, Charlotte quickly amassed a pile of books. "All of us used these books," she murmured, looking at the stack she'd created on the large table in the center of what had jointly been a room for learning and play. "Of course, Patrick had only started on them." She fell silent, her gaze abstract. Tears built in her eyes, then spilled over.

"Charlotte," Elizabeth ventured tentatively. "You do not have to give any of—"

"He died alone," Charlotte interrupted bitterly. "Patrick died alone. I was with each of my other family members when they died, but Patrick was alone. He was only seven. I was asleep. I should have been with him."

Jane moved to Charlotte's other side. "You could not have had three hours of sleep a day when—"

"When everyone in my family died? I do not care how much sleep I had. A seven-year-old should not die alone."

Angrily, she stormed from the room.

Elizabeth exchanged a look with her sister, having no idea if they should go after Charlotte. Jane offered a forlorn shrug. Neither of them had ever endured such grief. Elizabeth had no notion what to do, or if there was anything that could be done.

The following day Charlotte asked Elizabeth and Jane if they would return to organize the pile of books and kitchen items and see them taken to Miss Hervey and Oliver. When Elizabeth protested over the books, positing that Charlotte might want them for her own children someday, Charlotte leveled a cold look on her and merely repeated her request.

Once the gifts for Miss Hervey were put in order and sent with a servant, the two sisters found both Mr. Darcy and Mr. Wickham, and the four agreed to walk. Elizabeth felt a twinge of guilt for not returning directly to Longbourn to ask Charlotte to join them, but a part of her longed desperately for a walk without Charlotte's misery accompanying them.

They set out, Jane and Mr. Wickham ranging ahead as had become their custom, which amused Elizabeth. Between them, she had always been the faster walker. Still, if Jane's desire for private discourse with Mr. Wickham drove her to walk faster than was her wont, Elizabeth would not stop her.

"I arranged for two apple trees of different varieties to be planted at Miss Hervey's cottage," Mr. Darcy ventured. "They are the largest I was told are movable, which means they should be ready to bear fruit in two or three years."

"That was very thoughtful of you," Elizabeth said. "That will help Miss Hervey and Oliver." The day was colder than usual, and she pulled her cloak tighter about her.

"You seem troubled," Mr. Darcy observed softly.

Elizabeth sighed, her breath clouding the air. "Charlotte blames herself for not being with her youngest brother when he died."

"It is common to blame oneself in a tragedy, even though the situation is not under our control." He spoke with more knowledge than Elizabeth possessed.

A quick look showed his expression to be grave indeed. Pain welled in her for his loss of both his mother and father. She was assailed by the urge to take him into her arms. To hold him and assure him that all would be well. That he would not be alone.

Swallowing down that confusing well of emotions, she instead looked away.

"Wickham and your sister seem quite companionable," Mr. Darcy said quietly.

Looking ahead, Elizabeth watched Jane turn to Mr. Wickham with a warm smile, then laugh at something he said.

"Yes. They do." Did Mr. Darcy sound worried? Disapproving? Elizabeth could read nothing in his face or tone. "Has he said anything?"

"He says that he is helping her with her charities."

"Does he have any experience with charities?" Elizabeth asked, though that was in fact the least of her concerns.

"A great deal. He did most of the work in deciding where to distribute money both for my father and my uncle." Mr. Darcy still watched the two as they walked. "He is particularly astute at finding solutions that are not strictly monetary."

"Such as your apple trees."

"An idea I borrowed from Wickham," Mr. Darcy admitted.

"What else?" Elizabeth asked, studying the man beside her sister. Should Jane be opening her heart to hurt again so soon after discovering Mr. Bingley's unworthiness?

"The wife of one of my father's tenants was overwhelmed by raising four boys, ages four, two, and newborn twins. Wickham arranged for their holding to be combined with that of a widow with a large cottage but no surviving children, who was struggling to find someone to work the land for her. The widow helped with the children, and my tenant farmed both plots, and as the boys grew, they learned to work the land as well. Years later, when the widow died, her will asked that her farm be divided between the twins."

"And the families couldn't figure that out themselves?" she asked.

"It did not occur to them."

"It was good, then, that Mr. Wickham intervened," Elizabeth said, but Mr. Wickham's past good deeds did nothing to salve her present worry for Jane's battered heart. Some time ago, Mr. Darcy had asked her if Mr. Wickham was in danger of giving his heart where he could not hope for affection to be returned. Surely, she might now ask the same on Jane's behalf? "Is Mr. Wickham courting my sister?"

"I do not believe he is," Mr. Darcy said.

Elizabeth's heart sank with a flash of anger. "Why?"

"Wickham is…sensitive. He believes that she is mourning her affection for Mr. Bingley." Mr. Darcy slanted a look at Elizabeth. "In part because you told me she is."

Elizabeth stemmed her growing ire. Indeed, she had said as much. "She was. Or rather, as I believe I actually said, she was sad that the man she thought Mr. Bingley to be never existed."

"Was sad?" Mr. Darcy repeated.

"Yes, was. I believe she has come to terms with losing something she never really had, and even when she was enamored with the idea of Mr. Bingley, I cannot recall her seeming so happy."

"It is a wonderful thing to find someone who makes you happy."

Something in Mr. Darcy's tone snagged Elizabeth's attention, causing her to look at him.

The intensity of his gaze stole her breath. Confused, her cheeks heating, she looked away.

Did Mr. Darcy mean that she made him happy? He, she realized, made her so.

Chapter Twenty

Richard was returning from an early morning walk, taken to counter the hours he would soon spend seated for Sunday's sermon, when a lad from Meryton came up the lane. Intercepting him, Richard received a letter, for which he traded a few pennies. As the boy retreated, Richard turned the missive over to read, *To my esteemed nephews, Colonel Richard Fitzwilliam and Mr. Fitzwilliam Darcy, and their companion, Mr. George Wickham, residing in Lucas Lodge,* scrawled in Lady Catherine's hand.

Raising his eyebrows, for the missive appeared not to have been posted but rather to have come directly from the village, Richard cracked the seal.

> *I have taken accommodations in Meryton at what passes for an inn. You will all attend me after church.*

If Richard's eyebrows could go any higher, they would. What was Aunt Catherine doing in Meryton? Why had she not written of her intention to visit? Not that they could invite her to reside in Miss Lucas's home with them. Not only would that be unseemly as they were themselves guests, but the staff was too limited to meet Lady Catherine's needs.

Had she brought their cousin Anne with her? Richard turned the page over, though he knew the outer side contained only their names and location, and predictably learned nothing new.

He went in, joining Darcy and Wickham at a sufficient, if sparse, breakfast. After sitting and signaling his desire for coffee, Richard handed Darcy the note. "Did you know Aunt Catherine is in Meryton?"

Darcy shook his head, his eyes scanning the scant words, then handed the page to Wickham before saying, "I had no idea. What does she want?"

Richard shrugged. "Do not look to me for answers. Who can say what she is after?"

"Stirring the pot, undoubtedly," Wickham remarked and passed the letter back to Richard.

Tucking it away, Richard asked, "But why?"

"Because it entertains her?" Wickham spoke with no ire. Only wry humor for the habits of a woman he'd known his entire life.

Worry gnawed at Richard. "Have either of you written to her of late? Does she know about the investigation?"

"I have been corresponding with her, but you know neither of us would supply her with fuel for her meddling," Darcy said with a trace of reprimand.

"That does not mean your father hasn't," Wickham added to Richard.

Richard groaned. His aunt had almost certainly come to inquire into his investigation. She took a keen interest in the matter, having loved his sister well.

"It might be for the Bennets," Wickham said.

"The Bennets?" Richard frowned his confusion at that.

Darcy nodded. "I had nearly forgotten. Our aunt is the executor of their cousin Mr. Collins' will. He left each of the daughters a pound and Mr. and Mrs. Bennet each two pounds."

The hope they'd given Richard vanished. "If so, that will only be her excuse. Aunt Catherine would not have personally traveled all this way simply to dole out nine pounds."

"Whyever she is here, I imagine we will find out after church," Darcy said and sipped his coffee.

After taking their meal, they walked over to Longbourn to accompany the Bennets to church. Predictably, Mrs. Bennet had Darcy's carriage waiting, ready to take her, Mr. Bennet, and the three younger daughters. Also predictably, Miss Lucas, Miss Bennet, and Miss Elizabeth waited to walk with Richard, Darcy, and Wickham.

As they paired off, the other two men's affections being clear, leaving Miss Lucas to walk beside him, it occurred to Richard that he may be misleading her. It behooved him to ensure she did not believe him to be courting her simply because they often walked together, but how to go about that? Normally, he socialized in circles where his marital status was widely known. Usually, he was the one to start their conversations. Richard instead mulled over the perfect phrasing as they walked.

"Tell me of your family's estate," Miss Lucas said. "Mr. Wickham described it as quite lovely. He said he has spent some time there."

It was as Richard feared. Miss Lucas was developing expectations. "Yes. He was there for several years. After my Uncle Darcy died, my father convinced Wickham to give services in our family chapel. My late mother was unwell by that time and could not journey from the manor house. Wickham was a balm to her soul."

"Mr. Wickham is a clergyman?" Miss Lucas asked, startled.

In his preoccupation over how to gently dissuade Miss Lucas from aspiring to a match with him, Richard had forgotten both Wickham's masquerade as a soldier and his aversion to confessing his true vocation. "Ah, yes. I know he does not fit the common image, but he is, and those who know him well understand that the church is indeed his true calling." Richard realized he was babbling, startled by his breach of confidence, but soldiered on. "I suppose he was technically a curate. My father did pay him, and also supported him. Wickham had a room in our home and handled my mother's charities until her death. He also fulfilled certain social duties. Sometimes it is nice to have an extra man at a gathering."

Miss Lucas studied Mr. Wickham where he walked ahead of them with Miss Bennet. "He makes a very dashing officer. Many of the young ladies found him the most interesting officer in the militia." Somehow, Miss Lucas's tone indicated she was not one of them.

"For my father, indeed for old Mr. Darcy as well, Wickham was kind of a chameleon. He played whatever role was needed when guests came. He flirted outrageously with women who were decades older than he was. He discussed the Bible and Greek philosophers with the serious minded. He rode to the hounds and shot grouse, or fished with those who wanted companionship there. My mother's health kept her from being a proper hostess, and my father did not like to leave her side. Nor was my brother interested in taking on those duties. Wickham filled in."

"Was he good at all those things?"

"Good enough. He never tried to be the best. But guests do not want to spend time with someone who shoots better or rides better. They want someone who keeps up and enjoys himself."

"I hope his enjoyment was genuine and not a pretense," Miss Lucas said. "It can be tedious to pretend emotions one does not feel."

"Society often demands that we do that."

Miss Lucas sighed softly. "I have been doing too much of that. I pretend it helps when people offer me condolences, though it does not, especially condolences from those who ignored me before. I resent them and wonder how much my wealth has to do with their behavior."

"Nevertheless, from what I understand, you have done an excellent job of behaving properly."

"Tempting as it is to throw a temper tantrum or insist on solitude, there is no point to it. There is no benefit to me from indulging in bad behavior."

"Do you worry that your control means people believe you grieve less?"

"That is not my concern. Anyone who thinks that is free to do so. I am not going to put on a show for the benefit of others. My grief is for me to deal with. I appreciate kind words, but I also appreciate normal behavior. The Bennets have been wonderful to me." A smile softened Miss Lucas's features. "Their very normalness makes my life easier. They have not changed from who they were for my benefit."

"As others have?" Richard suggested.

Her features hardened once more. "Men are claiming undying love and women are claiming eternal friendship. But Mrs. Bennet is still self-centered. Lydia is still thoughtless. Jane is still good to everyone. Elizabeth is still my friend, no more nor less than before."

"It is fortunate that you found a refuge."

"I have, but I also have decisions to make. The protection the Bennets, you, Mr. Darcy, and Mr. Wickham have offered will not last forever." She shook her head. "I imagine I will, in fact, need to marry."

"I understand. There is something I should tell you, however. I am married and I love my wife."

She smiled slightly. "I know. I asked Jane to inquire after your matrimonial state from Mr. Wickham two days after making your acquaintance."

"Oh." Richard supposed that was flattering. "That is good. I worried I had given you false hope."

"No. You have, by your kindness, given me the very real hope that not all men are as horrible as the ones who have been seeking my time of late."

The distance between the parties who walked closed as they neared the church. They entered together, Richard searching for the carriage-carried Bennets as his eyes adjusted to the dimness of the indoors.

"Miss Lucas," a youthful voice called.

Richard turned to see a man of about twenty had entered the church behind them. The young Mr. Randolf Goulding, he thought, for he and Boyle had spoken to nearly everyone in Meryton at this point, both in official enquiries and unofficial gossip. Not that he was any closer to finding the poisoner, for all that.

"Miss Lucas," Randolf Goulding called again.

Miss Lucas, who had not turned the first time, continued to aim an angry, pinched expression away from the young man.

Randolf Goulding attempted to push his way into their group, to reach Miss Lucas's side. Richard turned fully around, blocking his way.

"Stand aside," Randolf Goulding demanded.

Richard regarded the young man coldly. "No. Miss Lucas can hear you. If she wishes to speak to you, it is up to her."

Randolf Goulding huffed. "I said, step aside."

"And I said no," Richard repeated, unimpressed and aware of a growing audience in the already half full church.

"You leave me no choice, sir." Randolf Goulding drew himself up and slapped Richard.

All around them, people gasped. Based on the pathetic nature of the blow, this youth, with his locally powerful father, had never exerted himself to more than ringing a bell to call a servant.

"Mr. Goulding," Richard said evenly. "You have known Miss Lucas for what I imagine is the entirety of your life, being, what, seven years her junior?" He cast her a questioning look.

"Yes. I can recall him in leading strings," Miss Lucas replied coolly. "He was a grubby, snot covered child."

Randolf Goulding's face reddened.

"Do you truly believe that Miss Lucas would be happy to have a duel fought over her?" Richard continued. "I am certain there are young ladies aplenty who would find the gesture romantic, but even after my short acquaintance with Miss Lucas, I know she is not such a one."

"You are refusing to fight me?" Randolf Goulding's voice dripped scorn.

"I am refusing to kill you."

Randolf Goulding's eyes went wide.

His words rimmed with ice, Richard elaborated, "You see, I have killed, Mr. Goulding. Both in the course of duels and in my service to the crown. If necessary, I will kill again, but I do not deem that to be necessary in your case. Not if you desist in tormenting Miss Lucas."

Randolf Goulding swallowed. His gaze darted about. Richard could see him weighing his honor against his life.

"Mr. Goulding," Miss Lucas said in a loud, clear voice. "I will never marry you. When I refused you before, that should have been enough."

"But you need to be protected," Randolf Goulding said almost pleadingly. "You must marry. I heard someone bribed a servant to tell them which bedroom window is yours."

Miss Lucas cast Richard a worried look.

"That has been dealt with," Darcy said firmly.

Interested, worried murmurs filled the church.

"What *have* you been doing with the miscreants?" Richard asked lightly.

Darcy shrugged. "Depending on my whim, anything from a stern reprimand to turning them over to the local authorities for time in the gaol, though in truth breaking into a home should have far more serious repercussions," he added in a dire voice.

Richard wondered if Darcy truly had seen any of the scoundrels locked away or if he'd said as much for dramatic effect. Or, taking in the worried looks exchanged by Miss Bennet, Miss Elizabeth, and Miss Lucas, were the words issued in the spirit of reassurance? If Darcy had indeed gone to the authorities, undoubtedly the local magistrate, Mr. Goulding, was more than pleased to lock away anyone attempting to secure Miss Lucas's hand.

Richard returned his attention to Randolf Goulding. "You see? Miss Lucas is protected. Your concern, while laudable, is misplaced."

"But I thank you for it," Miss Lucas added with only a trace of irony in her voice.

Taking the opportunity to retreat that their words offered, Randolf

Goulding bowed and scuttled away deeper into the church.

The six of them resumed their walk up the central aisle in the direction of the other Bennets, who watched with considerable interest. A man pushed past them, rushing ahead to where the priest, Mr. White, stood. Mr. Goulding Sr., Richard realized, watching the man. Had he been inside the church yet when his son issued his challenge?

Mr. Goulding spoke to Mr. White in a low voice, gesturing vehemently. Raising a complaint against Richard?

"I will not," Mr. White snapped, his words loud enough to carry. "She must consent, and she has not."

"You forget that I hired you," Mr. Goulding barked. "I will see you expelled as curate here. Leave."

His back stiff, Mr. White said, "You may issue all the threats you like. The banns will not be read."

"The banns won't be read?" an aggrieved voice cried. "They must be read. It is important."

A glance showed the complaint issued from Mr. Chamberlayne, who stood framed in the doorway of the church with a woman Richard did not know on his arm.

Mr. Goulding said angrily, "Mr. White, if you give the service without reading all the banns, I will send my servants to kick you and your children out of the parsonage this evening."

"On a Sunday?" Anger and scorn mingled in Wickham's voice. He stepped forward. "Mr. White, I will conduct the service to ease your conscience."

"Will you read the banns, Wickham?" Mr. Chamberlayne asked, sounding confused. "Will that, well, count? I need them to count."

"A soldier reading the banns?" Mr. Goulding scoffed. "This is a church, not a London stage."

"In fact, I am not a soldier." Wickham did not raise his voice, but nor did he attempt to speak quietly. "Or rather, my stint as a soldier was very abbreviated. I am, by vocation, a curate."

"Bravo," a voice called loudly from the front of the church.

Richard whirled. Beside him, Darcy groaned.

From the first pew, Lady Catherine rose, standing to her full formidable height. In a booming, commanding voice, she stated, "I am Lady Catherine de Bourgh of Rosings. I vouch for Mr. Wickham. He is a fully ordained member of the church and more than capable of giving a sermon, of leading a congregation, and certainly of reading banns." Lady Catherine looked about the church, then pinned Mr. Goulding with her gaze, daring him to speak against her.

"Ah, very well, then," Goulding mumbled. "Mr. Wickham may give the sermon, and Mr. White will not be cast out, but the banns must be read."

Throughout the church, people appeared confused and muttered to their neighbors. Wickham, with calm assurance, strode to the pulpit. In the sea of staring eyes, the ones that struck Richard most fully were Miss Bennet's. Her face held confusion and hurt.

"Please, friends," Wickham said as he took his place. "Take your seats so we may begin. God is patient, but such chaos on the Sabbath may be trying even to Him."

That earned some chuckles and the people of Meryton returned to their seats or moved to take them. Just before he sat beside Miss Lucas at the front of the church, Richard saw Mr. Bingley and Mrs. Hurst enter, arm in arm. He appeared a wraith of his former self, and Richard suspected their linked arms were more so she could support him than to adhere to social niceties. Mr. White settled into the pew beyond the two of them and Wickham looked up from the page before him.

"I have before me the banns." Without effort, Wickham pitched his voice to carry and yet, somehow, still remain conversational, rather than shouting.

Consulting the page, Wickham read banns first for two couples who were having them read for the third time. Then they were read for Mr. Benjamin Chamberlayne and Miss Margarette Haddington, much to Richard's surprise. Apparently, mourning was not the reason Miss Haddington had yet to marry Chamberlayne's brother. As Richard had forbidden him to leave, Chamberlayne had obviously brought his intended to him. A glance showed the couple sitting next to each other holding hands. Somehow, Richard could not picture the smiling young man beside Miss Haddington as a murderer. Mrs. Long, on Miss Haddington's other side, spoke briefly to her.

The next banns were for Mr. Simon Goulding and Miss Charlotte Lucas.

"I object," Miss Lucas said in a loud, firm voice.

"She cannot object," Mr. Goulding said smugly. "Only a parent or guardian can object, and I am her guardian."

Miss Lucas eyed him like something found on the bottom of her slipper. "You are not my guardian."

"The banns are not read for the marriage of Miss Charlotte Lucas and Mr. Simon Goulding," Mr. Wickham said in a calm voice.

Mr. Goulding surged to his feet. "I have the right to have the banns read."

"I think not," Darcy said, standing. "No woman should be forced into marriage."

"I am her guardian," Mr. Goulding reiterated.

Standing as well, though reluctantly, Mr. Phillips cleared his throat. "No. You are her trustee. Even if you were her guardian, you cannot legally force her into a marriage." He grimaced and sat back down.

"But I am her—"

"Trustee," Mr. Bennet said firmly, though he did not stand.

"And after the service, I will see that you are no longer even that," Miss Lucas said with exasperation.

Mr. Bennet cast Goulding a hard look. "I agree."

Mr. Phillips sighed.

"There are more banns to be read," Wickham said mildly.

With a final look of contempt for Goulding, Darcy retook his seat.

Wickham then read the banns for Mr. Randolf Goulding and Miss Charlotte Lucas.

"I object," Miss Lucas stated.

Mr. Goulding swiveled to glare at his son. "You are not even of age."

"I will be in two months and the banns are good for three," Randolf Goulding said. "But you cannot deny that if Miss Lucas agreed, you would give me permission to marry."

There was some chuckling in the congregation.

There were four more attempts at banns for Miss Lucas. By the time the reading of the banns was over, the congregation was amused and openly mocking the men involved.

Wickham shuffled the notes before him for a moment, then looked up. "Mr. White has a delightful sermon here on loving thy neighbor, but I believe I will take us in a different direction today."

Wickham proceeded to give a sermon without any notes, speaking fully from his heart and memory, and speaking well. Though Richard had heard Wickham give sermons before, he'd forgotten what a skilled orator he was. It was one of the finest sermons Richard had ever had the privilege of attending.

This was aided, in part, by Wickham's choice of topic. He selected *Matthew 5:4*, emphasizing, '*Blessed are they that mourn: for they shall be comforted.*' When he was finished, the men who had attempted to have the banns read slinked quickly out of the church.

Chapter Twenty-One

After a lovely sermon during which, more than once, Elizabeth glanced at Jane to see tears shimmering in her sister's eyes, Lady Catherine de Bourgh insisted she and the three gentlemen return to Longbourn. To Elizabeth's surprise, and worry, Jane asked to ride in the carriage, prompting Kitty and Lydia to join the gentlemen, Elizabeth, and Charlotte in walking back. The whole way, Lydia teased a preoccupied but convivial Mr. Wickham about masquerading as a redcoat.

Like a queen, Lady Catherine ordered them to her liking in the dining room, insisting on the middle seat on one long side of the table. Elizabeth's parents took their usual places at the head and foot, and the three gentlemen and Charlotte sat on Lady Catherine's side, leaving Elizabeth and her sisters to face them like some sort of strange tribunal. Mr. Wickham, Elizabeth noted, tried to catch Jane's eye but she kept her gaze on the hands she folded before her on the tabletop.

Once everyone was seated and offers of refreshments refused, Lady Catherine said, "Richard, is Boyle about?"

"He should be." Colonel Fitzwilliam signaled to a footman. "My batman, Boyle, is likely in the stable." He glanced around the table. "In anticipation of us joining you for a meal after church, I asked him to bring our mounts."

It interested Elizabeth that both Mr. Darcy and Lady Catherine took the time to know the names of servants, even ones who were not their own. Neither, at first impression, were the sort of person she would credit with such behavior.

"Very good." Lady Catherine produced a rolled sheaf of papers and a small purse from her rather voluminous gown. Unrolling the papers, she began smoothing them.

Elizabeth looked about but no one seemed inclined to speak while they waited for Colonel Fitzwilliam's batman. Down the table, Lydia whispered something to Kitty, slanting a look at Lady Catherine. Seated across from the lady as she was, Elizabeth sensed she took note, though she gave no reaction.

After what seemed like an eternity, during which even Elizabeth's mother remained silent as she cast awed looks at their guest, Boyle entered and bowed.

Lady Catherine looked up from her papers. "Ah, Boyle. Good. See that pens and ink are brought, then ensure that we are not overheard. You may listen."

"Yes, Lady Catherine." Boyle bowed and departed.

"I came here for two reasons," Lady Catherine said, studying everyone at the table in turn. "The first, the excuse, is to settle Mr. Collins' estate."

Boyle returned with ink, several pens, and a blotting pad. Opening the purse she'd set on the table, Lady Catherine proceeded to distribute the nine pounds Mr. Collins had collectively left them, handing them each a receipt to sign. Her thoroughness amused Elizabeth.

That finished, she set the pages out to dry and steepled her hands. "Now, I want a full report on this poisoning and the subsequent investigation."

Mr. Darcy leaned back in his chair to exchange a look with Colonel Fitzwilliam, who shrugged and nodded.

"Come now. I know most of it from my brother already," Lady Catherine snapped. "I simply wish to hear from those nearer the source."

"The soldiers were presumably poisoned by someone who walked in while the cook was sleeping," Mr. Darcy began.

"Sleeping?" Lady Catherine snapped, her eyes almost glowing with indignation.

"He was ordered to feign sleep," Colonel Fitzwilliam clarified. "After days of doing so, it seems he began sleeping for real. He paid with his life. He was one of those who consumed enough poison to die from the effect."

"Well then, God rest his soul," Lady Catherine said without a trace of irony. "Carry on, Darcy."

"Unfortunately, as the cook did not witness the poisoner, it could have been anyone," Mr. Darcy continued. "That is, except the men who were on maneuvers with Wickham and subsequently poisoned. Anyone else in the troop, and anyone in the village. Though fewer people had access to the kitchen at Netherfield Park, a great many did. As to what was poisoned there, we narrowed it down to the soup and at least one other dish."

"It was that spicy duck," Elizabeth's mother said firmly.

Colonel Fitzwilliam turned a questioning look on her. "How do you know that, madam?"

Mrs. Bennet shrugged. "I know my neighbors, and I know what they ate. It was the duck. My sister Phillips agrees."

"Mrs. Phillips was not even in attendance," Colonel Fitzwilliam protested.

"If Mrs. Bennet and Mrs. Phillips say it was the duck, it was," Elizabeth's father said firmly.

"Hm," Lady Catherine murmured. "Richard, I assume you have found no ties to France."

"I have not."

Lady Catherine nodded sharply. "Have you considered that this poisoning was merely a copy of the first, very publicly splashed about in all the papers?"

"We have." Colonel Fitzwilliam sounded grim.

"Sadly," Mr. Wickham said softly, "That only leaves us with more suspects."

Lydia leaned forward, opening her mouth to say something.

Lady Catherine held up a hand. "Think before you speak."

Lydia stared for a moment, closed her mouth, and sat back.

Elizabeth could not contain a smile. Despite the lady's hauteur, she half hoped Lady Catherine would stay for a long while. Anyone who could make Lydia think before she talked was welcome.

Lady Catherine looked about the table again. "When my brother wrote to me of the anonymous letter he received informing him that there would be another poisoning, I had high hopes that the deaths of my niece and her husband would finally be punished. Do you mean to tell me that even though you laid this trap, Richard, and you came here to offer assistance, Darcy, and you were brought into the militia troop as a malcontent and potential co-conspirator, Mr. Wickham, that you have made no progress in identifying the killer?"

Silence filled the room. Elizabeth stole looks about the table. Her mother, Mary, Kitty, and Lydia all looked confused. Jane still stared at her hands. Elizabeth's father appeared angry. As well he might be, with Meryton used, essentially, as bait and so many of his neighbors dead.

It was on Elizabeth's lips to explain to her father that Meryton was one of several towns chosen, and only because Netherfield Park had stood empty, and that the plan to catch the poisoner would have worked if only the dead cook had not fallen asleep. All the reasons she had already forgiven the three men who sat on Lady Catherine's side of the table. But something snagged at her mind. Something that had before, days ago.

"Your brother received the anonymous letter about the poisoning?" Elizabeth said slowly into the silence, addressing the austere woman across from her.

"He did," Lady Catherine said coolly.

"Your brother, the earl? Who is, insofar as anyone has mentioned, not in any way part of the military? His closest ties are through Colonel Fitzwilliam and the departed husband of his daughter?"

"Correct." Lady Catherine frowned at her now.

Undaunted, and uncertain that the frown even spoke of disapproval, Elizabeth said, "Why would someone write to an earl to warn him that a militia stationed in Meryton would be poisoned?"

"Because they knew about the death of my sister and her husband, which could be anyone," Colonel Fitzwilliam said glumly.

Elizabeth shook her head. "No. I mean, yes, but who would think to write to him first, rather than to, say, Colonel Forster, who was right here in Meryton with the troop? Or some other member of the King's forces?"

"Someone whose connection to the first poisoning is through my uncle," Mr. Darcy said, casting Elizabeth a look of admiration that called heat into her cheeks.

"Precisely."

Lady Catherine studied her with interest. "You mean to say, Miss Elizabeth, someone whose ties are to the *ton*, not the military. Who thinks through the lens of society, as it were."

"I do."

"If the porridge eaten by the men had not been poisoned, everyone would assume the poisoning was aimed at those attending the ball," Mr. Wickham said. "Without the note and the soldiers' deaths, officers would still have died, but there would have been no reason to assume they were the target."

Colonel Fitzwilliam's brows drew down in a frown. "So we should be asking, who at the ball did someone want dead?"

"And did they die?" Mr. Wickham added.

"Some people believe I have a motive," Charlotte said quietly.

Elizabeth shook her head. "You were never in the kitchen."

"Richard?" Lady Catherine asked.

Colonel Fitzwilliam cast Charlotte an apologetic look. "My inquiries show that Miss Lucas was at home when the soldiers' food could have been poisoned."

"But the ball was so chaotic," Elizabeth's mother said, wringing her hands. "How can we know who was meant to die?" She raised wide eyes to look down the table at Elizabeth's father. "Oh, it could be you, Mr. Bennet. It could be us."

"I cannot imagine it is any one of us or whoever it was would have tried again," Jane said softly, not looking up. "We would have once again been harmed."

Elizabeth surged to her feet at the same moment Mr. Darcy did, both of them blurting, "Mr. Bingley."

"Mr. Bingley is the poisoner?" Kitty and Lydia cried in horrified unison.

"Surely not Mr. Bingley," Mary protested.

Elizabeth rushed to the dining room door, saying, "No, Mr. Bingley *is* still being harmed. He is in danger." She wrenched the door open to the sight of Colonel Fitzwilliam's batman. "Please see the gentlemen's mounts saddled."

"Wait," Charlotte called in a loud voice. "Mr. Boyle, before you do that, please send in someone with paper. I need to write a letter."

Mr. Boyle nodded and hastened away.

"Who did it?" Mrs. Bennet asked. "And to whom are you writing? And why is Mr. Bingley in danger?"

"The poisoner is Mrs. Hurst," Charlotte replied. "And I am writing to Mr. Goulding. I will send him to Netherfield Park. He will listen to me."

"No, you will summon him here," Lady Catherine said firmly. "And Darcy, Miss Elizabeth, do sit down. This must be done correctly."

"Lady Catherine is right," Colonel Fitzwilliam said. "We must make every effort to gather evidence. Given warning, Mrs. Hurst will destroy any." But in seeming disparity with his words, he stood. "I will summon Colonel Forster." With that, Colonel Fitzwilliam left.

While they waited, Elizabeth's mother insisted on serving tea. Lady Catherine drank her cup, but Elizabeth was too agitated to do more than take a sip of hers. Jane refused to even have any. Kitty and Lydia drank theirs while cheerfully yammering about knowing a murderer. Mary excused herself, and soon sorrowful notes could be heard coming from the drawing room's pianoforte. Elizabeth's father continued to glower at Mr. Darcy and Mr. Wickham. When Colonel Fitzwilliam returned with Colonel Forster, Mr. Bennet included them in his ire.

Mr. Goulding arrived with a bouquet of flowers in hand, much to Elizabeth's disgust. As he stood in the doorway gaping into the full dining room, Lady Catherine said, "I understand that you are the magistrate here."

Mr. Goulding nodded.

"We have deduced that Mrs. Hurst is the poisoner. We want her arrested." Lady Catherine gestured to Colonel Forster. "The colonel will supply force, if it is necessary, but Netherfield Park should be searched for evidence. We would like to have a warrant so it can be done."

Goulding came into the room, laying the bouquet on the table. "Certainly, Lady Catherine. May I ask what you hope to find?"

"She is likely to still possess some of the poison," Mr. Darcy said. "We suspect she intended for three people to die; her husband, brother, and sister."

"That is despicable," Mr. Goulding said. Thoughtfully, he added, "But if they did, she would become very wealthy."

"I assume she has a personal maid," Lady Catherine said. "We should interview her as well."

Jane glanced up. "She was let go. Biddy Gibson. I have an address for her."

"Do you have the letter?" Mr. Darcy asked Colonel Fitzwilliam. "We should check her stationary and handwriting against it."

"Letter?" Mr. Goulding repeated. "What letter?"

Mr. Darcy darted a grimace at Elizabeth's father. "After the militia unit reached Meryton, the Earl of Matlock received an anonymous letter warning that a poisoning would take place here."

"A letter about which no one told us," Elizabeth's father said coldly. "Springing a trap about which we were also not informed."

Elizabeth looked down, aware that her father's anger was justified. Were she not so grateful to Mr. Darcy and Mr. Wickham for the care they'd shown Charlotte and, she admitted, so enamored with Mr. Darcy, she too would be angry.

"I see," Mr. Goulding said slowly. "Yes, well, we will sort that out later." He drew himself up. "It is getting late and it's Sunday, but I will find people to help."

"I can supply men," Colonel Forster reminded him.

Everyone looked about the table, faces set.

Chapter Twenty-Two

Grim guilt rode with Richard as he joined the other gentlemen and a contingent of Forster's men in their ride to Netherfield Park. When he, Forster, and Goulding knocked, the footman who answered the door stared out at the gathered force in confusion and attempted to turn them away on the grounds that Mr. Bingley was ill.

"We know he is," Richard snapped, much of his anger born of knowing that he was due the hard displeasure of Mr. Bennet, Mr. Goulding, and many others in the village. "That is why we are here."

Forster gestured and his men came forward to force the footman back and secure the door.

Gaining the entrance hall, Richard asked, "Where is Mr. Bingley?"

"In the back parlor, sir," the visibly nervous footman reported. "The smallest one, where the fire will do him the most good."

"Is Mrs. Hurst with him?"

"Y-yes, sir. She's serving him tea."

Richard exchanged a look with Forster before turning back to the footman. "You will lead me to them, quietly." He gestured to two of Forster's men. "You are with me."

"The rest of you will spread out and search the house," Colonel Forster ordered. "This is a gentleman's home so take care but be thorough. Bennet, Darcy, Wickham, please supervise. Anything suspicious is to be brought to them, men. Goulding, I believe we should take the honor of searching Mrs. Hurst's chamber."

Richard and the two of Forster's men he'd selected followed the footman deeper into the house. As they neared the little parlor, Mrs. Hurst's voice emerged, saying, "Come now, Charles, tea will do you good. Try just a few sips for me. I want to see you well again."

Could Mr. Bingley not hear the venom in his sister's voice, or did Richard imagine it?

He strode into the room to take in two startled faces. Mr. Bingley, ensconced in blankets and with a shawl about his shoulders, had a cup raised halfway to his mouth.

"Put the tea down, Mr. Bingley," Richard ordered.

Bingley blinked bloodshot eyes. "What? Why? What are you doing here?"

Richard answered the middle question. "Because it is most likely poisoned."

Mrs. Hurst gave a brittle chuckle. "Not this nonsense again. Are Mr. Darcy's friends ever going to stop bursting in on us with tales of poison? Really, gentlemen, this is too dreadful of you. My brother is unwell, as anyone can see." She stood. "Drink your tea, Charles, and I will deal with this."

"Set the tea down, Mr. Bingley." Richard turned to the two men. "Confine her somewhere. Do not harm her but use what force you must. She is not to speak to anyone until Mr. Goulding can interview her."

"I do not understand," Mr. Bingley said weakly, setting down his tea.

The two men marched forward.

"Do not touch me," Mrs. Hurst screeched. "Unhand me. Charles, do something."

Bingley struggled free of the blankets and to his feet.

Richard moved forward, raising a staying hand. "Sit back down, Mr. Bingley, and I will explain both why we are here and why you are so ill."

Bingley stared after his sister as the men dragged her from sight. "I—I do not understand. Why am I so sick?"

"Your sister, Mrs. Hurst, is the poisoner."

Bingley dropped back into his chair, but he was shaking his head. "No. Not Louisa. She lost so much. Hurst. Caroline." He looked up. "No. Louisa would never do such a thing." Absently, he reached for his tea.

Richard snatched the cup up and set it on the other side of the low table. Gesturing to the service there, he said, "None of this is to be touched until it can be examined." Taking in Bingley's startled, incredulous expression, he added, "If we are wrong, I will extend my deepest apologies, but I do not believe we are."

"We?" Bingley looked about as if he'd somehow missed another person.

"Colonel Forster and the local magistrate are searching her room." Richard decided not to mention the full-scale inspection of the house being overseen by the other gentlemen.

"That fool Goulding?" A touch of animation returned to Bingley's pale, pinched features. "You cannot take his word. He probably poisoned everyone so he could have Miss Lucas." Teeth gritted, Bingley stood once more. "Take yourself, Forster, his men, and Goulding from my house."

Richard eyed him pityingly. "Mr. Bingley, we have a warrant."

Bingley stared at him.

Carefully, clearly, Richard said, "Mrs. Hurst poisoned dozens of people. Killed nearly a score. Her husband died. Your younger sister, who by all reports was recovering, died. Now, look at you. I imagine that the more ill you become, the more care Mrs. Hurst takes of you. Bringing you broth. Fixing you tea."

"It…it is my grief overtaking me."

"When your parents died, did you nearly follow them?"

Bingley stared at him. "I did become ill when each of them died. Morose. Unconsolable for a time."

"But this ill? This physically ill?"

Bingley shook his head.

"Help us find the evidence," Richard urged. "If she is innocent, so be it, but if she's guilty, she should pay for her crimes."

Bingley shrugged free of the shawl that draped shoulders he now squared. "Come with me."

He led Richard to Mrs. Hurst's room where Forster, Goulding, and two officers were methodically going through Mrs. Hurst's possessions. Moving past them, Bingley picked up an innocent-looking footstool. It had what looked like a round, thick, solid wood top, decorated with both paint and a series of carved rings.

He proffered it to Forster, saying, "Hold the legs. If Louisa is hiding anything, it will be in here."

Forster grabbed onto the legs. Bingley took hold of the seat and twisted. The top came off.

They both peered inside. The compartment was lined with dull colored metal, presumably put there to conceal the fact that the stool was hollow. Inside rested a large bag that appeared nearly empty. Taking it, Richard crossed to the bed and spilled out a small amount of a finely chopped substance that was almost a powder. It could have been herbs or even mushrooms.

Richard looked back at Bingley. He hadn't realized the man could get any paler, but somehow Bingley had. On Mr. Goulding's orders, Mrs. Hurst was arrested. Her shouts of anger ricocheted through the house as they took her away.

***

Mr. Bingley came to Lucas Lodge early the next morning while Richard, Darcy, and Wickham lingered over breakfast. Richard had already taken his walk, which had proved informative, and Darcy had fed the chickens. Since the task could be easily delegated, Richard could only assume Darcy enjoyed tending the birds.

So ill did Bingley appear that all three of them moved to help him to a chair. With a glare, Bingley waved them off, taking a seat and asking, "What is the case against Louisa?"

"Would you care for coffee, Mr. Bingley?" Wickham asked, raising a hand to gesture to a waiting footman.

Bingley shook his head. "I would not."

"Tea? Anything to eat?" Wickham pressed, regarding the other man with clear worry.

Wickham's concern was understandable. Pale and drawn, with dark rings under his eyes and a coat that hung from his recently diminished frame, Bingley seemed to sway in his seat.

"I would like to hear the case against Louisa," he reiterated firmly.

Richard looked to Darcy, who nodded back to him, so he took the lead. "It has not been fully built yet, but both your tea and the powder found hidden in the footstool were used to lace food given to rats, and the rats died before dawn." Forster had sent word immediately, Boyle waking Richard even earlier than usual with the news.

Bingley winced, then nodded. "What else?"

"We checked both the handwriting and paper used in the anonymous letter claiming that the militia would be poisoned. Both are similar to examples of your sister's stationery and handwriting. Furthermore, there is a spelling error which we found duplicated in Mrs. Hurst's other correspondences."

"What was the spelling error?" Mr. Bingley asked, sounding defeated.

"The writer spelled 'repeat' ending in p-e-t-e."

Mr. Bingley drew in a sharp breath.

Richard forwent asking if that was a mistake Mrs. Hurst often made. "We will be checking with her maid to see if she knows about Mrs. Hurst obtaining poison."

Bingley nodded glumly.

"And going back over mine and Forster's notes, I noticed that several of the staff remarked on Mrs. Hurst's frequent visits to the kitchen."

"She...she was conscientious," Bingley whispered.

"She is noted to have asked questions that suggest a complete lack of knowledge as to what takes place in a kitchen."

"How does that matter?" Bingley asked.

"It indicates that while she made frequent visits to the kitchen at Netherfield Park, it was a new habit," Wickham explained.

Bingley turned to him in confusion.

"She wanted her new habit to appear normal so it would not draw suspicion," Darcy added.

"Are you really saying she planned in advance to kill all those people?" Mr. Bingley asked, his voice strangled.

"Yes," Richard said evenly, but with considerable sympathy for Bingley.

"She must have hit upon the idea when she learned the militia would be quartered in Meryton. My father received the anonymous letter warning of a poisoning, creating a situation where if members of the militia died, she would not be suspected." Richard drew in a breath and added another proverbial nail to Mrs. Hurst's coffin, for he had received new information while out on his habitual early morning walk. "And this morning, there was a witness who came forward. On the morning the troop was poisoned, someone passed by the Hervey farm within the appropriate window of time and was followed to Netherfield Park. That person, cloaked but presumably a woman because she was wearing a skirt, unlocked the servants' door to enter. The witness could not identify Mrs. Hurst, but it is suggestive."

Richard forbade mentioning that the witness in question was a ten-year-old boy, brought over to Lucas Lodge by his aunt, Miss Hervey, to tell the tale. "The only thing we do not know at this point is why? Yes, with all of you dead Mrs. Hurst would be wealthy, but is that truly why she wished to murder her entire family?"

Bingley looked away, his features pinched.

"Would you have eaten the duck if the salmon had not been available?" Darcy asked quietly.

Bingley scrubbed his hands over his face. "Yes. It is a family recipe, and a favorite of all of ours." He studied the tabletop for a long moment, then sighed. "Hurst was spending his money too rapidly. I know Mrs. Hurst was concerned about that."

She wasn't Louisa anymore, but Mrs. Hurst, Richard noted.

Bingley swallowed. "And Caroline?"

"We can only surmise that when she failed to die after the first poisoning, Mrs. Hurst poisoned her again, as she must have been poisoning you." Though, in truth, Richard feared it to be his desire to question Miss Bingley that forced Mrs. Hurst's hand, calling for Miss Bingley's suddenly rapid decline.

"But Caroline grew ill again and died so quickly." Bingley looked about the table. "I have simply been tired. And unable to eat much. Grief lays heavily upon me. That is just as likely the cause for my…my state of unwellness."

"Do you feel at all better today?" Richard asked.

Bingley shrugged. "I cannot tell. I could not sleep. I am exhausted."

Wickham watched him with sympathy.

"I suspect that Mrs. Hurst was poisoning you more slowly so as not to arouse suspicion," Richard said, though he wished he could give gentler news.

"I see." Bingley looked from face to face. "Is the case sound? Will she be convicted?"

"Discovering the poison hidden in her room was very damning."

A flash of stubbornness crossed Bingley's features. "I showed you where it was. I could have planted it there."

"Did you?" Darcy asked.

Bingley turned a look of mingled desperation and anger on him, then his shoulders slumped under his now too big coat. "No."

"We've summoned her personal maid, Biddy Gibson, from London," Richard said. "May we assume she will be able to give even more evidence against Mrs. Hurst?"

Bingley looked away, then muttered, "She did send Miss Gibson to collect a package from London. I assumed something for the…the ball." He closed his eyes again. "I saw Biddy carrying in a wrapped box and asked her what it was. She said she'd no idea but the mistress had insisted she go to a specific shop Mrs. Hurst had written to and return with the package post-haste." Bingley swallowed, looking nauseated. "I joked that it must be something special for the party. Miss Gibson said maybe the secret ingredient for th-the duck, because it was an herbalist's she was sent to."

Richard exchanged grim looks with Darcy and Wickham.

"I believe I will be going," Bingley said, standing. "I feel the need to lie down."

They all stood with him. Richard took in the worry and sympathy on Darcy's and Wickham's faces and knew his mirrored their expressions.

Halfway to the door, Bingley turned back. "I was going to leave without telling you this, but…Mrs. Hurst is five years older than I am. I suspect she thinks I don't remember, but as a child, she developed a fascination with herbs and mushrooms, both edible and poisonous."

Richard nodded. "Thank you."

"I will say as much in court if I must," Bingley added, then turned away.

Richard applauded the man for that, but he doubted it would be necessary. They had more than enough on Mrs. Hurst without forcing Bingley to testify against her. Richard sat back down with a sigh of his own.

"You are very glum for a man who has caught a murderer," Wickham said with forced lightness.

"My trap failed, and dozens of people died," Richard said quietly. "I should have had two cooks, both feigning sleep."

"Which would not have been believed," Darcy cut in.

"I should have thought of something," Richard snapped. "Some way to protect against this outcome." He shook his head. "In truth, I'd all but accepted that the deaths of Elinor and Christian were an accident, and the other two so-called poisonings simply bad luck with spoiled food. Putting out handpicked militias for bait, ensuring you were near one, Darcy, and other trusted allies among the *ton* the others, that was an act of desperation.

Even after the letter arrived and Wickham was sent here, I did not truly believe there would be another murder, let alone a mass poisoning."

Richard looked down at his plate, the food there no longer holding any appeal. "I will need to do something to make amends here in Meryton. Not that anything I can do will restore lives, but everyone who lost a family member must be compensated."

"Wickham and I will help you," Darcy said calmly, to which Wickham nodded. "Together, the three of us will see it done."

Chapter Twenty-Three

To Darcy's surprise, Mr. Bingley returned the following morning, again during breakfast. Declining any hospitality, he asked to speak with Darcy alone. Agreeing, Darcy left the table and escorted Mr. Bingley into a small parlor near the front of Lucas Lodge, where they would be able to speak without being overheard.

Dropping heavily into a chair, Mr. Bingley said, "Louisa is dead."

Darcy stared at him. "I am sorry," he ventured.

"She managed to hang herself sometime in the night."

"Then I am doubly sorry."

Mr. Bingley scrubbed his hands over his face. "In a way, I am relieved. She would have hung after the trial, regardless."

Darcy could think of nothing to say to that and so waited.

"I…I find myself full of guilt," Mr. Bingley said quietly. "I doubt the compartment inside the stool would have been found without my help. I condemned her."

"You may have added evidence, but we also had the letter sent to the Earl of Matlock, which decidedly matches her handwriting, and we will have the testimony of her maid and the young man who saw her sneak back to Netherfield Park on the morning the militia was poisoned. And once we spoke with Miss Gibson, we would have interviewed the shopkeeper to learn what Mrs. Hurst purchased from his shop. I believe, even without the contents of the stool, she would have been convicted."

"And what of the guilt I hold for the deaths she caused?" Mr. Bingley asked, raising stricken eyes.

"I can only hope it will fade in time." As Darcy hoped his guilt at being a part of Richard's trap would as well. "We must remind ourselves that we poisoned no one. Mrs. Hurst did this terrible thing. Her actions were her own." Or so Darcy kept telling himself.

Mr. Bingley stared at nothing for a long moment. "I delved into her finances. She keeps…kept detailed records. She and Hurst were in dun territory. He overspent so drastically that she was augmenting the household funds from her dowry, and that money had dwindled to a few hundred pounds. Soon, they would have been forced to retire to the country and live on his small family estate with his mother, who I know Louisa hated." Mr. Bingley shook his head. "I believe she was simply desperate. If only she had come to me. I could have helped."

"Her pride must have been such that she would not turn to her younger brother," Darcy observed.

Mr. Bingley nodded. He opened his mouth to speak, closed it again, then opened it to blurt, "And your pride, Mr. Darcy?"

"Mine?" Darcy asked, confused.

"Once, we were friends. Or rather, I thought we were. You told me that you do not care about my ties to trade, and until two days ago, you did not know of my ties to a murderer, yet you have made no effort to renew our friendship."

It was Darcy's turn to look away.

"What changed?" Bingley pressed.

Darcy could say that he'd been busy solving a crime and assisting Miss Lucas. He could claim that he had not wanted to intrude on Mr. Bingley's grief. Neither were the real reason he had not continued the acquaintance, though.

"Tell me," Mr. Bingley insisted. "I need to know the truth. Is it, after all, my ties to trade?"

Quietly, Darcy reiterated what he'd told Mr. Bingley before, concluding, "I judge people by who they are, not who their parents were."

"So you have said, but—"

Darcy held up a staying hand. "But upbringing matters. Our upbringing shapes who we are and how we behave." He met Mr. Bingley's gaze squarely. "I suspect you acted out of ignorance, but there were consequences to your actions."

"My actions?"

"You dismissed sick servants whose only crime was to eat food they were not supposed to eat."

"That is theft," Mr. Bingley said a touch hotly.

"If you had consulted with your housekeeper, you would have learned that extra soup was made as a treat for the staff."

Mr. Bingley stared at Darcy for a moment. "Caroline would never have authorized that."

"I do not believe she did."

A bit mulish, Mr. Bingley said, "Then it was still theft."

"Perhaps on the part of Mrs. Nicholls, but not on the part of those you dismissed."

Chagrin suffusing his features, Bingley protested, "I gave them their quarter's wages, and two pounds each, and saw that they got to London. Both of my sisters complained that they should have been dismissed without their wages. I was magnanimous."

For the first time, it occurred to Darcy that Mrs. Hurst had used Miss Bingley's desire to send away so much of the staff to remove both potential witnesses and her personal maid. Perhaps uncharitably, he wondered if Mrs. Hurst had argued for the harsher path, the withholding of wages, in the hope that most of the staff would die.

Deciding not to burden Mr. Bingley with such speculations, all Darcy said aloud was, "How long could you live in London on less than five pounds? For that matter, how long could you live on ten? Where would you eat? Sleep? Remember, your servants were ill. They couldn't walk for hours to find decent accommodations. Nor could they afford to hire someone to cart them about."

They may even have been so ill as to be insensible, and therefore unscrupulously robbed, but Darcy forwent adding that as well.

Mr. Bingley's face went red. He gritted his teeth, started to speak, then halted. After a long silence, the anger in his face faded. His hands white with strain where they gripped the arms of the chair he said, "I thought I was being generous."

"Generous would be caring for them until they recovered. Some of them died. Two have not been found."

Mr. Bingley blinked rapidly. "How do you know that?"

"Several concerned parties had them tracked down to see that they were cared for, although in some cases we were too late."

"We? You and Mr. Wickham?"

"Me and Miss Bennet. Not working together," Darcy added, as there was no point in tormenting Mr. Bingley with the implication that he and Miss Bennet were close. Darcy decided, as well, not to point out that he had also wished to interview the staff, in addition to seeing to their welfare, while Miss Bennet had thought solely of helping them.

Mr. Bingley looked away. Darcy wondered if he was considering the fact that Miss Bennet had looked at him differently of late, just as Darcy did. But then, everyone would see Mr. Bingley in a different light now that his sister's crime had been exposed. It must be a terrible burden to be the relation of a mass murderer.

Mr. Bingley stood abruptly, bringing Darcy to his feet.

"Mr. Darcy, I am off to London. I doubt I will see you again. As soon as Colonel Fitzwilliam is assured he has no more need of me, I will leave the London area. I am not certain where I will go, but I have money and enjoy society. In a different location with a different name, I can continue to do so. However, I will no longer attempt to join the *ton*. If our paths cross, I would prefer you not know me. I do not want to spend my life under the shadow of my sister's crime."

He bowed, Darcy mimicking the gesture, and left.

Darcy returned to the breakfast parlor and reported Mr. Bingley's news about Mrs. Hurst's death and her finances to Wickham and Richard. He did not mention the remainder of their conversation and they did not pry.

After breakfast, Darcy and Wickham set out for Longbourn to bring the news of Mrs. Hurst's demise to the Bennets. They found the family and Miss Lucas in the midst of their morning meal and joined them, though neither took more than coffee. As the hour was too early for calls, something none of the Bennets seemed to mind, for once Mrs. Bennet had not already heard, through her network of friends and relations, what they'd come to say.

Darcy concluded with, "Mr. Bingley is departing for London."

"When will he return?" Mrs. Bennet asked.

"I do not believe he means to."

"But who will hold another ball at Netherfield Park?" Miss Lydia cried. "We need another. The one we had hardly counted."

"I only danced with five officers," Miss Kitty said, then sneezed.

"You only danced with four," Miss Lydia snapped. "I danced with six."

"Yes, we require another ball," Mrs. Bennet said loudly over her daughters. She slanted a look at Wickham and added, "And Mr. Bingley was interested in Jane."

Miss Bennet's cheeks turned pink and she stared down at her plate.

"My dear," Mr. Bennet said, "With the entail broken, Jane should not be forced or even encouraged to marry the brother of a murderer. If she did, who else would marry into our family?"

Mrs. Bennet huffed. "I did not say Jane should marry him, but how will other young men understand her worth if she is not sought after." This time, she turned to eye Wickham directly.

Her face red, Miss Bennet came to her feet. "Excuse me."

Wickham started to stand.

"I will go after Jane," Miss Elizabeth said firmly, casting a glare at her mother before following Miss Bennet.

Mrs. Bennet merely shrugged. "Young people will get nowhere without encouragement."

Darcy took in the worry on Wickham's face and recalled the heartbreak on Miss Bennet's upon learning that Wickham was other than he'd claimed to be. Would Mrs. Bennet's encouragement be enough?

"Why is Jane so upset?" Miss Lydia asked in an aggrieved voice. "She had Mr. Bingley's affection, and now she's stolen Wickham's from me. She should be happy."

Wickham coughed, fixing his attention on his cup of coffee.

"If not a ball, we could have a recital," Miss Mary said into the silence that followed that.

"No one is having anything for some time," Mr. Bennet said firmly. "Not after the tragedy that took place at Netherfield Park." He leveled a look of displeasure on Darcy that bordered on dislike.

"About that," Darcy said, for things must be set right. Or rather, as right as they could be. "Colonel Fitzwilliam, Mr. Wickham, and I will be remaining in the community for the remainder of December to do our best to put right what may be put right. While we know that nothing can compensate for the losses to the community, we will do what we can." He turned to Miss Lucas. "If we may, we would like to pay you one month's rent for the use of Lucas Lodge. If not, we will find different accommodations."

"So you admit your culpability in what took place?" Mr. Bennet said before Miss Lucas could reply.

Darcy turned to Mr. Bennet. "With the knowledge that members of the militia and citizens around them were being targeted and poisoned, several traps were set, among them, the one here in Meryton." Darcy gestured to Wickham. "As soon as it appeared that the trap here had been sprung, Mr. Wickham was dispatched into the regiment to weed out the traitor. Arrangements were made to lure the poisoner in."

Gravely, Darcy held Mr. Bennet's angry gaze. "Would Mrs. Hurst have poisoned the food at the ball if a militia had not been stationed in Meryton? It could be that she would have. Or, one could argue that having the militia here put the notion of poisoning into her mind, and drew her to murder so many. We will never have the opportunity to ask her. All we do know is that we did our best to catch the poisoner, and to warn those at the ball the moment we knew of the poisoning."

Thoughtfulness overtook the displeasure on Mr. Bennet's face.

"We also know that we will strive to help this community in the aftermath of the recent tragedy," Wickham added, but his eyes were trained on the doorway through which the eldest two Bennet sisters had departed, not on Mr. Bennet.

"And the families of the soldiers who perished," Miss Mary said. "They will be helped as well, I hope?"

"Certainly," Darcy said. "That is always the case when Britain's troops die in the line of service." But he would speak to Richard to make certain they were compensated enough. They had, after all, been unwittingly used as a trap, even if that trap had never truly been sprung.

"This is all Mrs. Hurst's fault," Mrs. Bennet said loudly. "Oh, I can see the guilt in the both of you, Mr. Darcy, Mr. Wickham. I've seen it in the Colonel as well. But none of you are murderers. It's that Mrs. Hurst who killed people, and she's paid, and so it must all be forgotten." She turned a piercing look on her husband. "Forgiven and forgotten."

"Their sins and lawless acts I will remember no more," Miss Mary intoned.

Mr. Bennet shrugged and sipped his coffee.

"Lady Catherine de Bourgh is asking if you are at home," a maid's voice said from the doorway.

"They are certainly at home," the voice of Darcy's aunt groused, followed by the lady herself. "Richard informed me that you were both here, Darcy, Wickham." She nodded to the room. "Wickham, we must have words, and I have need to speak with you, Miss Lucas."

Miss Lucas's expression showed surprise. She started to stand.

Lady Catherine waved her down. "I believe what I will say should be said before most of those here, who have your best interest at heart." She turned to the side of the table where the youngest Bennet daughters sat. "Have you three finished eating?"

Miss Mary and Miss Kitty stood.

"I haven't," Miss Lydia said.

"You have," Lady Catherine stated.

Miss Lydia's eyes went wide. With a nod, she too rose. All three curtsied and departed.

"As it was a pleasure to see my youngest children cowed, I will forgo commenting on your right to order my household, Lady Catherine," Mr. Bennet said mildly.

"That is very kind of you, Mr. Bennet." Lady Catherine sat, taking the same seat she had the day they'd solved the murder.

Had Darcy detected amusement in his aunt's voice?

Lady Catherine gestured a footman over. "Tea, please, and a sweet roll." The man nodded and Lady Catherine turned back to address Miss Lucas with, "You are not in a position to make good decisions. Your life has been upended. You are grieving. You should do nothing that is irreversible."

"Such as marrying?" Miss Lucas asked.

"Precisely. You are beset by greedy, unscrupulous men who want to force you into a decision which should be made rationally and without pressure. There is no way you should be expected to make an irrevocable, life-altering decision at this time. You must find some way to take the time you need to grieve. Do not expect to recover quickly. You will be lucky if you are reasonably rational within a year."

A rare show of misery, pain and desperation overtook Miss Lucas's features. "But what am I to do? I cannot impose on the Bennets indefinitely, and come the end of December, Mr. Darcy, Mr. Wickham, and Colonel Fitzwilliam will depart."

"That, Miss Lucas, is one reason why I am here," Darcy's aunt said firmly. "Join me in London, where we will first purchase you some decent mourning clothes."

Miss Lucas looked down at her made over gown in surprise.

"If we suit each other, and I think we will, you will come with me to Rosings Park," Lady Cathrine continued. "You will be introduced as Mrs. Lucas for the respect and freedom that will offer, and touted as my paid companion."

Miss Lucas appeared alarmed.

"Oh, Charlotte, how wonderful for you," Mrs. Bennet exclaimed. "Just think, to live with a lady and the sister of an earl."

"Miss Lucas does not need to be a hired companion," Darcy said firmly.

Lady Catherine gestured as if waving Miss Lucas's and Darcy's concerns away. "That is why I said 'touted as.' I will treat you as a guest, Miss Lucas, except that once in a while, when the servants will overhear, I will have you fetch something."

Relaxing slightly, Miss Lucas said, "That does not sound too strenuous and, well, I am accustomed to being busy. I would like to be busy."

"What about Mrs. Jenkinson?" Darcy asked, referring to his cousin Anne's governess who, in more recent years, had become a companion to his cousin and aunt, Anne having outgrown the need of a governess.

Lady Catherine cast him a startled look. "Have I not told you?"

"Told me what?" Had some ill befallen Mrs. Jenkinson?

"Anne has decided she is in love. She is marrying one of our neighbors. Mrs. Jenkinson will receive her pension the day following the wedding."

Darcy gaped at his aunt. His cousin Anne marrying was definitely something she should have told him.

Ignoring his astonishment, Lady Catherine once again addressed Miss Lucas. "No one will wonder why I have hired a new companion, with my daughter wed and Mrs. Jenkinson retired."

"What if I join you in London and we do not suit?" Miss Lucas asked with no show of meekness.

Darcy's aunt shrugged. "If we do not suit, we do not suit. I will assist you in setting up a household in London, or Meryton or wherever you want."

"That is a very generous offer," Mr. Bennet drawled. "Why are you making it?"

Lady Catherine's face stilled, becoming grave. "I made a foolish decision after my husband died. I let Mr. Collins buy the living I hold. At the time, it felt as if there was so much to see to with Lewis gone that I was overwhelmed. I simply wanted the matter of the empty living settled. By the time I came to know what kind of man Mr. Collins was, it was too late. I sent him away, telling him to marry someone, hoping that a wife would occupy him so he would leave me alone. I could not stand his frequent visits. His sermons were bad enough." Lady Catherine shuddered.

Darcy stared at his aunt, startled anew. She always seemed so strong. So sure. He had not realized she'd required assistance after his uncle died. He would have offered his.

Not that Lady Catherine would have accepted.

"I thank you for your generous and kind offer, Lady Catherine," Miss Lucas said slowly. She looked to Mr. Bennet.

"You are welcome here for as long as you like, but I believe the offer to be well-meaning, honest, and a good solution," he said.

Miss Lucas's gaze went to the door through which Miss Elizabeth had departed, then she turned to Mrs. Bennet. "Mrs. Bennet? What is your opinion."

Surprise flitted across Mrs. Bennet's face. Rather than speak immediately, she furrowed her brow in concentration. "Will there be society for Charlotte should she wish it? In her guise as your companion, will she be permitted to visit others, or to invite guests?"

"Guests do not normally invite guests," Lady Catherine said, but she too appeared thoughtful. "There will be society, yes, and Miss Lucas may certainly travel, to an extent, without betraying the ruse. As to having guests, if it is someone not odious to me, I will invite them."

Mrs. Bennet nodded. "I believe you should accept, Charlotte, and if it doesn't work out, you are welcome to return to live with us."

Darcy could not help but wonder if the generosity of the offer was related to the additional visitors who would come because Miss Lucas was there.

"Then I accept." Miss Lucas mustered a weak smile. "Thank you, Lady Catherine. I believe you have offered the perfect solution."

"Certainly I have," Darcy's aunt said with a huff. "Now, Mr. Wickham."

Wickham, who'd been slowly turning his coffee cup in his hands, his gaze abstract, started. "Yes, Lady Catherine?"

"You will fill the Hunsford living. Mr. Hatter, curate of a nearby parish, has been assisting since Mr. Collin's demise, but you will be required to arrive in Hunsford in time for all Yuletide sermons. If you have unfinished matters here, you may employ my carriage to return weekly for up to a month following the Yuletide season."

Hope leaped in Darcy. He looked to his friend, praying Wickham would finally embrace his calling and accept Lady Catherine's offer.

Wickham set his coffee cup down. "That is very kind of you, Lady Catherine, but I fear it would not be in the best interest of the Hunsford congregation. Someone else would be far better suited to the task."

"I cannot imagine who," Mrs. Bennet said. "We all heard you speak on Sunday. You were very good, Mr. Wickham."

"Why would someone else be better?" Mr. Bennet asked, studying Wickham.

Miss Lucas looked on with interest.

"Well, simply because, ah—" Wickham fumbled.

"You are under no obligation to explain yourself," Darcy interrupted firmly.

"He is ashamed," Lady Catherine stated, her gaze locked on Wickham. "On the evening that Mr. Wickham was ordained, my foolish brother-by-marriage enlightened him to his parentage."

"That is enough," Darcy cut in.

Ignoring Darcy, Lady Catherine leveled a finger at Wickham. "This man was born a bastard, the child of a barmaid and an unknown traveler. His mother was a fifteen-year-old orphan raised in the inn. Nothing is known of his father at all. The Wickhams adopted him as a babe and raised him as their own."

Darcy stared at her, shocked that she would be so cruel.

Wickham, his face white with strain, swallowed. "Why are you doing this?" he asked in a quiet, beseeching voice.

"Because I have watched you hide yourself away in service to my kin when you should be leading a congregation. I have watched you, time and time again, sabotage your happiness because you do not believe you are worthy. Of a living. Of regard." She gestured to the doorway. "Of love."

Wickham swiveled to face the doorway. Darcy followed his gaze to find Miss Bennet and Miss Elizabeth standing there, their faces slack with shock.

"It ends now," Lady Catherine declared. "Everyone will know the truth of your parentage and you will see that those who are worthy of your friendship will not care, just as Darcy does not, as his parents and yours did not, and as neither I, my husband, nor my brother ever have."

Wickham surged to his feet. "If you will all excuse me," he said in a voice tight with strain. Gaze downturned, he crossed the room and pressed past Miss Bennet and Miss Elizabeth, who stepped aside. A moment later the front door could be heard to open and then close firmly.

Covering her mouth, her eyes stricken, Miss Bennet hurried away. Her rapid footfalls pattered up the staircase.

Miss Elizabeth, still appearing stunned, murmured, "I should follow her," yet did not move from her place just inside the doorway.

"That was cruel," Darcy gritted out, glaring at his aunt.

"That was necessary," Lady Catherine said firmly.

Her absolute conviction did nothing to quell Darcy's anger.

"Whatever else that was, it was certainly entertaining," Mr. Bennet said to no one in particular.

Chapter Twenty-Four

Darcy came down to breakfast the morning following Lady Catherine's public exposure of Wickham's past to find his friend seated at the table, coffee at his elbow and a ledger and ink before him. Wickham, who Darcy had not seen since his abrupt departure from Longbourn the day before, appeared composed. Darcy knew him well enough to observe the strain about his eyes and mouth, though.

Taking the seat across from Wickham, Darcy ventured, "Has Richard breakfasted or not yet returned from his walk?"

"He has already walked and broken his fast, and I believe is now in Meryton working on reports with Colonel Forster."

Which meant that Richard had not slept well, Darcy concluded. Most likely because he was awash in the same guilt that Darcy and Wickham were.

Wickham made a note in his ledger, then dipped the pen he held back into the ink. "I believe the first priority is to find Mr. Robinson a nanny. We could approach Mrs. Clarke. She lost both her husband and son. She is alone now and without occupation."

"Does she require occupation?"

Wickham shrugged. "Not in order to live, but possibly in order to move past her grief."

"And what do you require to move past your guilt at being born?"

Wickham's head snapped up, his face white as he stared at Darcy. A drop of ink splashed onto the ledger. Wickham shook his head. "I would rather not discuss that."

"And yet, we must."

"Must we?"

"It is time we did," Darcy said firmly.

Sighing, Wickham carefully cleaned the pen and set it aside. He then capped the inkwell. "Very well. What would you have me say?"

"It is more what I would have you do, which is to realize that the circumstances of your birth are not your fault, and do not reflect on the person you are. I believe Miss Bennet can come to see that, and so must you."

"Miss Bennet?" Wickham looked away. "What has she to do with anything?"

"Do you not care for her?" Darcy asked, surprised.

"I admit I do."

"Do you not wish to offer for her?"

Wickham grimaced, not an auspicious reply. "What man would not wish to offer for her? She is…she is perfect."

Darcy had no trouble not wanting to offer for Miss Bennet, but refrained from saying so. "Then may I assume you have not offered for her because of some ridiculous notion that you are unworthy?"

"Ridiculous?" Anger touched Wickham's voice. "She is the daughter of a gentleman. I am no one. Not even the son of a steward."

"You are who you make of yourself."

"That is an interesting belief for a man who defines himself by being a Darcy," Wickham snapped. "A man who grew up destined to be master of Pemberley."

Chagrin shot through Darcy. "That is different."

"Is it? Why?" Wickham leaned forward in his chair. "Because being a Darcy is a good thing, and being the bastard son of a fifteen-year-old barmaid and some passerby is not?"

Darcy ground his teeth, wishing he were the better arguer of the two. Especially as he was in the right. "What if I were a pathetic excuse for a gentleman? If I gambled Pemberley into ruin, chased after every skirt I saw, and left a string of bastards in my wake? Would my heritage as a Darcy still make me a good man?"

"It would still make you a respected, and respectable, gentleman," Wickham countered.

"You were raised with every advantage given me." Darcy struggled not to raise his voice, for this was not an argument to be won by volume. "We are the same."

"No. You are Mr. Fitzwilliam Darcy of Pemberley. I am no one. My parents did not even officially adopt me and, by all reports, my mother was simply labeled 'Smith' when the innkeeper took her in. Henrietta Smith. That is my only parent."

That sparked an idea in Darcy. "Very well. Miss Henrietta Smith is your mother. What do we know of her?"

Wickham stared at him for a long moment, lines creasing his brow, then said, "As I said. She was a fifteen-year-old orphan when my parents met her."

"We know she loved you enough to want to give you a good life. We know she was a conscientious and kind nanny, beloved by my parents and yours." Softly, Darcy added, "We know she died saving my life. Not only died saving it but chose to save mine over her own."

Wickham looked away, blinking rapidly.

"In short, we know she was a good and noble woman who made the very best of the terrible circumstances to which she was reduced." Darcy leaned forward now, too, driving his point home. "And yet you, given so much better circumstances, are flittering about from task to task, refusing to claim the happiness she wanted for you. Is that any way to honor your mother?"

Wickham stared at him, his mouth pinched and his eyes wide.

Darcy stood. "Think on that while you make notes in your ledger."

Pushing in his chair he stormed from the room. In short order, he was outside, long strides carrying him he knew not where. He did not know why he was so very angry, or even with whom, but tumult roiled through him as he strode rapidly in the cold morning air.

He'd regained his composure by the time he saw a pair of figures moving nearer, farther up the path he followed. The path to Longbourn, he realized, and the figures were Miss Elizabeth and Miss Bennet. It did not surprise him that his feet had carried him in Miss Elizabeth's direction.

He met them with a bow. "Miss Bennet. Miss Elizabeth."

"Mr. Darcy. How fortuitous. We were on our way to Lucas Lodge," Miss Elizabeth said by way of a greeting.

"I would be pleased to escort you."

Smiling, Miss Elizabeth fell in beside him, Miss Bennet on her other side.

They strode in silence for a time, their pace far slower than the one Darcy had employed up to then, until Miss Elizabeth ventured, "It is rather early for a walk, which I know is an odd observation as we, too, are out walking."

Darcy weighed his answers, then decided on the truth. Ill-mannered, perhaps, but he wanted to get to the bottom of Miss Bennet's feelings for Wickham. If he managed to convince Wickham to try for happiness and she was unreceptive, Darcy's efforts would all be for naught. Wickham would retreat into his shell of unworthiness again.

"To be truthful, Wickham and I had somewhat of a row." He slanted a look at Miss Bennet as he spoke.

"A row?" Miss Elizabeth echoed in surprise.

"Oh dear." Miss Bennet's worry was such that Darcy could not imagine it being much more keenly felt if he'd said, 'I shot Wickham in the arm.'

"Yes." Taking a girding breath, Darcy forged ahead. "Over his…" He could not quite bring forth the words, 'Inability to seek happiness.' "Because he has not yet accepted my aunt's offer of the living in Hunsford."

"It is all true, then?" Miss Bennet asked, her voice broken.

Darcy had hoped for a more promising reaction from her. "The story of Wickham's birth?"

She shook her head. "No. What Lady Cathrine said about Mr. Wickham's inability to seek happiness."

"Jane and I care nothing about the circumstances of Mr. Wickham's birth," Miss Elizabeth said staunchly.

Did that mean that others in the Bennet household did? Darcy considered his answer carefully. He may not need to convince the two ladies who walked with him of Wickham's worthiness, but he wanted that worthiness known. Especially if others in their household required convincing.

He halted in the middle of the path and began peeling off his gloves.

They both turned back to look at him.

"Mr. Darcy?" Miss Elizabeth asked.

Shoving his gloves into a pocket, Darcy held out his hand, palm down. "You have likely noted the scar on my hand?" Though decades old and faded with age, a long, wide, jagged-edged slash of whiter skin still cut across the back of his right hand.

Miss Elizabeth nodded, but Miss Bennet stared at his hand in surprise.

"I received this scar when I was not quite four." Darcy dropped his arm. "Men were working on Pemberley's roof after a storm. Wickham and I were playing too close to the house, and our nanny, the young woman who gave birth to Wickham, was worried something might fall off the roof and harm us." Darcy's throat tightened and he cleared it. "She called him and he went to her, but I was, apparently, too busy gathering up our toys to heed her. She came to collect me. A pile of loose tiles fell and she pushed me out of the way, and somehow I injured my hand. The tiles landed on her, killing her." Meeting Miss Bennet's gaze, Darcy said quite clearly, so there could be no mistake, "Wickham's mother sacrificed her life to save mine. That is the person she was. That is who he is."

Miss Bennet smiled at him. "I thank you for telling me that story, Mr. Darcy, but I already know what sort of person Mr. Wickham is. I simply did not know why he refused to properly court me. At first, I thought it was out of respect for my one-time hopes regarding Mr. Bingley."

"At first, it in part was," Darcy felt obliged to say.

"But Elizabeth told me of your conversation regarding that." Miss Bennet cast her sister a grateful look. "And yet Mr. Wickham was still withdrawn." She looked down. "I could only assume his attentiveness to me was another ruse. One he politely refrained from taking too far."

"I can assure you that his affection for you is very real," Darcy said.

Miss Bennet raised her head to reveal a radiant smile. "Thank you, Mr. Darcy. If you will excuse me." She dipped a quick curtsy and hurried away in the direction of Lucas Lodge.

Miss Elizabeth watched her sister's departing form, her expression amused. "You have made Jane very happy, Mr. Darcy."

"Have I?"

"Most assuredly." Miss Elizabeth turned her cheerful expression back to him.

"And what of those others in your household you alluded to?" he could not help but ask. "Those who may not be pleased to see Miss Bennet in a union with a man who has no lineage, only a living in Hunsford to his name?"

Miss Elizabeth squared her shoulders, as if girding for an argument. "To them I will say that Jane's happiness means more than Mr. Wickham's origins, especially now that the entail is broken. There is no reason that Jane must marry a wealthy, landed man."

"Before the entail was broken, she needed to do so, then?"

"I would not have said so," Miss Elizabeth said fiercely. "There is, after all, no reason to think we will not all marry, and do so while our father lives."

"I have every hope that you, in particular, will wed, Miss Elizabeth," Darcy said, the words welling up from his heart and into the December air between them. "And do so soon."

She drew in a quick breath, fury departing as she studied his face. "You do?"

Darcy flexed his fingers, acutely aware that with his gloves still in his pocket, he could cup her cheek and feel the velvety softness of her skin, if she would permit him to. "I do, and while I am pleased to have assisted Miss Bennet, I must admit that her happiness is of far less concern to me than yours."

"Than mine?" Miss Elizabeth's question came out a mere whisper.

"Indeed."

"You once said that you chose me to insult at the assembly because you felt me able to withstand your words."

He nodded. "Because you were the most beautiful woman in the room. In any room."

She studied his face, her wide eyes questioning.

"Perhaps I also did so to safeguard my heart," Darcy admitted.

"Your heart?" Miss Elizabeth repeated. "Did it need guarding?"

"I did not realize so at the time, but a piece of me must have known, even then, that I was in danger of falling in love with you."

A gasp escaped her lips. "Is love so very dangerous, Mr. Darcy?"

"I did not journey to Meryton to seek a wife. I came here to catch a murderer."

"And so you have. One might say that danger has passed."

"One might." If he tried to kiss her, would she permit it or move away? If she shared even a tenth of his feelings, he would know happiness.

She moved a half step closer on the path. "And do you still deem falling in love a danger?"

"If it is, I have succumbed, and only you can save me." He watched the rapid rise and fall of her breath. The butterfly wing flutter of her pulse in her long, elegant neck.

She reached for him even as he did for her, their lips meeting.

It was a tender, sweet kiss, for Darcy did not want to press her, and when he raised his head, it was to find her cheeks a bright pink. He could not help but imagine his kiss had been her first.

Elizabeth brought her hands up to her cheeks, her smile wide. "That was…" She trailed off. Mischief glinted in her eyes. "That was tolerable."

Darcy chuckled. "I am certain I deserve that."

"I am certain as well."

He reached for her, his hands closing loosely on her waist. "Perhaps I can do better."

Elizabeth cocked her chin, her eyes bright. "There is only one way we will find out."

Darcy pulled her to him.

Some time later, a throat cleared behind him. Reluctantly, he relinquished Elizabeth's lips. She blinked up at him, dazed. Seeming to realize she'd slid her hands inside his coat, she yanked them out, her cheeks blazing.

With a rueful smile, she murmured, "I believe we have been found out."

Darcy stared down at her. As lovely as she always was, she had never before looked so beautiful. "That is fortuitous, for I want the whole world to know that I love you."

"It seems as if the two of you have an announcement to make," Wickham's voice said behind him.

Capturing Elizabeth's hand in his, Darcy turned to grin at his friend, only to find that Wickham was not alone. He, too, held the hand of a Bennet sister. "As do you?"

Miss Bennet smiled up at Wickham. "As do we," she agreed.

Darcy had not thought his heart could hold more joy, but somehow it could. "May I suggest we make our way to Longbourn to speak with Mr. Bennet?"

"You may," Wickham agreed.

Together, the four of them set out down the trail, contentment and happiness their new companions.

Epilogue

Darcy sat beside his beautiful wife, watching their children sleep in the seat across from them as they journeyed to London. Rather, their son and younger daughter slept. Jane, their eldest at eight, read a small volume she'd brought with her for the purpose, her grasp of the written word far outstripping Darcy's at her age. He smiled, certain Jane got her keen wit from her mother.

He was surprised any of them had found sleep, for all were very excited to arrive. Jane so she could see her favorite cousin, Elinor, Richard and Vivian's daughter. Only six month's Jane's senior, she was the younger girl's dearest friend. He wondered how the two would get on with young George and Thomas this year. The Wickham's twin boys were a year younger than Jane, and tormented her and Elinor marvelously. Darcy and Elizabeth's son, little Fitz, liked to trail after the twins and mimic them, turning on his sister in favor of being included in the older boys' pranks.

Nor would Darcy and Elizabeth's daughter Frances be without a playmate, though at three she may not appreciate her companions as much as she would in a few years' time. Darcy and Elizabeth were certain that, in the years to come, little Frances would become quite close with Georgiana's daughter and Charlotte's.

Charlotte finally marrying four years ago had been a surprise to everyone, and her daughter a gift to them all. She had often said she was in no hurry to find a husband, content in her role as Lady Catherine's companion and happy to play with Darcy and Elizabeth's children, and his cousin Anne's growing brood. None of them had even realized that Charlotte had taken a fancy to Lord Green, a childless, widowed earl of Lady Catherine's acquaintance, until the union was announced.

Jane lowered her book, looking up to find he watched her. Darcy smiled at his eldest.

"Papa, can we not stay in London for the whole month?"

"We have been over this, Janie. We are expected at Longbourn for Christmas," he said for what he imagined to be the fiftieth time.

"And you know your grandparents have finally finished the new wing," Elizabeth added, as she usually did. "They want to show off the addition to

Longbourn."

Jane swung her feet, her legs not yet long enough to reach the floor. "But I want to stay in London with Elinor."

Elizabeth cast their daughter a commiserative look but said, "You have plenty of cousins to play with at Longbourn."

True enough, as Elizabeth's younger sisters had all married and each had at least two children already, and would likely have more. Especially Kitty, who'd become round and cheerful with motherhood, and never coughed anymore.

"Yes, but they are all babies, except George and Tom, and they are horrible. They run and yell and swing sticks." Jane angled her pert little nose into the air. "They are savages."

"What did we say about calling people names?" Elizabeth said sternly.

Jane let out a huffing sigh. "Not to." Wrinkling her nose, Jane gave her mother a glare and raised her book back up before her face.

Elizabeth shook her head, her expression amused.

Darcy captured her hand and kissed it.

When they arrived in London, Darcy was immediately informed that his agent waited for him. Leaving Elizabeth to see the children settled, he went to his office to discover what the man deemed so urgent.

Simmons, his agent, rose when Darcy entered. "I'm sorry to bother you immediately upon your arrival, sir, but there is something that needs your attention."

Darcy nodded acknowledgement of that and took the seat at his desk, knowing that Simmons wouldn't bother him unnecessarily. "What seems to be the issue?"

Simmons moved to the seat across from him. "It is the house you recently inherited from your father's cousin."

It was a decent enough dwelling, holding eight families in reasonable comfort, though Darcy had not yet had time to assess it in detail. He wondered what the trouble with it could be.

"The bakery next door caught on fire, and it spread to your property," Simmons continued. "I am afraid the house is ruined. Little is left. Everyone made it out, but they lost most of their possessions."

Darcy grimaced. "That is tragic. What have you done to take care of the displaced tenants?"

"Me? Nothing," his agent said, then held up a hand to forestall Darcy's anger. "But everyone has a roof over their head and food. Also, they were given money to buy clothing for their immediate needs. It was all accomplished before I even got word of the fire."

"What charity acted so quickly?" Darcy asked, impressed. He would have to make a donation.

Simmons shook his head. "Not a charity. One man. A Mr. Charles from Bristol. A cab was taking him and his wife to their hotel when they saw the fire. He redirected the cab to a bank. He apparently went in, withdrew money, and came back and arranged everything."

"Mr. Charles?" Darcy sorted through his acquaintances and could not recall ever hearing of such a person. "Do we know him?"

"I don't know anything about him, but I thought you might want to thank him." Simmons fished a page from his pocket. "I tracked him to this hotel, but he will be leaving London in a few days."

"Thank you. I do indeed wish to thank him." And to meet this very generous gentleman.

The following afternoon, Darcy sought out Mr. Charles at his hotel and was escorted into a room that outstripped the occupants. Neither Mr. Charles nor his wife dressed as if they possessed the sort of wealth required to blithely withdraw and distribute the level of funds that Mr. Charles had when seeing to Darcy's newly inherited tenants. More than not-showy, their clothing was unfashionable and unadorned. Mr. Charles had a short beard, and his hair was straight and flat, with no effort made to liven it to the current style. Mrs. Charles wore a simple bun.

Yet the hotel was one of the more luxurious in London, and the room a suite.

"Would you care for tea, Mr. Darcy?" Mrs. Charles asked in a soft voice.

"Yes, thank you."

Darcy sat and engaged in typical talk of the weather and speculation on when Parliament might sit until tea arrived. After being served his, he broached the topic for which he'd come. "I would like to thank you for assisting my tenants with such rapidity and thoroughness. I would be more than pleased to reimburse you."

"That is kind of you, Mr. Darcy," Mr. Charles replied. "But I would not think of accepting your money."

Darcy had not expected that. "But those tenants are my responsibility. I insist."

Under his beard, Mr. Charles' mouth twitched but Darcy could not tell if it was with amusement or anger. "Be that as it may, the funds are little to us."

"That is not my concern," Darcy protested. "It was kind of you to step in, and your alacrity does you great credit, but I, too, possess the funds to see to the welfare of those in my care."

"As you say, it is not a question of money," Mr. Charles said easily. "It is a question of helping others. My wife and I take great pleasure in doing so." Clear blue eyes pinned Darcy's. "Would you deny me that pleasure?"

Darcy could swear he knew that look. That light, easy voice. "I suppose

I will not. Short of bringing the funds here and secreting them in your luggage, I have no recourse."

"Then we are in agreement," Mr. Charles said. Now, he was definitely smiling beneath his beard.

"I did not believe we would ever meet again," Darcy said quietly, when he finally realized who he was talking to. "I was curious as to where you disappeared to."

Mr. Charles grinned, his teeth flashing white. "Then I have hidden well."

Darcy slanted a look at Mrs. Charles, but she seemed unperturbed.

"Do not worry, Mr. Darcy." She took a sip of her tea. "I am aware of my husband's past. He told me everything after he proposed."

Darcy raised an eyebrow at that. Had the so-called Mr. Charles trapped this woman into marriage?

Mrs. Charles exchanged an amused look with her husband and continued, "He told me after I accepted his proposal but before we announced our engagement to anyone, so that I could beg off if I elected to." She turned a warm look on Mr. Charles. "I did not elect to."

"Did you know they were my tenants when you assisted them?" Darcy could not help but ask.

Mr. Charles shook his head. "I did not. Had I, I may not have, feeling secure in the knowledge that you would."

Mrs. Charles reached to squeeze her husband's hand. "I fell in love with Mr. Charles because of his kind heart. He was always so active in all the local charities, and yet he never sought credit."

Under his beard, Mr. Charles colored slightly. "Yes, well, I spent a lot of time thinking on the value of money. What it means to people. How far they might go to possess it. How much some of them require it." He shrugged, looking away.

Mrs. Charles patted his hand again. "He even gives the income he receives from renting the Hursts' home to charity."

"Renting the Hursts' home?" Darcy repeated. He had not thought to ever hear that name again. Indeed, had hoped not to.

Mr. Charles grimaced. "Sadly, I inherited their London property. It is heavily mortgaged, but it rents for more than the mortgage payments." He looked down. "I have no desire to keep what it earns."

"Understandably." Darcy would not wish to, either. He cleared his throat. "Well, I cannot but thank you for your assistance, then, Mr. Charles, Mrs. Charles. I, and my tenants, are very grateful."

"Think nothing of it," Mr. Charles said.

They returned the talk to inconsequential things as Darcy finished his tea. When he rose, Mr. Charles walked him to the door.

"It is my understanding that you married Miss Elizabeth Bennet," Mr.

Charles said softly.

Darcy nodded. "I did."

"I hope you know every happiness."

"We do." Darcy could not hold in a smile at the thought of his lovely wife and three beautiful children.

"And that Mr. Wickham married Miss Bennet."

"Mrs. Charles seems quite lovely and dedicated to you," Darcy said, rather than answer that Wickham and Jane were exceedingly happy, he as a curate and she as the wife of one.

Mr. Charles smiled. "She is, and I, too, am very happy."

Darcy clasped his arm. "I am glad to hear that." He started to turn away, but halted, unable to resist asking, "Is it Charles Charles, then?"

Mr. Charles chuckled. "No. Mathew Charles, but I wanted an excuse to answer to the name, as I felt certain I would do so by mistake."

Darcy nodded. "A good plan. Well, then, Mr. Mathew Charles, I wish you well. Until we meet again."

Mr. Charles dipped his head. "Until we meet again, Mr. Darcy."

As Darcy left the hotel, he reflected on the vagaries of life. Elizabeth often found amusement in them. He could not wait to tell her this one.

~ The End ~

About the Authors

Renata McMann

Renata McMann is the pen name of Teresa McCullough, someone who likes to rewrite public domain works. She is fond of thinking, "What if?" To learn more about Renata's work and collaborations, visit **www.renatamcmann.com**.

Summer Hanford

Starting in 2014, Summer was offered the privilege of partnering with fan fiction author Renata McMann on her well-loved *Pride and Prejudice* variations. More information on these works is available at **www.renatamcmann.com**.

Summer is currently partnering with McMann as well as writing solo works in Regency Romance and Epic Fantasy. She lives in the Finger Lakes Region of New York with her husband and compulsory, deliberately spoiled, cat. The newest addition to their household, an energetic setter-shepherd mix, has been trying, and failing, for six years to gain acceptance from the cat, but is adored by the humans. For more about Summer, visit **www.summerhanford.com**.

Get Your Thank You Gifts! Sign Up for Our Mailing List Today!

Visit: **www.renatamcmann.com/news/**

THE FAKE DEGREE

Almost true, almost fatal, almost………

A fiction based on real lives

Bir Singh Yadav

EKA PUBLISHERS
#118 Ushodaya Enclave, PO Miyapur
Hyderabad 500049 (India)
ekapresshyderabad@gmail.com
+91 8008101590

www.ekapress.org

First Published in India by Eka Publishers 2020

ISBN: 978-81-944712-0-2
FICTION

The right of Bir Singh Yadav to be identified as the author of this work has been
asserted by him.

Edited by Smriti
Printed and bound in India by Eka Publishers